THIEF

LOVE ME WITH LIES

Books by Tarryn Fisher

LOVE ME WITH LIES SERIES

The Opportunist
Dirty Red
Thief

Mud Vein

Marrow

*F*ck Love*

Bad Mommy

Atheists Who Kneel and Pray

NEVER NEVER SERIES

THIEF

LOVE ME WITH LIES

NEW YORK TIMES BESTSELLING AUTHOR
TARRYN FISHER

Visit my website at www.tarrynfisher.com
Cover Designer: Sarah Hansen, www.okaycreations.com
Editors: Lori Sabin and
Erica Russikoff, www.ericaedits.com
Interior Designer: Jovana Shirley,
www.unforeseenediting.com

For the Passionate Little Nutcases—
This one is for you.

ONE

PRESENT

Olivia. I've lost her three times. The first was to impatience. The second was to a lie so dense we couldn't work our way through it, and the third time—this time—I've lost her to Noah.

Noah. He's a good guy. I checked him out. Extensively. But, he could be the Crown Prince of England and he still wouldn't be good enough for her. Olivia is a piece of art. You have to know how to interpret her, how to see the beauty under the harsh lines of her personality. When I think of him having her in ways I can't, I want to pound my fist into his face until there's nothing left.

She's mine. She always has been; she always will be. We've been running in opposite directions for the last ten years, and we collide at every turn. Sometimes, it's because we're looking for each other, other times it's fate.

She has the kind of love that can stain your soul, make you beg not to have one, just to escape the spell she's put you under. I've tried to break myself of her over and over, but it's pointless. I've got more of her in my veins than blood.

I see her now; she's on TV. All seventy-two inches of the screen are filled with Olivia: black hair, ambivalent eyes, ruby-red fingernails tap, tap, tapping on the table in front of her. Channel six news is covering the story. Dobson Scott Orchard, a notorious rapist who kidnapped eight girls in a twelve-year span, is on trial…and Olivia is defending him. It turns my stomach. Why she would take this man's case is beyond even my understanding of her. Perhaps her contempt for herself propels her toward defending worthless criminals. She defended my wife once and won the case that could have put her behind bars for twenty years. Now, she sits calmly next to her client, every so often leaning over to say something in his ear as they wait for the jury to enter the room with their verdict. I am on my second Scotch. I don't know if I'm nervous for her or about her. My eyes drift to her hands—you can always tell what Olivia is feeling by her hands. They've stopped tapping and are fisted, her tiny wrists resting on the edge of the table like they're chained there. I have a bird's-eye view of her wedding band. I pour myself another Scotch, shoot it, and toss the bottle aside. The screen switches to a media room where a reporter is talking about the mere six hours that the jury deliberated—what it means for the verdict. Suddenly, he jerks in his seat like someone has shocked him. *The jury has entered the courtroom, where in a few minutes the judge will read the verdict. Let's go there now.*

I sit forward in my seat, my elbows resting on my knees. My legs are bouncing—a nervous habit—and I wish I had another finger of Scotch. The entire courtroom is on its feet. Dobson looms over Olivia, who looks like a tiny porcelain doll next to him. She is wearing a blue silk blouse—my favorite shade. Her hair is clipped back, but the waves are escaping the pins and falling around her face. She's so beautiful; I drop my head to avoid the memories. They come anyway. Her hair dominates every one of them, wild and long. I see it on my pillow, I see it in my hands, I see it in the pool where I first kissed her. It's the first thing you notice about her: tiny girl, surrounded by a mass of wavy, dark hair. After we broke up, she cut it. I almost didn't recognize her in the music store where we ran into each other. My shock at how she'd changed aided my lie. I wanted to know the Olivia who cut her hair and cut through a room using only her lies. Lies—it sounds demented to want a woman's lies. But, Olivia loves you with her lies. She lies about how she's feeling, how she's hurting, how she wants you when she tells you she doesn't. She lies to protect you and herself.

I watch as she impatiently swipes a strand of it behind her ear. To the untrained eye, this is a normal female gesture, but I see the way her wrist yanks back. She is agitated.

I smile. It drops from my face as soon as the judge reads *not guilty by reason of insanity*. By God—she did it. I run all ten fingers through my hair. I don't know whether I want to shake her or congratulate her. She collapses in her seat, wearing her shock in her eyebrows. Everyone is embracing, patting her on the back. More of her hair bounces loose as she sustains the congratulations. Dobson will be sent to an institute for the mentally disturbed, rather than federal prison. I wait to see if she will embrace him, but she keeps her distance, only offering him a tight smile. The camera pivots to the prosecutor's face; he looks enraged. Everyone looks enraged. She's making enemies—it's her specialty. I want to protect her, but she's not mine. I hope Noah's up for the task.

I grab my keys and go for a jog. The air is thick with humidity; it pulses around me, distracting me from my thoughts. Drenched as soon as I leave my condo, I turn left out of my building and head for the beach. It's peak hour for traffic. I cut through the bumpers, ignoring the agitated eyes that follow me across the street. Mercedes, BMWs, Audis—the people in my neighborhood are not short on cash. It feels good to run. My condo is a mile from the beach. You have to cross two waterways to get there. I glance at the yachts as I dodge a couple strollers and think about my boat. It's been a while since I worked on it. Maybe that's what I need—a day with the boat. When I reach the water, I make a sharp left and run along the shore. This is where I deal with my anger.

I run until I can't. Then I sit in the sand, breathing hard. I have to pull myself together. If I wade in this sewer of emotion for much longer, I might never come out. Pulling my cell from my pocket, I hit the home button. My mother answers, breathless, like she's been on her elliptical. We pass through the niceties. No matter what the situation, no matter how desperate my voice could be, my mother will politely inquire how I am and then give me a brief update on her roses. I wait until she's finished, and then say in a more strangled voice than I intend, "I'm going to take the job in London."

There is a moment of shocked silence before she responds. Her voice is overly happy. "Caleb, it's the right thing. Thank God it came around again. You turned it down the last time for that girl; what a mistake that wa—"

I cut her off, tell her I'll call tomorrow after I've spoken to the London office. I take one more look at the ocean before I head home. Tomorrow I'm going to London.

But, I don't.

I wake up to pounding. At first I think it's the construction going on in my building. 760 is remodeling their kitchen. I crush my head beneath my pillow. It does nothing to mute the sound. Swearing, I toss it aside. The pounding sounds closer to home. I roll onto my back and listen. The room rocks on its axis. Too much Scotch—again. The pounding is coming from my front door. I swing my legs over the side of the bed and pull on a pair of grey pajama pants I find lying on the floor. I cross my living room, kicking aside shoes and piles of clothes that have been gathering for weeks. I fling open the door, and everything freezes. Breath...beats of heart...thought.

Neither of us says a word as we size each other up. Then she pushes past me and starts pacing my living room, like showing up here is the most natural thing in the world. I'm still standing at the open door, watching her in confusion, when she turns the full battery of her eyes on me. It takes me a minute to speak, to realize this is really happening. I can hear someone using a drill in the condo upstairs. I can see a bird making its way across the sky, just outside my window, but I tell myself that my senses are lying in regards to her. She's not really here after all these years.

"What are you doing here, Duchess?"

I take her in, absorb her. She looks manic; her hair is braided down her back, but there are pieces of it that have come loose all around her face. Her eyes are lined in kohl, drenched in emotion. I've never seen her wear her makeup like that before. She throws her arms wide; it's an angry gesture. I brace myself for the string of expletives that usually come with her anger.

"What? You don't clean anymore?"

Not what I was expecting. I kick the door shut with my foot and run a hand along the back of my neck. I haven't shaved in three days, and all I'm wearing is a pair of pajama pants. My house looks like a college dorm.

I edge my way to the sofa as if this isn't my living room and I sit down, uncomfortable. I watch her pace.

Suddenly, she stops. "I let him loose. I put him back on the street. He's a fucking psycho!" She slaps a fist into her open palm on the last word. Her foot touches an empty bottle of Scotch, and it rolls across the hardwood. We both follow it with our eyes until it disappears under the table.

"What the fuck is wrong with you?" she asks, looking around.

I lean back and link my hands behind my neck. I trace her gaze to the disaster that is my condo.

"You should have thought of that before you took the case."

She looks ready to punch me. Her eyes start at my hair, work down to my beard, linger on my chest, and scoop back up to my face. All of a sudden, she's sober. I see it fill her eyes, the realization that she came here and she shouldn't have. We both make our move at the same time. She bolts for the door; I jump up and block her.

She keeps her distance, tucking her bottom lip under her teeth, kohl eyes looking less sure.

"Your move," I say.

I see her throat spasm as she swallows her thoughts, swallows ten years of us.

"All right…all right!" she says finally. She walks back around the couch and sits down on the recliner. We've begun our usual game of cat and mouse. I'm comfortable with this.

I sit on the love seat and stare at her expectantly. She uses her thumb to spin her wedding band. When she sees me watching, she stops. I almost laugh when she pulls up the foot of the recliner and slouches backwards like she belongs here.

"Do you have a Coke?"

I stand up and get her a bottle from my fridge. I don't drink Coke, but I always have it in my fridge. Maybe it's for her. I don't know. She pops the cap, pressing the bottle against her lips and chugging. She loves the burn.

When she's done, she wipes the back of her hand across her mouth and stares at me like I'm the snake. *She's the snake.*

"Should we try being friends?"

I open my hands and tilt my head like I don't know what she's talking about. I do. We can't stay away, so what's the alternative? She hiccups from the Coke.

"You know, I've never met anyone that can say as much as you, without a single word coming out of his mouth," she snaps.

I grin. Usually, if I let her talk without interrupting her, she'll tell me more than she intended.

"I hate myself. I might as well have been the one to put Casey fucking Anthony back on the street."

"Where's Noah?"

"Germany."

I raise my eyebrows. "He was out of the country for the verdict?"

"Shut up. We didn't know how long they'd take to deliberate."

"You should be celebrating." I lean back and sling both arms across the back of the couch.

She starts to cry, stoic-faced, tears pouring like an open tap.

I stay where I am. I want to comfort her, but when I touch her, it's hard to stop.

"You remember that time in college when you started crying because you thought you were going to fail that test, and the professor thought you were having a seizure?"

She cracks up. I relax.

"You did your job, Duchess," I say softly. "You did it well."

She nods, gets up. Our time is over.

"Caleb…I—"

I shake my head. I don't want her to say she's sorry for coming, or that it won't happen again.

I walk her to the door.

"Am I supposed to say I'm sorry for what happened with Leah?" She looks at me through her lashes. Her tears have clumped her mascara together. On another woman it would look sloppy; on Olivia it looks like sex.

"I wouldn't believe you if you did."

She smiles; it starts in her eyes and spreads slowly to her lips.

"Come over for dinner. Noah's always wanted to meet you." She must see the skepticism on my face, because she laughs. "He's great. Really. Bring a date?"

I run my hand over my face and shake my head. "Dinner with your husband is not on my bucket list."

"Neither was defending your ex-wife in a lawsuit."

I flinch. "Ouch."

"See you next Tuesday at seven?" She winks at me and practically skips out of my condo.

I don't agree, but she knows I'll be there.

Damn. I'm whipped.

TWO

PRESENT

I call my date. She's running behind schedule as usual. I've seen her twice a week for the last three months. It came as a surprise how much I enjoy her company, especially after what happened with Leah. I felt done with women for a while, but I guess I'm an addict.

We agree to meet at Olivia's instead of driving together. I text her Olivia's address while I trim the beard down to a goatee. I go for James Dean and wear blue jeans and a white shirt. There is still a tan line where my wedding band used to be. For the first month after the divorce, I found myself constantly feeling for the ring, having a moment of panic every time I saw my empty finger and thinking that I'd lost it. The truth always choked me, like a mouth full of cotton. I lost my marriage, not my ring, and it had been my fault. Forever became five years; until death do us part became irreconcilable differences. I still miss it, or maybe the idea of it. My mother always said I was born to be married. I rub at the empty spot as I wait for the elevator in her building.

She's still in the same condo. I came here once during Leah's trial. It's about three times the size of mine, with floor-to-ceiling windows that overlook the ocean. She's a show-off. Olivia doesn't even like the ocean. The closest I've ever seen her get is to stick in her big toe. She's on the top floor. I clutch the bottle of wine as the elevator pings and the door slides open. She's the only one on this floor.

I take inventory of the hallway: a pair of men's tennis shoes—his, a plant—his, a plaque on the door that says *Go Away!*—hers. I eye it all warily. I would have to be on my best behavior—no flirting, no touching, no undressing her with my eyes. I'd just have to focus on my date, and that shouldn't be a problem. I smile to myself as I anticipate Olivia's reaction. The door opens before I can reach for the bell. A man fills the space. We stare at each other for a good ten seconds, and I have a brief moment of awkwardness. Did she forget to tell him that I was coming? Then he runs a hand through his semi-damp hair, and his face moves into a smile.

"Caleb," he says.

Haon

I give him a once-over. He's a few inches shorter than I am, but he's stockier—well built. Dark hair, cut short—there is grey at his temples. I peg him at about thirty-five, though I know from the P.I. I hired that he's thirty-nine. He's Jewish; if his look didn't tell me that, the Star of David around his neck would have. He's a good-looking guy.

"Noah." He holds out his hand. I grin as I shake it. The irony that both of our hands have touched his wife gives me a bit of a mean edge.

"She sent me out here to get these," he says, scooping up the tennis shoes.

"Don't let her know that you saw them. She's a Nazi about mess."

I laugh at the fact that her Jewish husband is calling her a Nazi and follow him inside. I blink at the foyer. It's different from the last time I was here. She's replaced all the cold white and black with warm colors. It looks like a home—wood floors, rugs, knickknacks. Jealousy rips through me, and I push it aside as she comes trotting out of the kitchen pulling off an apron.

She tosses it aside and hugs me. For a scat of a second it feels right, her coming toward me with such determination. Then she holds her body stiff, instead of letting it melt into me. I can't help but feel thwarted. I have to taper my smile, which always spreads hard and fast when she's near. Noah is watching us, so I hand her the wine.

"Hello, Du—Olivia. I wasn't sure what was for dinner, so I brought red."

"Malbec," she says, grinning at Noah. "Your favorite." I see genuine affection in her eyes when she looks at him. I wonder if that's how I looked at Leah, and how Olivia stood it for all those months during the trial.

"We're having lamb," she says. "So, it's just perfect."

The doorbell rings. I immediately feel more cheerful. Olivia's head shoots toward me and she looks in my eyes, trying to decide what I'm up to. I allow a slow smile to spread across my face. I'm finally going to get my answer. She either feels what I do or she doesn't. Noah retreats a few steps to open it, and we stay with our eyes locked. Her body is frozen, tense, anticipating what I am about to deliver. I hear my date's voice behind me. Olivia's eyes skirt past me to where Noah is temporarily blocking her view of my date, then he steps aside, and I see what I was waiting for. Olivia shocked, Olivia disarmed, Olivia angry. The color drains from her face, and her hand shoots up to her collarbone to grab at her necklace—a simple diamond on a chain. Noah arrives at my shoulder, and I turn to smile at Jessica. Jessica Alexander.

"Jess, you remember Olivia," I say. She nods and genuinely beams at the raven-haired villain that knocked her out of my life like she was a bowling pin. "Hello, stranger," she says. She lurches forward and embraces Olivia in a surprise hug. "Long time, no see."

Jessica Alexander found me on Facebook. She messaged me to say she was living in the Miami area again and wanted to get together for drinks. I was drunk when I read the message and responded with my number. We met up the next day at Bar Louie. She looked the same: long hair, long legs, short skirt. My college taste still appealed to me, and so did her personality—which was surprisingly even sweeter than I remembered. I needed a nice, long dose of sweet after the last two vipers I loved. Neither of us brought up the baby, but I did tell her about Estella. What I gathered was that she had no idea about Olivia's part in our breakup. We saw each other regularly after that. We have yet to share a bed.

I watch Olivia's face over Jess's shoulder. She has always had a knack for self-control. And then she does the damnedest thing. She laughs and hugs Jess back, like they're old friends. I'm in such a state of shock I almost take a step back. Noah is watching everything unfold with mild curiosity. We are all just characters to him, no doubt.

"Come in, come in." She ushers us into the living room and shoots me a triumphant look. I realize that she's not a better person, just a better actress.

Touché. There is still fun to be had.

Jess runs off to help Olivia in the kitchen, which leaves Noah and me with a plate of Brie and crackers. We do the small talk thing for about ten minutes. The go-to topic for men is sports—Marlins, Heat, Dolphins... quarterbacks, starters, pitchers—things I don't fucking care about anymore.

"Are you uncomfortable?"

I look at him in surprise. *He knows. Well, shit.* But, the honesty sets me at ease at least.

"Wouldn't you be?" I accept the whiskey he hands me. Single malt, black label—decent.

He sits down across from me and grins. "Sure."

I don't bother him, so how much could he really know? Unless...unless he's so secure in their relationship he feels like there is nothing to worry about. I sit back and eye the situation with new perspective. He's not the jealous type, obviously.

"If you don't have a problem with it, I don't either," I say.

He throws his ankle across his knee and settles back in his chair. "Did you have me checked out?"

"Background check in three different countries." I take a sip and curl my tongue around the flavor.

Noah nods like he expected this. "Find anything you didn't like?"

I shrug. "You married my first love; I already didn't like you."

He tucks in one corner of his mouth in a knowing smile and nods slowly.

"You care about her, Caleb. That's fine with me. You and I won't have a problem as long as you keep your hands off of my wife."

The girls come in. We stand. Olivia can sense there has been an exchange. Her ever-cold eyes travel between the two of us.

Choose me.

Her gaze lands on Noah. Their intimacy makes me jealous. Rageful. I grind my teeth until Olivia notices. I stop as soon as her eyes trace my jaw, but it's too late. She's seen what I'm feeling.

A perfect eyebrow arches up.

God. I hate it when she does that.

I want to spank her.

The lamb is overcooked and the asparagus is mushy. I am so impressed that her spiteful little hands are now cooking; I clean my plate and have seconds. She drinks three glasses of wine so casually I wonder if it has become a habit or if this dinner is making her nervous. We talk about her clients, and she has everyone laughing. Noah is clearly infatuated by her. He watches everything she does with a slight smile on his lips. It reminds me of myself. She asks

Jessica questions about what she has been doing with her life. It makes me uncomfortable. I am careful not to speak only to her, not to look at her too much, not to look away when she interacts with Noah, because it bothers me. It's hard not to study their dynamic. She is genuinely fond of him. I notice that her personality is softer when he's around. She has not cussed once since I stepped through their door—which is the longest her mouth has ever been clean in the history of Olivia.

Her mouth.

Noah is one of those rare personalities that has a calming effect on a potentially tripe situation. I can't help but like the guy even though he has my girl. He has the balls to threaten me too.

As we say our goodbyes in their foyer, Olivia refuses to meet my eyes. She looks exhausted, like the night has taken its toll on her emotionally. She stands close to Noah, and I see her reach for his hand. I want to know what she's feeling. I want to be the one to comfort her.

Jess comes home with me and spends the night. My mother has left four messages asking about my move to London.

I wake up to the smell of bacon. I can hear the clang of pots and water running in the sink. I walk naked to the kitchen. Jess is making breakfast. I lean over the counter and watch her. I was married to a woman for five years and rarely did I see her crack an egg. She's wearing one of my T-shirts. Her hair is pulled up in a messy knot. It's very sexy. I eye her legs; they go on forever. I'm a leg guy. The scene in *Pretty Woman* where Vivian is telling Richard the exact measurement of her legs is one of the best scenes in the movie. A lot can be forgiven if a woman has a great set of legs.

Jessica's are unparalleled.

I sit as she hands me a mug of coffee and smiles shyly like we've never done this before. I really like her. I loved her once; it would be easy to fall into this woman again. She's beautiful—more beautiful than Leah, more beautiful than Olivia. *Can anyone be more beautiful than Olivia?*

"I didn't want to wake you," she says. "So I kept myself busy with feeding you."

"Feeding me," I repeat. I like that.

"I like doing things for you." She smiles coyly. "I've missed you, Caleb."

I blink at her. What would have happened if she had told me she was pregnant, instead of going to get an abortion? We'd have a ten-year-old.

I pull her to me and kiss her. She never fights, never acts like she doesn't want me. I take her to the couch and we let the toast burn.

Later, I'm sitting at the café down the street, drinking espresso. Jess had to go to work. My phone pings, signaling a text message.

O: Well?

I smile to myself and finish my espresso before answering.

Well, what?

There is a long pause. She's thinking about how to suck the information out of me without sounding like she cares.

O: Don't play games!

I remember the last time you asked me not to do that. I think we were in an orange grove.

O: Fuck you. What did you think of Noah?

Nice

What did you think of Jess?

O: Same stupid slut

I crack up. The other patrons of the café turn to see what I'm laughing at.

I gather up my things to leave. She always did get right to the point. I am almost to my car when my phone pings again.

O: Don't fall in love with her.

I stare at that message for a long time. One minute—three. What does she want from me? I don't respond. I feel like she's punched me.

And that's it. I don't hear from her for another year.

THREE

PAST

The first time I saw her—my God—it was like I'd never seen another woman in all my life. It was the way she walked that caught my eye. She moved like water: fluid, determined. Everything else blended together in a blur and all I saw was her. The only solid in all that color. I smiled when she stopped under this grotesque, twisted-looking tree and gave it the single dirtiest look I had ever seen. I'd never even noticed the tree before, though it was one of those things that when you see it, you wonder how you'd ever missed it. One of my friends punched me on the arm to get my attention. We'd been talking about basketball. The coach put half the team on suspension for smoking pot, and now we had to get through the last few games with our best players benched for the rest of the season. But the conversation had ended for me the minute I saw her. They followed my eyes, gave each other knowing looks. I had somewhat of a reputation in regards to women. They were still calling out remarks when I stepped under the tree. Her back was to me. She had the type of hair you wanted to wrap your hands in—dark and wild, all the way to her tiny waist. My first words to her should have been: *Will you marry me?* Instead, I went with: "Why are you angry with the tree?"

She spun on me so fast I drew back. She set me on my axis, wobbling and unsure. These were all feelings I was not well acquainted with. The rest of our exchange pockmarked my ego.

"Just a question, Sunshine, don't attack." Holy shit, she was hostile.

"Can I help you with something?" she snapped.

"I was interested in finding out why this tree made you frown." It was lame, but what the hell else was I supposed to say? She'd either had a really bad day, or she was always like this, and either way I was compelled to stand in the shade and talk to her.

Suddenly, she looked tired. "Are you trying to flirt with me?"

Damn. This had turned into one of the strangest female encounters I'd ever had. So, I told her my name.

"I'm sorry, what?"

"My name…" I offered her my hand. I just wanted to touch her. She was ice cold. It was like her personality seeped out of her skin. She pulled her little hand away too quickly.

"Yes, I was trying to flirt with you, until you shot me down, that is." I don't think in all the days I'd been alive and breathing, I'd ever shaken hands with a girl I wanted. It was awkward. For her too. Her brow creased, and she looked around the parking lot like she wanted someone to come save her.

"Listen, I'd love to stand around and feed into your ego with chitchattery, but I have to go."

Chitchattery. She just made up a word and used it in a sentence to insult me. God. Who the hell was this woman? And if I could get her to stop being hostile, what would she taste like? She had already started walking away. I had to do something or say something that would at least make her remember me. So, I decided to insult her back.

"If you were born an animal, you'd be a llama," I called after her. It was true. I happened to really like llamas. They were reserved and they always gave you the stink eye. When you pissed them off, they spat at you. I'd seen it happen to my brother at a petting zoo once. That's when they became my favorite animal. But, she didn't know that. She just knew I was comparing her to an animal. And it pissed her off.

"I'll see you around," I said, before turning away. And I would. I was going to chase this chilly, abrasive woman. I'd chase her all the way to her fucking ice palace and melt it down if I had to. I was used to women wanting me; she wanted nothing to do with me—wouldn't even tell me her name. As I watched her walk away I knew two things: I wanted her, and it was going to be a lot of work.

No one knew who she was. I was completely baffled by it. The girl was so high above anything I'd ever seen, I thought every guy on campus would respond to my description—wicked dark hair, seething eyes, a waist small enough to wrap your hands around. I had to use my connections in the admissions office with a girl I'd dated in high school who still had a thing for me.

"Caleb, I'm not allowed to do this," she said, leaning over the counter. I ignored her attempt at getting me to look at her cleavage.

"Just this once, Rey." That's all it took.

"Okay, building?"

I'd seen her walking into Conner's.

"There are over five hundred girls in Conner's. You're going to have to be more specific."

"Sophomore," I said, guessing.

She typed something into her keyboard. "Great, now we have two hundred."

I racked my brain for something else. Blue jeans, white shirt, black fingernail polish. I could take a guess at her major.

"Try pre-law or philosophy," I said. She had one of those combative personalities that lawyers specialized in. But, she was staring up at a tree, deep in thought…

Rey looked around and then quickly spun the monitor toward me. I glanced through the column of photographs. There were about thirty to a page. She scrolled and my eyes searched.

"Hurry up, Casanova. I could get in trouble for this, you know."

"She's not there," I said after a few seconds. I tried to look nonchalant. "Oh well, guess I'm out of luck this time. Thanks anyway."

Rey opened her mouth to say something, but I gave her a quick wave and jogged out. Her picture had been there, third from the top. I hadn't wanted to put her on Rey's radar—she had the bad habit of spreading rumors about the girls I liked.

Olivia Kaspen. *Aivilo.* What a perfect little name for a perfect little snob. I smiled all the way back to the dorms.

I looked for her everywhere. She didn't go to the gym. She was never in the cafeteria or at any of our home games. I went back to the spot I first saw her and hung out outside of her dorm. Nothing. She was either a first-class hermit or I'd imagined the whole thing. Olivia Kaspen. A cross between Snow White and The Evil Queen. I had to find her.

I wasn't smiling a week later. I'd spotted her in the stands at one of our last games of the season. We'd made it to the playoffs and were leading the game by ten points. The minute I saw her, I was distracted. I kept glancing up into the stands where she was sitting, clutching a styrofoam cup between her hands. One thing was clear—she wasn't looking at me. I don't know what possessed me to believe that I could impress her with my game play, but I tried. The visiting team went on a ten-nothing run. The game was tied. I stood at the free-throw line, and to this day I don't know what possessed me to pull the little stunt that cost us the game. I jogged over to my coach. Normally a stunt like that would have gotten me kicked off the team, but I happened to be the BMOC and it helped that he was a family friend.

"I can't focus. I have to take care of something," I told him.

"Caleb, you have to be fucking with me right now."

"Coach," I said quietly. "Give me two minutes."

He narrowed his eyes and stared at me over his glasses. "Is this about that girl?"

My blood ran cold. My coach was an insightful guy, but—

"The one who's missing?" he finished.

I stared at him blankly. Laura? We'd dated, but not seriously. I wondered if my parents had said something to him. My mother was friends with her mother. She had been enthusiastic when we'd started dating, but Laura was all looks and no personality. We had fizzled out almost immediately. Before I could correct him, he said, "Go. Hurry up."

He called a time out and put the team in a huddle.

I took the stairs two at a time. The closer I got, the paler she got, and she was already pretty pale. When I crouched down next to her, her eyes were wide and she looked ready to bolt.

"Olivia," I said. "Olivia Kaspen."

She looked momentarily shocked. She composed herself quickly. Her eyes danced around my face before she leaned toward me and said, "Bravo, you found out my name." Then in a lower voice, "What the hell are you doing?"

"You're quite the mystery on campus," I said, tracing the outline of her lips with my eyes. I'd never seen such sensual lips in all my life. How had it taken me this long to find those lips?

"Are you going to be making a point any time soon, or are you holding up the game to brag about your detective skills?"

Oh my God. How could I not laugh at that? I wanted to tell her right then and there that she was going to marry me, but I was pretty sure she'd slap me if I did. I decided to turn on the charm. It would have worked with any other girl. But, damn if she shot me down.

"If I make this shot, will you go out with me?"

She all but rolled her eyes. The look on her pretty little face was of absolute disgust. Then she stole my line and called me a peacock.

"It took you all week to think up that one, didn't it?" I said, smirking. I was fairly certain at that point she was playing hard to get.

"Sure," she said, shrugging.

"So then, it's fair to say that you were thinking about me all week?"

When I was a kid I watched a helluva lot of Looney Tunes. Smoke was always coming out of the characters' noses when they were angry. Usually, it lifted them right off the ground. The expression on Olivia's face was that of smoke coming out of her nose.

"No…and…no, I will not go out with you." She wasn't looking at me anymore. I wanted to grab her chin and steer her face back to mine.

"Why not?" My first inclination was to say: *Why the hell not?*

"Because I am a llama and you are a bird and WE are not compatible."

"Okay," I breathed. "Then what will it take?" I was completely out of my element—begging a girl to go on a date with me. This was fucked up.

"Miss it."

I stared into her cold, blue eyes and knew I'd just met the kind of girl books are written about. There was no one like her.

"Miss it," she said again, "and I'll go out with you."

I didn't say another word. I was in shock. I jogged back to the court, my mind so stuffed with opposing thoughts I figured I'd die of a brain explosion before I got to make the shot. I wasn't going to do it. It was crazy. She was crazy. Fuck. That. Shit.

But, when I stood at the free-throw line, ball in hand, I had a couple seconds of deep thought. I was angry. I should have done what came naturally, which was to win the game, but I kept seeing her face. The way she looked down her nose at me and said, "Miss it." There had been something in her eyes that I couldn't shake. She asked me to do the impossible. She set the bar high and she expected me to fail.

I raised the ball, my palms curved around it like it was an extension of my body. How many hours did I spend playing basketball each week? Twenty…thirty? It was nothing for me to make this basket—I could do it with my eyes closed. But, something about the look on her face tied an invisible string around my wrist, making me clutch the ball harder than I normally would. I could see the sad victory on her face, like she had resigned herself to all men being disappointments. She was wrong if she thought that she could predict what I was going to do. If I wanted her…

I wanted her.

I missed the shot.

I was in way over my head.

FOUR
PAST

I missed a shot. People looked at me like I'd gunned down a gym full of people instead of shooting an air ball. My mother was always teasing me, telling me that I didn't take anything seriously. It was a joke in my family—my lack of dedication to anything. I was good at most everything I did, but I didn't love any of it. Not basketball or finance, or boating, or the money that came so easily to my family. It all made me feel empty. My friends—the ones I'd grown up with—spent their time and money getting box seats or floor seats at baseball games and football games and basketball games. I'd go to the goddamn games and enjoy them, but at the end of the day, there wasn't a damn thing that filled me. I started reading books about philosophy. I even took a couple classes my sophomore year. I liked it. Philosophy gave me something to believe in. But, Olivia Kaspen stepped into my life, and for the first time, I was dedicated to something. Her philosophy. Her emotional makeup. I was taking her seriously. All five feet, two inches of her. She was mouthy and condescending and she never smiled, but I liked her. I wanted to give her something. So I missed the shot.

"Is it true?"

I looked up from my plate of pancakes. Desiree, one of the cheerleaders, slid into the seat opposite me. She was wearing her makeup from the night before and my buddy, Kiel's jersey. Why did girls want to wear a guy's jersey? *Eerised.*

"Is what true?"

"You missed the shot for a girl?"

"Where did you hear that?" I pushed my plate away and took a sip of tea.

"Everyone is talking about it." She smirked at me and ripped off a piece of my pancake, sliding it between her teeth.

I looked at her through narrowed eyes. I was having a hard time pulling off this charming act when my palms were sweating. "Who are they saying I did it for?" If people found out it was Olivia I'd missed the shot for, things would get very uncomfortable for her.

Desiree sucked the syrup from her fingers. "Oh, there are rumors. Who knows if they're true? You know how people can be."

I shrugged, trying to be nonchalant, but my shoulders were tense.

"Humor me, Des."

She pursed her lips and leaned forward. "A pre-law major. No one really knows who she is. Some people say they saw you talking to her before you missed the shot."

"Maybe my game was just off," I said, setting my mug down and standing up.

Desiree smiled up at me. "Maybe. But, your game has never been off before. If you ask me, it's kind of romantic."

"Romantic?" I repeated.

"Yeah. She must be pretty hot."

I leaned down until both of my hands were flat on the table, and Desiree and I were at eye level.

"Does that really sound like something I would do, Des?"

She looked at me for a long minute before shaking her head.

"No, actually."

"Well, there you have your answer."

I left, wiping my palms on my pant legs. How many people had seen me speaking to Olivia? It was stupid…careless, but then I could have never anticipated her challenge. If things had gone my way, she would have agreed to a date for *making* the shot. Everyone would have walked away a winner, aka I would have walked away the winner.

I couldn't help but smile as I jogged down the stairs in front of the dining hall. Forget it. Girls rarely surprised me. I would have missed that shot five hundred times for a date with her.

I'd never felt anything like her.

Olivia burned. When she walked into a room you could feel her fire. It rolled off of her in waves. She was angry and passionate and fearless. She burned hot enough to keep everyone away. It was a good trick, except I played with fire.

Bang, bang, she shot me down.

"I just don't think we're compatible."

She was afraid of me. I knew it the moment we locked eyes that first day, under the tree. She might not have known her type, but I knew it.

I almost laughed. She delivered those words in her clipped, matter-of-fact voice, her eyes dancing everywhere but my face. We'd been on our first date the week before. I'd practically conned her into it, sending the very basketball that I'd used to procure the date, to her dorm room with a note to meet me in the library. The library had gone well. She wore this long sleeve, black lace shirt that was so tight, I could see every curve, not to mention her ivory skin peeking through all of the eyelets in the lace. I wanted to kiss her, right there, in the stacks. I would have pushed her up against the Dickens' section if I hadn't thought it would scare her away. Reluctantly, she agreed to the date. I took her to Jaxson's, my favorite ice cream place. At the start of the evening, she'd been standoffish, but then she opened up and told me things about her past. I thought things had gone great. Until…

I just don't think we're compatible.

"That's not how it feels to me," I said. Our chemistry was palatable. She was either in denial or lying her ass off. I'd bet anything it was the latter.

She blinked at me—fast little blinks, like bird wings.

"Um, well, I'm sorry. I guess we're just on two different wavelengths." She dragged out *wavelengths*, as if she wasn't sure that was the right word to use. We were actually on the same wavelength—I wanted her and she wanted me, but I wasn't going to be the one to point that out. Olivia didn't know she wanted me yet.

"No, that's not what I meant. I know you like me just as much as I like you. But, it's your choice, and I am a gentleman. You want me to back off? Okay. Goodbye, Olivia."

Before I could grab her, before I could shake sense into her, I walked away.

Don't walk away! Fight her on this!

That's what I was thinking. But, the last thing I wanted to do was chase after someone who didn't want me…or didn't know they wanted me.

I went back to my dorm room and drank warm beer. Rejected for the first time—it wasn't pretty. It was pretty fucked up, actually. Or at least that's what I thought then. I'd done everything she'd asked me to do. My teammates were barely talking to me, my coach had put me on suspension, and my heart was hurting. *Hurting.* How could I be feeling this way over someone I'd just met?

I took a sip of my beer, pulled out my Statistics textbook, and stared at the page for thirty minutes without ever seeing anything. No, that's not true. I was seeing Olivia Kaspen.

I saw her everywhere. I pretended not to. I pretended that she was just another girl, not the girl I wanted. My friends thought I'd lost it. I wanted her because I couldn't have her—that was the consensus. Maybe it was true. They had taken to slapping me on the back and pointing out random girls on campus who would sleep with me. Sex therapy, they called it. I tried it once or twice, but it was ineffective. I was benched, rejected, and drunk on a girl I'd only kissed once. When someone mentioned that she was probably a lesbian, I pounced on the idea. Then, just months after she told me that we weren't compatible, she started seeing the biggest load of douchebags I had ever laid eyes on. I fucking hated them. So, I moved on. She wasn't what I thought she was.

Then I met Jessica. The first thing she ever said to me was, "Damn, I don't know if I want to lick you or marry you."

I'd said, "How about both?" And that was it. We were together. Jessica Alexander was sexy and kind and ditzy—my type exactly. She was smart too, but you'd never know it from the way she babbled on and on about insignificant things like clothes and movies. I liked being with her. I liked having sex with her. She took away the constant edge I felt. Olivia gradually receded to the back of my mind. I could joke about it after a while. In retrospect, it seemed funny that I'd become so obsessed with a girl I barely knew. Then right when everything was going my way, I found out that Jessica was pregnant and had an abortion behind my back. She wasn't the one to tell me. That's what killed me. She made the decision without me. That was my baby—mine. I wanted that baby. I would have taken the baby even if Jessica didn't want it. I punched a tree, sprained my wrist, and went into dating hibernation.

After my parents divorced, my mother wanted to move to America. She was born in Michigan. Her father—my grandfather—met my grandmother at Cambridge where he was studying abroad. When they got married, they moved back to the States for a while and had my mother. But, when my grandmother was homesick, my grandfather sold their land and house, and moved back to England for her. My parents ran in the same social circles and they happened to happen. She nixed the "Sams and Alfreds and Charlies" and gave my brother and me American-sounding names. When she caught him cheating for the third time, she packed us up and moved us to America. I took it way harder than my brother. I blamed my mother for a while, until I flew to England for my dad's fourth marriage. When I saw him taking vows for the fourth time, I *got it.* I wasn't even sure what this wife's name was. Elizabeth? Victoria? I was pretty sure it was a Queen of England. But, I knew I didn't believe in divorce. You couldn't make vows and just break them. If I married a woman, I was going to stay married. I wouldn't treat marriage like a lease. Ever.

I wanted to marry Jessica. I mean, it's not like I bought her a ring, but I saw her fitting into my world. My mother liked her; Jessica loved me. It was so easy. But, when I found out she had an abortion and didn't even bother telling me she was pregnant, I lost it. I at least wanted a say with my child.

Then Olivia came back. She came back, dancing like a siren. I knew exactly what she was doing the night she came to my frat house and cocked her finger at me from the dance floor. If she hadn't come to me, I would have gone to her. *Forget all you know*—I said to myself. *This is the one you belong with.* I don't know how I knew that. Maybe our souls touched underneath that tree. Maybe I decided to love her. Maybe love wasn't our choice. But when I looked at that woman, I saw myself differently. And it wasn't in a good light. Not a thing would keep me from her. And that could make a person do things they never thought themselves capable of. What I felt for her scared the hell out of me. It was a consuming obsession.

In truth, I'd barely touched on the obsession. That was still coming.

FIVE

PRESENT

"Pass the butter, please."

Damn.

I pass her the butter, but not before I assess the density of that request. When you're passing a woman butter across the table, you're in something serious. I grab her tanned arm as she reaches for it and kiss the inside of her wrist. She smells like clean linen. She smiles at me—she's always smiling. She has dimples; the deeper she smiles, the deeper they cut. Jessica and I don't officially live together, but we alternate between each other's places. Mostly we are here, but that's because I like my own bed. I watch her butter her toast while she plays on her iPad. We have a nice little thing going on. I still feel like a barren wasteland on the inside, but she makes it better.

"Pass the salt, please." I test this out. See how it feels. She passes the saltshaker without looking up, and I frown. Everyone knows you don't pass the salt without the pepper. They're a pair. Even if someone only asks for one, you pass both. Now I'm going to have to break up with her.

Kidding.

We get ready for work and kiss at the bottom of the elevator.

"Caleb," she says, as I'm walking away.

"Yeah?"

"I love you."

Wow. Okay.

"Jess," I say. "I—"

"You don't have to say it back." She smiles. "I just want you to know."

"All right," I say, slowly. "I'll see you tonight, yeah?"

She nods.

Eight months, one week—that's how long it has been since she spent the night at my place for the first time. *Acissej*—it doesn't really roll off the tongue like some of them do. What she just said feels strange, but I can't pinpoint why. Maybe it's time to move in together. I climb into my car and put the AC on full blast. She likes my facial hair. Leah wouldn't tolerate facial hair. She said it chaffed her face. When she used the word *chaffed* I wanted to divorce her. Or maybe I just always wanted to divorce her. When I think about Leah, I feel sick. Not because of her—she has very little power over me anymore. It's that little girl.

I pull my thoughts away from that. When I get to work, my mother is at the office, visiting Steve.

"He's never home anymore, and you hardly come to visit," she says, hugging me. "I have to come here to see my two boys."

She doesn't mention my brother. She's just as pissed at him as I am for sleeping with my ex-wife. Leah dropped that little bomb on me the same night she told me I wasn't a father. I'd be lying if I hadn't thought a million times over that Estella might be his. That hurts the most.

"How's Jessica?" my mother asks.

I half smile and sort through the papers on my desk. She has taken a seat in my office, so I know she's here to chat. If I don't give her something, she won't go away.

"She told me she loved me this morning."

"Well, did you say it back?"

"No."

She's quiet for a few minutes.

"I really liked Leah," she says. "When you lost your memory, she really just stuck with you. As a mother, I appreciated that." She sighs. "But, I know you still love *that* girl."

My turn to sigh.

"I don't know what you're talking about. And even if I did, I wouldn't want to talk about it. So talk about something else. How are your roses?"

"Don't even," she says. "Jessica is great, Caleb. Really, she is. But, she wants a commitment. You do know that, don't you?"

"Yes."

"Do you want to be married again? Have…children?"

I flinch.

"Not really."

"You can't let one woman steal who you are."

I appreciate my mother, I do. But, she has no idea what she's talking about. My heart is still broken. I'm trying to figure out how to live without what I really want. That includes letting go of old dreams and making some new ones. I think, anyway.

"I don't want those things anymore," I say firmly.

"I saw Estella."

I freeze.

"What?"

"At the mall. I ran into Leah and she was with her."

I'm quiet. I don't know what to say. How is she? Was she talking? What does she look like?

I run a hand across the back of my neck and stare at the armrest on her chair.

"She was my granddaughter. I love her." Her voice drops off at the end, and for the first time, I consider my mother's feelings in all of this. She lost Estella too.

"She's yours, Caleb. I feel it."

"Mother, stop it…"

"No, I won't. You get a paternity test. There is something not right."

I stop what I'm doing and sit down. "Why would she lie to me about that? She loses child support, babysitting, and claim on me, by lying."

"Oh, Caleb. Leah is the type of girl who values revenge more than practicality."

I get goosebumps. Honest to God.

I shake my head. "You want that to be true. I do too. But, it's not. There is a good chance she *is* your grandchild. Talk to your son."

She pulls her mouth tight. It makes her look older.

"Just think about it," she says. "If she refuses, you can get the court to order one." She leans forward. "Caleb, she has your nose."

"Fuck. Okay, we're done here." I never curse in front of her. I stand up and walk her to the door. Before I push her out, I kiss her on the cheek. "You're a good mother. But, I'm a grown-up. Go meddle in Seth's life."

She smiles, pats my cheek, and looks more worried than before.

"Goodbye, my son."

SIX

PAST

I had her. It wasn't a firm grip, but I finally had her. We fell into a relationship easily. The day-to-day routine was light and airy. We played, we kissed, we talked for hours about things that mattered and things that didn't. I could never predict what she was going to say next. I liked that. She was so different from the girls I was used to. Even Jessica—who was the closest thing I'd come to falling in love—had never elicited the feelings from me that Olivia did.

There was one day in particular when we were talking about how many kids we wanted—or maybe I was talking about it. Olivia shied away from the future.

"Five—I want five."

She raised an eyebrow and crinkled her nose. "That's too many. What if your wife doesn't want that many?"

We had taken a drive to the beach and were lying on a blanket pretending to look at the stars, but mostly we were looking at each other.

"I guess you and I can come to a compromise."

She started blinking rapidly as if something had flown in her eye.

"I don't want children," she said, looking away.

"Yes, you do."

She hated when I did that—told her she was wrong about her own thoughts.

I leaned up on my elbows and looked at the water to avoid the dirty look she was giving me.

"You're not going to mess them up," I said. "You're not going to be like your father, and you will not land up like your mother because I will never leave you."

"I'll die of cancer then."

"No, you won't. We'll have you checked regularly."

"How do you always fucking know what I'm thinking?"

I looked over at her. She was sitting up with her knees pulled to her chest and her head resting on her knees. Her hair was piled on top of her head in a large, almost comical knot. I wanted to pull it out and let it tumble down her back, but she looked so cute, I left it.

"I see you, even when you think I'm not looking. I'm probably more obsessed with you than is healthy."

She tried to swallow her smile, but I saw it pinching the corners of her mouth. I tackled her to her back. She giggled. She hardly ever giggled…I could probably count the number of times I'd heard that sound on my two hands.

"You don't give an inch. That's why I like you, Olivia—no middle name—Kaspen. You make me work for every smile, every giggle…"

She shook her head. "I don't giggle."

"Really?" My fingers crept up her ribs. I tickled her. She giggled so hard, I was laughing too.

When we sobered up, she lay with her head on my chest. Her next words took me by surprise. I lay as still as I could, barely breathing, afraid that if I moved she would stop speaking her heart.

"My mom wanted six children. She only got me, and that sucks for her because I was a total weirdo."

"You were not," I said.

She twisted her head up to look at me.

"I used to line my lips in black eyeliner and sit cross-legged on the kitchen table…meditating."

"Not that bad," I said. "Crying out for attention."

"Okay, when I was twelve I started writing letters to my birth mother because I wanted to be adopted."

I shook my head. "Your childhood sucked; you wanted a new reality."

She snorted air through her nose. "I thought a mermaid lived in my shower drain, and I used to call her Sarah and talk to her."

"Active imagination," I countered. She was becoming more insistent, her little body wriggling in my grip.

"I used to make paper out of dryer lint."

"Nerdy."

"I wanted to be one with nature, so I started boiling grass and drinking it with a little bit of dirt for sugar."

I paused. "Okay, that's weird."

"Thank you!" she said. Then, she got serious again. "My mom just loved me through all of it."

My arms tightened around her. I was afraid the wind, the water…life would take her away from me. I didn't want her to blow away.

"When she was in the hospital toward the end, she was in a lot of pain, but all she did was worry about me," she paused, laughed a little. "She had no hair. Her head looked like a shiny egg and it was always cold. I tried to knit her a hat, but it was terrible, full of holes, but of course she wore it anyway."

I could hear her tears. My heart was aching like she had it between her fist.

"She was always asking me, *'Are you hungry? Are you tired? Are you sad?'*" Her voice cracked. I ran my hand up her back, trying to comfort her, knowing I couldn't.

"I would have switched places with her."

Her sob ripped me open, spilled everything out. I sat us both up and held her in my lap as she cried.

Her pain was so jagged. You couldn't touch her without it slicing through you too. I wanted to fold myself around her and absorb the rest of the blows life would deliver.

That was the exact moment my heart threaded with hers. It was as if someone reached down with a sewing needle and stitched my soul to hers. How could one woman be so sharp and so vulnerable at the same time? Whatever would happen to her would happen to me. Whatever pain she would feel, I would feel it too. I wanted it—that was the surprising part. Selfish, self-centered Caleb Drake loved a girl so much he could already feel himself changing to accommodate her needs.

I fell.

Hard.

For the rest of this life and probably the next.

I wanted her—every last inch of her stubborn, combative, catty heart.

A few months after that, I told her I loved her for the first time. I'd loved her for a while, but I knew she wasn't ready to hear it. The minute the words were out of my mouth, she looked like she wanted to stuff them back in. Her nostrils started flaring and her skin flushed. She couldn't say it back. I was disappointed, but not surprised. I knew she loved me, but I wanted to hear it. The more she rejected me, the more aggressively I fought to tear down her walls. I pushed too far sometimes…like the camping trip. I tried to prove to her that she wasn't as autonomous as she thought. I wanted to show her that it was okay to be vulnerable and to want me. For someone like Olivia, sex was directly tied to her emotions. She tried to pretend that sex wasn't important to her—that she could have a healthy relationship without it. But, her body was her playing card. The longer she held out with sex, the longer she held onto her power.

When I walked into that tent, I was determined to strip her of her power.

"You are master of your own body, yes?"

She jutted her chin defiantly.

"Yes."

"Then you won't have a problem controlling it."

I could see the uncertainty in her eyes as I moved toward her. If she wanted to play games, I was going to play harder. She was out of her league. For the last year, I'd had to fight away every desire, every need I had. All I wanted was three words. Three words she wouldn't give me, and now she was going to pay.

She tried to walk away, but I grabbed her by the wrist and pulled her back.

The restraint I'd held back for a year sat precariously on the edge of a cliff. I let it dangle there for a minute before I shoved it off and kissed her. I kissed her like I would have kissed an experienced girl. I kissed her like I kissed her the first time, in the pool—before I knew she was so broken. She responded better than I thought. It was almost as if she'd been waiting for me to kiss her like that. She tried pushing me away a couple of times, but it was halfhearted. And even then, she never stopped kissing me. Her mind was at war with itself. I decided to give her a little help. Ripping away from her, I grabbed her flimsy T-shirt and ripped it off, neck to seam. It tore like paper. Her mouth dropped open, as I pulled the remaining fabric from her arms and tossed it aside. I pulled her toward me again and kissed her as my fingers found the clasp on her bra and flicked it off. She was against me now, skin to skin. I yanked her pants down and she keened into my mouth like it was the best and worst thing I'd ever done.

She was panting into my mouth—God I was so turned on. I slowed down a little. I wanted to take my time kissing all the places I'd always wanted to and had never been allowed—the space between her breasts, the insides of her thighs, the commas on her lower back.

She had a sweet spot right above her collarbone where her neck dipped. I listened to her intake of breath in satisfaction and worked my way down. I'd just reached her perfect nipples when she leaned into me like her lust was too heavy and she couldn't stand. I put her on the ground and lowered myself on top of her. I was sucking on her nipples and letting my hand slide up the inside of her thigh. She was wearing black lace panties; they stood out against her creamy skin. My hand stopped when it reached the junction of her thighs. I wanted her to want it. I let my thumb brush across the lace and she bucked underneath me. I wondered if anyone else had ever touched her there. I was having a hard time controlling myself. I breathed into her hair. It smelled like fresh laundry.

"Are you still in control?"

She nodded. I could feel her shaking and I wanted to call *bullshit.*

"Stop me," I said. "If you're in control, then stop me."

I pulled off the sweatpants that were still lingering around her ankles. She looked up at me with glassy eyes, like stopping me was the last thing she wanted to do.

That's when I snapped out of it. My game was turning toxic. I breathed in hard through my nose. I could take her now. She'd let me. But, that wouldn't be fair. I was manipulating her. She'd be angry with me after—she'd fold in on herself and I'd lose her. I just needed her to acknowledge me.

"Who owns you?"

She licked her lips. Her hands were locked on my arms. I could feel slight pressure as she pulled me toward her. She was silently asking me. I held back—she'd taught me how. She shook her head, not understanding.

I hunted her eyes down, forced her to see me.

I put a hand over her chest. I could feel her heart...pounding for me.

I want her. I want her. I want her. Please, Olivia. Please let me have you...

"Who owns you?"

Her eyes liquefied. She understood. Her body went limp.

"You," she said softly.

Her vulnerability, her body, her hair—it was all turning me on. I had never in my life wanted a woman more than I wanted her.

I threw my head back, closed my eyes, and rolled off of her.

Don't look at her. If you look at her again you'll land up inside of her.

"Thank you."

And then I left as quickly as I could to take a cold, cold shower.

She wouldn't look at me for a week after.

SEVEN

PRESENT

My cell phone rings. I crack open an eye. There is no light filtering through the blinds, which means it's either too fucking late or too fucking early to be calling. I hit answer and crush the phone to my ear.

"'Lo."

"Caleb?"

I sit up in bed and glance over at Jessica to see if I've woken her. She's sleeping on her stomach, her face hidden by her hair.

"Yeah?" I rub my eyes and pull my knees up.

"It's me."

It takes me a few beats to figure out who "me" is.

"Olivia?"

I glance at the clock and see it's 4:49. I swing my legs over the side of the bed, holding the phone between my shoulder and ear. Before she says another word, I have my pants on and am reaching for my shoes.

"Caleb, I'm sorry…I didn't know who to call."

"Don't say sorry, just tell me what's up."

"It's Dobson," she says. Her words are jumbled and rushed. "He's been sending me letters for a year. He broke out of Selbet last night. The police think he's coming here."

I break away from my phone to pull a shirt over my head.

"Where's Noah?"

There is silence on the other end of the line and I think she's hung up.

"Olivia?"

"Not here."

"All right," I say. "All right. I'll be there in thirty minutes."

I wake Jessica up and tell her where I'm going.

"Do you want me to come with you?" she asks, barely opening her eyes.

"No, it's fine."

I kiss her temple and she collapses back against her pillow in relief. I can smell salt in the air when I step out of the elevator and into the garage. You can always smell the ocean the strongest earlier in the day when the car exhausts and general human pollution hasn't woken up for the workday yet.

It takes me thirty minutes to reach Sunny Isles Beach where her condo rises above all of the others, one side overlooking the city, and the other overlooking the ocean. It's the only residential building with reflective glass on the outside. When I walk into the lobby, the night manager looks me over like he's deciding if my name is Dobson and I've just escaped from crazy town.

"Mrs. Kaspen has given us strict orders that no one is to be let up," he says.

"Call her," I say, pointing at the phone.

Just then I hear her voice behind me. "It's all right, Nick."

I turn, and she's walking toward me. She's dressed in white yoga pants and a matching hoodie. She has the hood pulled over her hair, but some of her waves are peeking through, framing her anxious face. I do what comes naturally. I cross to where she is in two strides and pull her against me. She buries her face in my chest so that she can barely breathe and hooks her arms up instead of around. This is how we've always hugged. She called it the Upper Cut. In college she would always say, *"Upper-cut me, Caleb."* People would look at us like I was getting ready to hit her.

"Are you afraid?" I say to the top of her head.

She nods into my chest. "Dis is wot I ucking get." She's muffled, so I lift her chin. Her mouth is a few inches away from mine. I remember how soft her lips are and have to fight back the urge to taste her. Which brings me to the most important question.

"Where is your husband, Olivia?"

She looks so sad, I almost regret asking.

"Don't ask me that today, okay?"

"Okay," I say, staring into her eyes. "You wanna go get some breakfrast?" She cracks a smile at my mispronunciation of the word. We used to say it like that.

We.

Used to.

She looks nervously toward the entrance of the building.

"Duchess," I say, squeezing her arms. "I got you." I give her a small smile.

"That's good," she nods, "because if he gets me, I'm in a lot of fucking trouble."

I laugh at her dry humor and steer her toward the door.

We are met head-on by Cammie.

"WTF!" she says, throwing her hands in the air. "I didn't know this was a fucked-up relationship reunion."

Olivia covers her eyes. "Don't judge me."

Cammie smacks me on the butt and hugs Olivia. "I told you I'd come right away, you didn't have to call him."

"I called him first," she says. "He makes me feel safer than you do."

"It's his massive penis, isn't it? He could just smack Dobson with it and he'd—"

"Let's take my car," I say, opening the door. Cammie climbs past me and stretches out on the backseat. "Hi, Cammie."

She gives me a smile and I shake my head. Olivia's best friend is her polar opposite. The two of them together were always a strange thing to behold. It was like watching a rainstorm when there were no clouds in the sky. One minute they were fighting, the next clutching each other in desperation.

"Well, look at us," Cammie says. "All together again, like ten fucking years of lies and bullshit never happened."

I look at her in my rearview mirror. "Angry much?"

"Nope, nope—I'm fine. Are you fine? I'm fine." She folds her arms across her chest and looks out the window.

I glance at Olivia, who is staring out of her window, too distracted to pay attention.

"Can we just not fight tonight, Cam," she says, halfheartedly. "He's here because I asked him to be."

I frown. I know better than to ask what is happening between the two of them. It could result in a screaming match. I turn into the parking lot of a Waffle House. Olivia watches my hand as I shift gears.

"So, did you tell him about Noah, O?"

"Shut up, Cammie," she snaps. I look at her out of the corner of my eye, curiosity piqued.

"Tell me what?"

Olivia suddenly spins around in her seat and points a finger at Cammie. "I will destroy you."

"Why would you do that when you're so good at destroying yourself?"

I open my door. "Waffles. Mmmm." A few more snide remarks fly back and forth until I cut them off.

"No one speaks until you've had five bites of food each."

When they were twenty they'd start fighting as soon as their blood sugar was low. Ten years later and not much has changed. You keep them fed, or they'll take you out. Like Gremlins.

They are both sour-faced and obedient until the waitress drops off our meals. I cut into my omelet and watch as they slowly come out of their funk. In a few minutes they're laughing and taking bites of each other's food.

"What are the police saying, Olivia?"

She sets down her fork and wipes her mouth. "After I won the case, he was convinced it was because I loved him and we were supposed to be together. So, I guess he broke out, and he's coming to claim his bride."

"Seems like that happens a lot," Cammie says through a mouthful of waffle. "Your ex-clients becoming obsessed with you and self-destructing." She sucks syrup off the tip of her finger and stares pointedly at me.

I kick Cammie under the table.

"Ow!"

Olivia props her chin in her hands. "Don't you wish Dobson loved Leah instead?"

I try not to laugh—I really do. But, those little quips of hers…she's just so damn—

Cammie gives me a dirty look. "Stop looking at her like that."

I don't respond, because I know exactly what she's talking about. I wink at Olivia. My ex-wife accused me of the same thing. When I look at her, I can't seem to look away. It's been that way since the first day I saw her under the tree. All other beauty, since then, has reminded me of her. No matter what it is, it's just a reflection of Olivia. The little witch has me spellbound.

I catch Olivia's eyes and we stay there for a good six seconds, locked in a gaze so intimate my stomach hurts when we look away. I see her throat working as she tries to swallow her emotion. I know what she's thinking.

Why?

I think that every day.

I pay the check and we climb back into my car. The girls don't want to go back to Olivia's.

"Caleb, he could crush you," Cammie says. "I've seen him in person. No offense, but I don't think you could take him. He'd. Crush. You."

Olivia's head is between her knees. She doesn't want to joke about something so serious, but it's hard with Cammie and me making light of everything. I see her back shaking in silent laughter. I reach over and snap her bra.

"You too, Duchess? You don't think I could take care of Dobbie?"

"Dobbie was torturing small animals by the time he could walk. I once saw him bite the head off of a mouse and eat it."

I make a face. "Really?"

"No. But, he eats his meat *very* rare."

I snicker. "Is it true what they said about his mother? Her molesting all those kids in that church?"

Olivia picks at some fluff on her pant leg and shrugs. "It would seem so, yes. He spoke many times about the things his mother would do to him. It makes sense—his need to, um…force women to love him after having a mother like that."

"Damn," says Cammie from the backseat. "I thought having daddy issues messed you up."

"Was he ever aggressive toward you?" I glance at her from the corner of my eye.

"No, no, he was very quiet. Almost gentlemanly. The girls told me that he would ask permission before raping them. That's sick, isn't it? Let me rape you… I'll ask first and kill you if you say no, but let me ask anyway."

The corner of her mouth dips in and she shakes her head. "People are so messed up. All of us. We just hurt each other."

"Some of us a little more so, don't you think? For instance, our good friend Dobson could have become an advocate for abused children rather than becoming a serial rapist."

"Yeah," she says. "His mind was broken. Not all abuse victims have the strength to make it through what he went through and come out with their brains all in one piece."

I love her. God, I love her so much.

"Can we just *not* go back to my place?" she says. "It feels weird being there."

"What about Cammie's?" I suggest.

Cammie shakes her head. "I'm staying with my boyfriend while I close on my new house. Olivia hates him."

I look at my watch. Jessica will be at my place until she leaves for work in a few hours. She only stays over a couple nights a week, but even so, I don't like the idea of taking Olivia somewhere I have had sex with other women.

"We could get a hotel," I say. "Hide out until they catch him."

Olivia shakes her head. "No, who knows how long that will be? Just take me home, it's okay."

I can see the fear on her face, and I want to ask again where Noah is.

"I have an idea," I say. When they press me, I won't tell them what it is. It's a ridiculous idea, but I like it. I make a U-turn and slide my car between the early morning traffic, heading back to her building.

"Do you want to grab some clothes?" She nods.

We make a brief stop at her building. I go up to her condo, in case Dobson is watching, and grab a duffel bag out of her closet. I open a couple drawers in her dresser until I find underwear. I stuff it into the bag. Next, I go to her closet and randomly choose a few items for her and Cammie. Before I leave, I stop at the other closet. *His.*

I pull open the door, not knowing what to expect. His clothes are there, all neatly on their hangers. I slam the door shut a little harder than I intended. I make one more stop in the living room. There is a table where he kept his whiskey in a decanter. The bottle is empty. I open it and hold it upside down.

Dry.

How long has he been gone? Why? Why didn't she tell me?

I don't say anything when I climb back into the car. Cammie is snoring softly in the backseat.

I pass her the bag and she mouths *thank you.*

Anything, Duchess, anything.

EIGHT

PAST

Soap sprayed on my windshield and the car vibrated as the jets beat water across the windows. Olivia pulled away from my mouth and glanced over her shoulder. I kissed down the elegant lines of her neck then laced my fingers into the back of her hair, steering her mouth back to mine. Things were getting out of control—for Olivia. For me, this was normal. A girl straddled on my lap, wearing a skirt…in the car wash…things could only get better from here. Not with Olivia. Things would not get better from here. Despite the fact that she was my girlfriend…and I loved her, and I wanted her naked and on top of me, I didn't want to take something from her that she wasn't ready to give.

I grabbed her by the waist and replanted her in her own seat. Then I gripped the steering wheel and thought about my great aunt Ina. Aunt Ina was sixty-seven years old and she had warts…gross…nasty…protruding—warts. I thought about her chins and her cankles and the hair that grew out of her arm wart. Aunt Ina seemed to do the trick. I felt slightly more in control.

Olivia huffed in the seat next to me. "Why do you always do that? I was having fun."

I kept my eyes closed and leaned my head back. "Duchess, do you want to have sex?"

Her answer came quickly. "No."

"So what's the point of doing that?"

She paused to think. "I don't know. Everyone else messes around. Why can't we just…you know?"

"No, I don't know," I said, turning to look at her. "Why don't you inform me what exactly it is that you have in mind?"

She blushed. "Can't we just compromise?" she whispered this without looking at me.

"I'm twenty-three years old. I've been having sex since I was fifteen. I think I am compromising. If you're asking me to feel you up like I'm a fifteen-year-old boy, I'm not going to do it."

"I know," she said weakly. "I'm sorry—I just can't."

Her voice pulled me out of my selfishness. It wasn't her fault. I'd already waited a year. I would wait another—I wanted to wait. She was worth it.

I wanted her.

"The thing with messing around is—you slowly work your way toward sex. It starts with hands and then mouths and then before you know it you're doing all three, all the time."

She blushed.

"Once you start, you don't stop. It's a slow decline toward sex. So, if you're really not ready to have sex, don't start doing the other stuff. That's all I'm saying."

I opened the bottle of water that was sitting in my cup holder and took a sip. The car wash rattled around us, strips of soapy rubber slapping the metal. I felt those slaps.

She climbed back into my lap. *God, I hope she can't feel my erection.* She put a hand on each side of my face and pressed her nose against mine. Her nose was cold. This was the softer side of Olivia. It was the side that caused me to want to stand over her like a dominating alpha male and bare my teeth at anyone who came near her.

"I'm sorry, Caleb. I'm sorry I'm so messed up."

My hands went back to her waist. "You're not messed up; you're just sexually repressed."

She giggled. It was so girly and soft. When a woman made that sound, I couldn't help but smile.

I looked down at her toned legs. All I would have to do was unzip my pants; she was already right—

"You're going to have to go back to your seat." My voice was gruff.

She scuttled back looking guilty.

We sat in silence for a few minutes as the dryers came on. I watched the drops of water shimmy across the windshield until they disappeared. What had I gotten myself into? I'd fallen in love with someone I couldn't fix. My coach called me a fixer. It started my sophomore year when I saw a couple of the freshmen on the team struggling with their game. I worked with them on the side until their defense improved. Coach always used my side projects as starters. My junior year I had ten guys come to me on the side and ask for private practice sessions. I don't know why, but I was good at it. Now, my need to fix things had transferred onto the women I was attracted to. I thought back to my ex-girlfriend, Jessica. She had been perfect, until…

I clenched my teeth. Maybe that's why things hadn't worked out between us. She was too perfect. Olivia was so beautifully broken. The hairline cracks in her personality were more pieces of art than flaws. I loved flawed art. Michelangelo's statue of Lorenzo with its warped base that rose to accommodate his foot, the Mona Lisa's missing eyebrows. Flaws were seriously underrated. They were beautiful if you looked at them just so.

I knew I was lying to myself by thinking I could fix her. But, it was too late. I didn't know how to let go. She broke the silence first.

"I wish I knew what you were thinking," she said.

"There's always the option of asking me." I put the car in gear and pulled forward. She watched my hand on the stick shift—she always did that.

Car wash—over. Pounding need to be inside of her—not over.

"I feel like you're always trying to sneak into my mind. You're like Peter Pan—always climbing in windows and causing trouble."

She scrunched up her nose. "Did you really just call me Peter Pan?"

"I've called you worse." I eased the car into the traffic.

"A llama," she said. "I loved that."

I laughed at her obvious sarcasm, and the lust spell was broken. I was back to just needing to be with her.

"Peter Pan wants to sneak into your mind and know what you're thinking," she tried again. She was looking at me so earnestly, I gave in.

We pulled up at a red light. I reached over and grabbed her hand. Okay, if she wanted my thoughts, I was going to give them to her. Maybe it would do her good to be inside the mind of a normal adult male. Maybe she'd play with said "normal adult male" with a little more caution. I raised her fingers to my lips and kissed them. I conjured up an image of her on my lap and my voice dropped low so she knew I meant business.

"If you climb into my lap while wearing a skirt and kiss me like that again, I'm going to pull off your panties and fuck you."

Her face blanched. Good. I needed her to be scared enough to not do that again. I wasn't Superman. I was a man—a man that very much wanted to make love to his girlfriend.

She didn't let go of my hand; if anything her hold on it tightened. I looked at her out of the corner of my eye. She was biting her bottom lip, staring straight out of the windshield with glassy eyes.

I choked back a laugh. *By God, I think I actually turned her on.* My little Duchess—always the surprise.

From that day on, "Peter Pan" was our code word for—*what are you thinking?*

"Peter Pan."

"Leave me alone."

"You invented this game."

We were lying on her floor, supposedly having a study session. Her lips were still a little swollen from our kissing session.

"I'm covered in Cheeto dust and trying to study. You're annoying me because for the last forty minutes you've been staring at me, and it's breaking my concentration." She put another Cheeto in her mouth and let it melt. I grabbed her hand and stuck one of her fingers between my lips, sucking the Cheeto dust off. It was a new Oliviaism.

Her eyes glazed for a second, and I dropped her hand.

"Since when do you read the paper?" It was slightly buried underneath her body. She raised her ribcage to let me pull it out and I rolled onto my back.

"I saw it when I was checking out at the grocery store." She looked half guilty. I unfolded it and looked at the front page.

"Laura," I said. I didn't mean to say it out loud, but seeing her picture caught me by surprise. I got a sick feeling in my stomach whenever I thought about it.

"New leads in the Laura Hilberson case," I read. The paper said that one of her credit cards had been used at a gas station in Mississippi. Since the gas station had no video surveillance, they weren't able to get a shot of who was using the card. The teenager behind the counter was high at the time and didn't remember anything at all.

"You dated her," Olivia said. I nodded. She pushed her textbook aside and rested her head on her fist. "So, what was she like? Do you think she would just disappear? Do you think someone took her?"

I scratched my belly. "It was like a week. I didn't know her very well." *That isn't true. Why am I lying?*

Olivia knew I was lying.

"Tell me," she says.

"There's nothing to tell, Duchess."

"Caleb, you're one of the most perceptive humans I've ever met. Are you really telling me that you have no insight into this situation?"

My brain locked and I wasn't sure which way to send my tongue. This was such a touchy subject. I was about to tell another lie—or maybe it was the truth—when Cammie came barreling into the room, saving me.

"Oh my God! Did you guys have sex?"

I propped my hands behind my head to watch as they started their usual playful arguing.

Where was Laura? This was crazy.

Laura Hilberson was a compulsive liar. I knew it within three dates. She was a pretty girl, shy for the most part, but everyone seemed to know who she was. It might have been because her parents owned a yacht and she invited everyone on the weekends. Our college was a private one. Olivia was one of the handful of students who attended on full scholarship. No one else really needed a scholarship.

I asked Laura out after we were assigned to a group project in Speech class. Date one included her telling me about her best friend dying from a four-wheeler accident three years earlier. She cried when she told me, saying she was closer to the girl than she was to her siblings. When I asked her how many brothers and sisters she had, she paused only briefly before saying—eight. Eight siblings. *Wow!* I thought. Her parents must be stretched pretty thin. How did they even manage to hug everyone in one day?

Date two was spent on her parents' yacht. For all their money, they were simple people. Her mother made us sandwiches for lunch—one slice of turkey, white bread, and a tomato. They spoke about their church and the mission trips Laura had gone on throughout high school. When I asked if any of her siblings went with her, they stared at me blankly. Laura saw a school of dolphins just then and we all were distracted with watching them play in the water. Later we went back to their house so I could pick up my car. They lived in a modest two-story, the only indication of their money really being the yacht, which they called their splurge.

She showed me around the house while her mother got us some Cokes from the garage fridge. I counted the bedrooms: one, two, three, four. Each one had a queen, except for Laura's—she said she preferred a twin. When I asked where everyone slept, she said that most of her siblings were older than her and had already moved out.

My internal alarm really went off when I said goodbye to her family in the foyer. On the wall to the right of the front door was a huge montage of family pictures. Grandparents, Christmases, birthday parties—my eyes scanned each one as we chatted about school and upcoming finals. When I finally said goodbye, I walked to my car knowing two things: Laura was an only child, and Laura was a compulsive liar.

Date three should never have happened. I was thoroughly turned off after I figured everything out. It was a group date and I landed up paired with Laura. We went on a road trip to see the Yankees play the Rays. Everyone knew it would be an embarrassing game for the Rays, but we wanted to get out of town and have some fun before finals killed us. Laura drove with me and one other couple. She sat in the front seat chatting about her last trip to Tampa, when her sister got lost at the beach and her parents had to call the police.

"I thought you were the youngest," I said.

"It was a long time ago. I think she was only five," she said.

"So, that made you how old?"

"Three," she answered quickly.

"You have a memory of that happening?"

She paused. "No. But, my parents tell me about it all the time."

"Is your sister in college now?"

"No. She's in the military."

"What branch?"

"She's a Navy SEAL."

My eyebrows went up. I checked my rearview mirror to see if John and Amy heard her in the backseat.

They were both slumped over, sleeping.

Damn.

It was dark. I was glad she couldn't fully see the expression on my face. There were no women in the Navy SEALs. I may not be fully American, but it was a pretty well known fact. Or at least I thought it was.

"Well, that's impressive," I said, for lack of anything better. "You must be proud." *Or lying.*

For the remainder of the drive, I asked what each of her siblings did, and she had an answer each time.

At that point I was simply doing it for amusement. At the baseball game the next day, I wedged myself between two of my friends so I wouldn't have to sit next to her. The lies were exhausting me. But, that night I went back for more.

I asked her about her mission trips, trying to decode some of her psychology. Christians weren't supposed to lie—not this big anyway. This was delusion. Maybe she wasn't right in the head. She acted normal socially. *God.* This was blowing my mind. It made me wish I'd done what I'd wanted and studied psychology instead of business. I asked one of the girls in our group about her later that week.

"She's cool," she said. "Kind of quiet."

"Yeah. It's probably because of being the youngest of all those siblings," I said.

Tori screwed up her face. "She only has two—a brother and a sister. They're both studying abroad."

Oh hell no.

I'd never spoken to Laura again. I couldn't figure out if she knew she was lying, or if she did it because her brain was cracked. Or, maybe she thought it was fun. Who the hell knows? I didn't hang around to find out. When they said she was missing, I immediately thought she disappeared on purpose. Then I felt guilty for thinking that.

She'd probably been abducted and there I was making up stories to suit my interpretation of her.

They found her at the Miami International Airport. When the papers started reporting about her abduction by a man named Devon, I tried not to question it. Tried. Olivia was fascinated with the case. She read everything she could. I don't know if it was because she was studying law or because she had a personal tie to Laura. I kept my opinions to myself and hoped she was okay.

Then there was a night after Estella was born. I was making dinner, and the news was playing softly on the television. I heard her name. Softly, but my ears were tuned to that name. I came out of the kitchen to find Leah trying to change the channel.

"Don't," I said. Olivia was on my flatscreen, walking with a man I presumed to be Dobson Orchard. She waved away from the press and got in a car with him.

No, Olivia.

I wanted to tell her to stay away from this case. To stay away from him. I wanted to touch her silky, black hair and wrap her in my protection. My mouth was dry by the time the news went to commercial.

That's when I realized they'd flashed Laura's picture, describing her as one of his first victims. Dobson/Devon…

Forget it, I thought. She'd been drugged. Maybe she got the name wrong. Maybe the news did. Maybe she jumped on the Dobson train because she wanted the ride. When she was in college she was looking to be a part of something, a family of eight. Maybe, just maybe, she found it in the faces of Dobson's abducted, assaulted victims. Fuck if I didn't pick the strangest women to spend time with.

NINE

PRESENT

"Where are we?" Cammie sits up, rubbing her eyes.

"Naples." I pull down a heavily wooded street, and she looks around in alarm.

"What the hell, Drake?"

Olivia, who has been quiet the whole drive, looks impassively out the window. I'm worried about her. She hasn't asked once where we're going. Either she trusts me, or she doesn't care. I'm good with both.

The road curves, and I pull down a much smaller street. The houses here are spaced further apart. There are ten of them, all sitting around a lake and surrounded by their own five acres. The closest neighbors own horses. I can see them grazing behind white picket fences. As we drive past, Olivia's head cranes to get a better look.

I smile to myself. She's not a hundred percent zoned out.

I stop the car outside an ornate white gate and reach into my glove box to find the automatic opener. My hand grazes her knee and she jumps.

"It's good to know I still have that effect on you," I say, pointing the device at the gate. It swings open just as her hand shoots out and smacks me on the chest.

I grab her hand before she can pull away and hold it right over my heart. She doesn't fight me.

Cammie sniffs in the backseat, and I let her go.

The driveway is paved with creamy, brown brick. We follow it for two hundred yards until we reach the house. I throw the car into park; Olivia watches my hand.

I watch her watch my hand. When she looks up, I smile.

"Where are we?"

"Naples," I repeat, throwing open my door. I lean the seat forward to let Cammie out and walk around to open the door for Olivia.

She gets out and stretches her arms above her head, looking at the house.

I wait for her reaction.

"It's beautiful," she says. I grin and my hammering heart calms down.

"Who does it belong to?"

"Me."

She raises her eyebrows and follows me up the stairs. The house is three stories, brick-faced with a turret and a widow's walk that has the most astonishing view of the lake. As we approach the front door, she gasps.

The knocker sits on a solid wood door and is in the shape of a crown.

I stop at the door and look at her.

"And you."

Her nostrils flare, her eyelashes beat, and her mouth puckers into a little frown.

I turn the key in the lock. We walk into our house.

It is unbearably hot. I head straight for the thermostat. Cammie swears colorfully, and I'm glad they can't see my face.

The house is fully furnished. I have someone come in once a month to dust and clean the pool—which has never been used. I move from room to room, opening the shades. The girls follow behind me.

When we reach the kitchen, Olivia wraps her arms around her body and looks around.

"Like it?" I ask, watching her face.

"You designed this yourself, didn't you?"

I like that she knows me so well. My ex-wife liked everything to be modern: stainless steel, sterile white, and tile. Everything in my house is warm. The kitchen is rustic. There is a lot of stone and copper and hardwood. I made the decorator use a lot of red, because the color reminds me of Olivia. Leah has red hair, but Olivia has a red personality. And as far as I'm concerned, red belongs to the love of my life.

Cammie wanders around the living room, eventually plopping herself down on the couch and turning on the television. Olivia and I stand side by side, watching her. This was not how I intended for her to see this.

"Want me to show you the rest of your house?"

She nods and I lead her out of the kitchen and toward the curving staircase.

"Leah—"

"No," I say. "I don't want to talk about Leah."

"Fine," she says.

"Where's Noah?"

She looks away. "Please stop asking me that."

"Why?"

"Because it hurts to answer."

I consider her for a moment and nod. "You're going to have to tell me eventually."

"Eventually," she sighs. "That word is so *us*, isn't it? Eventually, you'll tell me you're faking your amnesia. Eventually, I'll tell you that I'm pretending not to know you. Eventually, we'll come back together, fall apart, come back together."

I watch her study my wall art, riveted by her words. She says things that genuinely move me. She lets her soul slip through her lips, and it's always raw and incredibly sad.

"Caleb, what is this house?"

I stand behind her as she lurks in the doorway to the master bedroom and tug on the ends of her hair.

"I was building it for you. I was going to bring you here the night I proposed. It was only an empty lot, but I wanted to show you what we could build together."

She blows air through her nose and shakes her head. It's the way she fights tears.

"You were going to ask me to marry you?"

I briefly consider telling her about the night she walked in on me at the office, but I don't want to overload her emotionally.

"Why did you keep building? Furnish it?"

"A project, Duchess," I say softly. "I needed something to fix."

She laughs. "You couldn't fix me—or that dirty redhead. So you went for a house?"

"It's a lot more rewarding."

She snorts. I would have preferred a giggle.

She flips on the light switch and walks carefully into the bedroom, like the floor could fall out from beneath her at any minute.

"Have you ever slept here?"

I watch as she runs a finger along the plush, white comforter and sits on the edge of the bed. She bounces a few times and I smile.

"No."

She lies down on her back and then suddenly rolls twice across the bed until she's on her feet on the other side. It's something a little kid would do. As always, when the word *kid* pops in my head, my stomach clenches painfully.

Estella

My heart falls and then rises slightly when she smiles at me.

"It's kind of girly in here," she says.

A corner of my mouth shoots up. "Well, I did intend on sharing it with a woman."

She puckers her lips and nods. "Peacock blue—it's very fitting."

There is a vase of peacock feathers on the dresser. The corners of her mouth tilt up as she remembers something from long ago.

I show her the rest of the bedrooms and then take her up the narrow flight of stairs to the attic, which I converted into a library. She exclaims excitedly when she sees the books, and I have to practically drag her up the narrow flight of stairs to the widow's walk. She has two books in her hands, but when she emerges into the sunshine, she sets them down on one of the lawn chairs, her eyes wide.

"Oh my God," she says. She throws her arms up in the air and spins around. "It's so beautiful. I'd be up here all the time if—"

We both turn away at the same time. I walk over to look at the trees; she stays near the lake.

If…

"If you hadn't lied to me," she sighs.

Had I really *not* expected that? She's queen of the jab. I laugh really hard. I laugh so hard—Cammie slides the back door open and peeks her head out. When she sees us, she shakes her head and retreats back inside. I feel like I've just been scolded.

I glance at Olivia. She's getting her book and settling down in one of the lawn chairs. "I'll just be up here if you need me, Drake."

I walk over and kiss the top of her head. "Okay, Duchess. I'll go make lunch. Don't let anyone steal you."

They catch Dobson in Olivia's building two days later. He was coming for her. I want to kill Noah. What if she hadn't called me? Dobson avoided the police for almost a decade. Could he have gotten past them and to Olivia? I don't even want to think about it. When we get the call, I know it's time for me to take her back, but we linger for an extra day. Even Cammie doesn't seem eager to leave. On the fourth day, I bring up leaving just as we're finishing our dinner of grilled salmon and asparagus. Cammie politely excuses herself from the picnic table and goes inside the house. Olivia picks at the lettuce on her plate and works at avoiding my eyes.

"Do you not feel ready?" I ask her.

"It's not that," she says. "It's just been—"

"Nice," I finish for her. She nods.

"You can come stay at my place for a few days," I offer.

She glares at me.

"Would I sleep between you and Jessica?"

I smirk. "How do you know I'm still seeing Jessica?"

She sighs. "I keep tabs on you."

"You stalk me," I say. When she doesn't respond, I touch the top of her hand with my finger, tracing a vein.

"It's okay. I stalk you too."

"Are things the same with Jessica? Like they used to be in college?"

"Are you asking me if I'm in love with her?"

"Does it sound like I'm asking you that?"

I cover my face with my hands and sigh dramatically. "If you want to ask me personal and extremely uncomfortable questions, go ahead. I'll tell you anything you want to know. But, for the love of God—just ask a direct question."

"Fine," she says. "Are you in love with Jessica?"

"No."

She looks surprised. "Were you before? In college, I mean?"

"No."

"Would you have married her if she'd kept the baby?"

"Yes."

She bites her bottom lip and her eyes get watery.

"You didn't make Jessica have an abortion, Olivia."

The tears roll.

"Yeah, I did. I drove her to the clinic. I could have talked her out of it and I didn't. On a deep level I knew you would have married her if you found out she was pregnant. I could have told her that and she might not have gone through with it."

"Jessica doesn't want children," I say. "She never has. It's sort of a deal-breaker between the two of us."

She wipes her face with her sleeve and sniffs. It's pathetic and cute.

"But you're together. What's the point of your relationship if it isn't going anywhere?"

I laugh and catch a tear off of her chin with my fingertip.

"That's so you. You don't do anything without purpose. It's why you wouldn't give me a shot in the first place. You didn't see yourself marrying me, so you wouldn't even have a conversation with me."

She shrugs and half smiles. "You don't know me, fool."

"Oh, but I do. You had to see me make an ass of myself before you'd even consider going on a date with me."

"What's your point, Drake?"

"Jessica broke up with someone before she moved back here. I got a divorce. We are both a little messed up in the head, and we like being around each other."

"And you like fucking," she said.

"Yeah. We like fucking. You jealous?"

She rolls her eyes, but I know.

It's getting dark. The sun is burning a hole through our sky, making it orange and yellow as it dips below the trees.

"You know," I say, leaning across the table and taking her hand. "I could have sex with a thousand women, and it wouldn't feel like it did that night in the orange grove."

She rips her hand away and turns her entire body around so she can watch the sun set. I smile at the back of her head and start collecting the plates.

"Denial's an ugly thing, Duchess."

TEN

PAST

"Let me see that one."

He reached into the spotless glass case and pulled out something a little more striking than the last. Engagement rings all looked the same after a while. I remember when I was a kid I would say my name over and over until it sounded more like a blur of noise rather than a name. He pushed another bauble over the counter, this one larger than the last. It laid on a square of black velvet. I picked it up and stuck it on my pinkie to get a good look.

"That's three carats, colorless with a VVS2 rating," Thomas said. *Samoht*

"It's beautiful, it really is. I think I'm just looking for something more…unique." I pushed it back at him.

"Tell me about her," he said. "Maybe I can get a better feel for the right ring."

I grinned. "She's fiercely independent. Never wants help from anyone, not even me. She likes nice things, but she's ashamed of it. She doesn't want to seem shallow. And she's not. God, she's perceptive…and she knows herself. And she's kind. Only she doesn't know she's kind. She perceives herself as cold, but she has such a good heart."

When I looked at him, his eyebrows were slightly raised. We laughed at the same time. I leaned over the counter and covered my face with both hands.

"Well, you're definitely in love," he said.

"Yes, I am."

He walked a few steps away and came back with another ring.

"This is from our pricier collection. It's still a solitaire. But, as you can see, the band is quite unique."

I took the ring. The center stone was oval in shape with the diamond set east to west. A deviation from the norm—I already thought she'd like it. When I looked closer, I noticed that the band had branches and tiny leaves etched in the white gold. The ring had a style common to those worn a century ago. Modern and antique. Just like Olivia.

"This is it," I said. "It's perfect since we met under a tree."

I left the store and walked into the overly warm humidity. Living in Florida felt like you were perpetually existing in a bowl of pea soup. Today, however, I didn't care. I was smiling. I had a ring in my pocket. Olivia's ring. Everyone would think I was crazy for asking a girl to marry me when I hadn't even had sex with her. That's why I didn't bother telling anyone my plans. If my family and friends couldn't be supportive, then they wouldn't be included. I didn't need to have sex with her to know how I felt. She could refuse to have sex with me every day for the rest of our lives and I still would choose her. That's how deep I was *in* this.

The plans were in motion. In six weeks I would ask Olivia—no—I would *tell* Olivia to marry me. She would probably say no, but I'd just keep asking—or telling. That's what happened when you were possessed by a woman. All of a sudden you stopped running from love and started breaking all of your own rules…making a fool of yourself. I was okay with that.

I called her cell, tried to keep my voice even.

"Hi," she breathed.

"Hey, baby."

There was always a brief pause after we said our hellos. I liked to think of it as the saturation. She told me once that every time she saw my name on her caller ID she got butterflies. I got this swelling ache in my chest. It was a good ache—like a heart orgasm.

"I'm making plans for a few weeks from now. I thought we could go away for a couple of days—Daytona maybe."

She sounded excited. "I've never been there."

"It's more beach. Another corner of the same ol' same ol' Florida. I want to take you to Europe. But, for now, Daytona."

"Caleb, yeah, I'd like that. Daytona and Europe."

"Okay," I said, smiling.

"Okay," she repeated.

"Hey," she said after a few seconds. "Don't get separate rooms."

I think I tripped over the curb.

"What?"

She laughed.

"Byyye, Caleb."

"Bye, Duchess."

I was grinning from ear to ear.

After we hung up, I stopped for an espresso at an outdoor café. I wiped sweat from my forehead as I called a hotel and made reservations. One room: king bed, Jacuzzi tub, view of the ocean. Then I called a florist and ordered three-dozen gardenias. They asked for the delivery address of the hotel and I had to hang up to find it before calling them back. I was laughing in between calls. Out loud.

People kept staring, but I couldn't help it. This was crazy and it made me so happy. I called Cammie, and then thinking better of it, I hung up. Cammie was the closest thing Olivia had to family, but her idea of secret keeping was…not to keep a secret. I wished there was a father to ask—no, I didn't. I would have punched her father, probably on numerous occasions. My final call was to an old friend who could help me with the last part of my plan. The best part. I wasn't just going to give her a ring; she needed more than that to see how serious I was.

I stood up and dropped money on the table. Then I headed to my mother's house. Hopefully, there were plenty of sedatives at the Drake mansion. She was going to need them.

"Caleb, it's a mistake." My mother's face was ashen. She was tugging on the locket she wore around her neck. A sure sign that she was about to crumble emotionally.

I laughed at her. I didn't like to be disrespectful, but I didn't like anyone telling me Olivia was a mistake either. I pulled the ring box from her fingers and snapped it closed.

"I'm not here for your opinion. I'm here because you're my mother and I want to keep you involved in my life. However, that is subject to change if you insist on treating Olivia as if she isn't good enough for me."

"She—"

"—Is," I said firmly. "In college I was the asshole that slept with everyone because I could. I've been with many women, and she is the only one who makes me want to be a better person…and a better person for her. I don't even need to be good; I just need to be good for her."

My mother stared at me blankly.

"Forget it," I said, standing up. She grabbed my arm.

"Have you told your father?"

I felt myself flinch. "No, why would I do that?"

"Your brother?" she asked.

I shook my head.

"They'll confirm what I'm saying. You're young."

"I wouldn't be too young if I'd bought this ring for Sidney, would I?"

She bit her bottom lip and I pulled my arm from her grasp.

"My father is so against commitment he's managed to date a new woman every month for the last ten years. Seth is so reclusive and neurotic; he'd rather be alone for the rest of his life than have someone leave a dish in the sink. I don't think I'll be going to either for relationship advice. And just for the record, it's your job to be supportive of me. Everyone told you not to divorce my father and marry Steve. Had you listened to them, where would you be now?"

She was panting by the time I finished saying that. I glanced at the door. I needed out of here, fast. I wanted to be with Olivia. See her face, kiss her.

"Caleb."

I glanced down at my mother. She had been a good mother to my brother and me. Good enough to leave my father when she saw how damaging his influence on us had been. To others she was not a particularly kind woman, but I understood that. She was verbally cutting and critical. It was common among the wealthy. I never expected her to embrace Olivia. But, I had hoped for a less trite reaction. Maybe even forced happiness for my sake. I was growing weary of her pronounced cattiness.

She placed her hand on my arm again, squeezing lightly. "I know you think I'm shallow. I probably am. Women in my generation were taught not to think too deeply about our feelings, and to do what needed to be done without dissecting it emotionally. But, I am more perceptive than you think. She will be your destruction. She's not healthy."

I gently removed her hand from my arm. "Then let her destroy me."

ELEVEN

PRESENT

I take Cammie home first. When she steps out of the car, she kisses my cheek and holds my eyes for a second longer than is normal. I know she's sorry. After all these years of Olivia and me, how can she not be? I nod at her and she tucks her lips in and smiles. When I get back in, Olivia is watching me.

"Sometimes, I feel like you and Cammie speak without speaking," she says.

"Maybe we do."

The rest of the ride is quiet. It reminds me of our drive back from the camping trip, when there was so much to say and no courage to say it. We're so much older now, so much has happened. It shouldn't be this hard.

I carry her bag upstairs. She holds the front door open for me when we get to her floor, so I step past her and walk into the foyer. Once again I feel Noah's absence. It feels like she's been living here on her own. The air is warm. I can smell traces of her perfume in certain spots. She turns on the air conditioner and we move into the kitchen.

"Tea?" she asks.

"Please."

I can pretend for a few minutes that this is our house and she's making me tea like she does every morning. I watch her put the kettle on and get the tea bags. She rubs the back of her neck and tucks a foot behind her knee while she waits for the water to boil. Then she carries a glass jar of sugar cubes and a small milk jug to the table and sets them down in front of me. I turn away and pretend I wasn't watching her. This pierces my heart a little bit. We always said we'd have sugar cubes instead of plain sugar. She fetches two teacups from the cabinet, stretching on her tiptoes to reach them. I watch her face as she drops four cubes into my cup. She stirs it for me and pours in the milk. I reach for the cup before she pulls her hand away, and our fingers touch. Her eyes dart to mine. Dart away. She drinks her tea with only one cube of sugar. We find the tabletop increasingly interesting as the minutes pass. Finally, I set my cup down. It clinks against the saucer. There is a storm brewing between us. Maybe that's why we are savoring the calm. I stand up and take both of our cups to the sink. I wash them and set them in the drying rack.

"I still want you," I say. I surprise myself by saying this out loud. I don't know if she's having the same reaction because my back is to her.

"Fuck you."

Surprise, surprise.

She can't hide from me with her dirty mouth. I see how she looks at me. I feel the sting of regret when our skin accidentally touches.

"I built you that house," I say, turning around. "I kept it even after I got married. I hired a landscaper and a pool guy. I've had a cleaning service go in once a month. Why would I do that?"

"Because you're a nostalgic fool who only lets go of the past long enough to marry another woman."

"You're right. I am a fool. But, as you can see, I'm a fool who never quite let go."

"Let go."

I shake my head. "Uh-uh. This time you found *me*, remember?"

She turns a little red.

"Tell me why you called me."

"Who else do I know?"

"Your husband, for one."

She looks away.

"Fine," she finally says. "I was scared. You were the first one I thought to call."

"Because…"

"Goddammit, Caleb!" She slams her fist on the table and the fruit bowl wobbles.

"Because…" I say again. Does she think she scares me with her little temper tantrums? She does a little.

"You're always wanting to overtalk everything."

"There is no such thing as overtalking something. Lack of communication is the problem."

"You should have been a shrink."

"I know. Don't change the subject."

She bites on her thumbnail.

"Because you're my hiding place. I go to you when I'm messed up."

My tongue twists, knots, freezes. What am I supposed to say to that? I never expected that. Maybe more swearing. More denial.

Then I go nuts. Really crazy. It's the tension of wanting her and wanting her to admit that she wants me.

My hands are behind my neck as I pace her small kitchen. I want to hit something. Throw a chair through the glass box that is her condo. I stop suddenly and face her.

"You leave him, Olivia. You leave him or this is the end."

"The. End. Of. WHAT?" She leans over the counter, her fingers splayed out like her anger. Her words punch. "We've never had a beginning, or a middle, or a fucking *minute* to be in love. You think I want this? He hasn't done anything wrong!"

"Bullshit! He married you and he knew you were in love with me."

She draws back, looks unsure. I watch her walk the length of her kitchen, one hand on top of her head, the other on her hip. When she stops and faces me, her face is contorted.

"I love him."

I cross the kitchen in two seconds. I grab her upper arm so she can't get away and lean down until I'm right in her face. She has to see truth. My voice sounds more animal than human—a growl.

"More than me?"

The light drains from her eyes and she tries to look away.

I shake her. "More than me?"

"I don't love anything more than I love you."

My fingers tighten on her arm. "Then why are we playing these stupid games?"

She rips her arm away from me, her eyes flashing.

"You left me in Rome!" She shoves me and I stumble back. "You left me for that redheaded bitch. Do you know how much that hurt? I came to tell you how I felt, and you walked away from me."

Olivia rarely shows her hurt. It's so unusual I'm not sure how to deal with it.

"She was unstable. Her sister shot herself. She swallowed a bottle of sleeping pills, for God's sake! I was trying to save her. You didn't need me. Ever. You made a point of showing me that you didn't need me."

She wanders over to the sink, picks up a glass, fills it with water, takes a sip, and throws it at my head. I duck and it hits the wall, shattering into a thousand pieces. I glance at the wall where the glass struck, then back at Olivia.

"Giving me a concussion is not going to solve our problems."

"You were a fucking coward. If you had just talked to me that day in the record store, without the lies, we wouldn't be here."

Her shoulders—which a second ago had been tensed in battle stance—go limp. A single sob escapes her lips. She reaches a hand up to catch it, but it's too late.

"You got married…you had a baby…" Her tears are flowing freely, mingling with her mascara and tracking black across her cheeks. "You were supposed to marry me. That was supposed to be my baby." She drops to the sofa behind her and wraps her arms around herself.

Her tiny frame is racked with sobs. Her hair has cascaded over her face and she bends her head with the purpose of veiling her face.

I go to her. I scoop her up and carry her over to the counter, setting her down so we're eye to eye. She is trying to hide behind her hair. It's almost to her waist again, like it was when I met her. I pull the hair tie from her wrist and divide her hair into three pieces.

"Is it weird that I know how to do a braid?"

She laughs in between her crying and watches me. I tie off the braid with the hair tie and flip it over her shoulder. Now I can see her.

Her voice is raspy when she speaks. "I hate that you always make jokes when I'm trying to feel sorry for myself."

"I hate that I always make you cry." I rub little circles on her wrist with my thumb. I want to touch her more, but I know I shouldn't.

"Duchess, it wasn't your fault. It was mine. I thought that if we had a clean slate…" My voice trails off because there is no such thing as a clean slate. I know that now. You just embrace your dirty slate and build over it. I kiss her wrist. "Let me carry you out. I'll never let you touch the ground. I was made to carry you, Olivia. You're fucking heavy with all of your guilt and self-loathing. But, I can do it. Because I love you."

She has her pinky pressed against her lips as if she's trying to hold everything in. This is a new Oliviaism. I like it. I pull her pinky away from her lips, and instead of dropping her hand, I lace my fingers through hers. *God, how long has it been since I've held her hand?* I feel like a little boy. I fight back the smile that is trying to take over my face.

"Tell me," I say. "Peter Pan…"

"Noah," she breathes.

"Where is he, Duchess?"

"He's in Munich right now. Last week, Stockholm, the week before that, Amsterdam." She looks away. "We're not…we're taking a break."

I shake my head. "A break from what? Marriage or each other?"

"We like each other. Marriage, I guess."

"Fuck, that doesn't even make sense," I say. "If we were married I wouldn't let you out of my bed, never mind my sight."

She pulls a face. "What's that supposed to mean?"

"There are guys like me out there, and I wouldn't let them get near you. What's he playing at?"

She's quiet for a long time. Then she blurts:

"He doesn't want children."

Estella's face blurs my vision before I ask…

"Why not?"

She shrugs, trying to pretend like it's nothing. "His sister has Cystic Fibrosis. He's a carrier. He's seen how much she's suffered and he doesn't want to bring children into the world with the risk of them having it."

I can see how much it bothers her. Her mouth is pinched and her eyes are darting around the tabletop as if she's searching for a crumb.

I swallow. This is a touchy subject for me too.

"Did you know that before you married him?"

She nods. "I didn't want children before I married him."

I stand up. I don't want to hear her talk about how Noah made her want things that I couldn't make her want. I must look sulky because she rolls her eyes.

"Sit down," she snaps. "I see you still play footsie with your inner child."

I walk to the floor-to-ceiling window that circles her living room and look out. I ask the question I don't want to ask, but I can't *not* know. I am jealous.

"What changed your mind?"

"I've changed, Caleb." She gets up and comes to stand next to me. I glance at her and see that her arms are crossed over her chest. She is wearing a long sleeve, grey cotton shirt and black pants that sit low on her hips so that a few inches of flesh are exposed. Her hair is loosely braided over her shoulder. She stares out at the traffic that is zooming below us. She looks badass. I smirk and shake my head.

"I never felt worthy enough to have babies. Duh—right? I have all those super cool daddy issues."

"Aw, man. Are you still working through those?"

She grins.

"Little bit here and there. I can have sex now."

I cock up one corner of my mouth and narrow my eyes. "I'm pretty sure I cured you of that."

Her eyelashes beat so rapidly they could blow out a match. She chews on her lip to keep from smiling.

I tilt my head back and laugh. We both get such a kick out of making each other uncomfortable. *God, I love this woman.*

"You did though," she says. "Despite what you think, it wasn't because of your bedroom moves. It was what you did to get me back."

I raise my eyebrows.

"The amnesia?" I'm surprised.

She nods slowly. She's still looking out the window, but my body is pivoted toward her now.

"You're not that person…the one who lies and does crazy things. That's me. I couldn't believe you did that."

"You are crazy."

She shoots me an annoyed look.

"You broke your own moral code. I figured if someone like you would fight for me, I might actually be worth something."

I look at her earnestly. I don't want to say too much or too little.

"You are worth fighting for. I haven't given up yet."

Her head snaps up. She looks alarmed.

"Well, you should. I'm married."

"Yeah, you got married, didn't you? But, you only did it because you thought we were over—and we're not over. We'll never be over. If you think that little piece of metal on your finger can shield off your feelings for me, you're wrong. I wore one for five years and there wasn't a day that went by when I wasn't wishing it were you."

I look at her lips, lips that I want to kiss. I turn and grab my keys to leave before we can start fighting—or kissing. She stays at the window. Before I walk out of the living room, I say her name.

"Olivia."

She looks at me over her shoulder. Her braid swings across her back like a pendulum.

"Your marriage won't last. Tell Noah the truth; be fair. When you do, come find me, and I'll give you that baby."

I don't stay to watch her reaction.

I feel guilty that I'm offering my ex-girlfriend a baby when my current girlfriend is probably at my house, waiting for me—wanting me to offer her a marriage. My life comes into focus when I walk through my front door. There is music playing loudly from my stereo. I walk over and turn it down. Jessica is at the stove, flipping something in a frying pan. It amazes me that she wants to cook even when she's not at work. You'd think she'd be sick of it by now. I sit at a barstool and watch her until she turns around.

She must see something on my face. She sets down the wooden spoon she is holding and wipes her hands on a dishtowel before walking over to me. I can see the sauce of whatever she is cooking pooling on the counter under the spoon. I don't know why, but I can't stop looking at that spoon.

I grind my teeth as she walks toward me. I don't want to hurt her, but if I do what I did with Leah, I'll land up staying just to protect her heart. It'll be halfhearted, because the only thing I want in life is to protect Olivia's heart.

When she reaches for me, I grab her hands and hold them. She can see the breakup in my eyes; she shakes her head before I've opened my mouth.

"I'm still in love with Olivia," I say. "It's never going to be fair to anyone I'm with. I don't want to give you pieces of me."

Her tears pool and then spill.

"I think I knew that," she says, nodding. "Not the cause, but you're different. I thought it was because of what happened with Leah and Estella."

I flinch.

"I'm so sorry, Jessica."

"She's a bitch, Caleb. You know that, right?"

"Jess—"

"No, listen to me. She's a bad person. She defends bad people. Then out of the blue, she calls you in the middle of the night and wants you to come rescue her. She's cunning."

I rub my forehead.

"It's not like that. She's not like that. She's married, Jessica. I don't get to be with her. I just don't want to be with anyone else."

I look at the spoon and then I force myself to look at Jessica.

"I'd want to have children."

She backs up a step. "You said you didn't."

I nod. "Yes, I spoke out of hurt. Because of what happened with…Estella." It's the first time I've said her name in a very long time. It hurts.

"I've always wanted a family. But, I don't want to be married to someone and pretend I don't want kids."

She shakes her head; it starts slowly and then speeds up.

"I have to go," she says. She runs to the room to grab her things. I don't stop her. There is no point. Once again, I've hurt someone because of my feelings for Olivia. *When will it stop? Will it ever stop?* I can't do this to anyone again. It's got to be Olivia or nothing for me.

TWELVE

PAST

Four o'clock, five o'clock, six o'clock, seven. I still wasn't out of the building. I'd been waiting four hours for papers. Papers! As if the rest of my life depended on me signing my name to a piece of paper. I glanced at the clock. I was supposed to be at Olivia's an hour ago. I checked my phone. She hadn't called. Maybe she was still busy packing.

"Caleb," my co-worker, Neal, stuck his head through the door, "you sticking around for the party?"

I grinned. "No, I have somewhere to be tonight."

He raised his eyebrows. "You have somewhere better to be than a dinner your boss is throwing for potential clients?"

"My boss is also my stepfather," I said, typing into my keyboard. "Pretty sure I can swing it." My secretary popped her head next to Neal's.

"Caleb, Sidney Orrico is here. She says she has some things for you to sign."

I jumped out of my chair. "Send her in."

Neal raised his eyebrows, but his head disappeared and was replaced by Sidney's.

"Hey you," she said.

I stood up and walked around the desk to greet her.

Sidney Orrico: brown curls, dimples, blue eyes, long legs. We were neighbors, we went to the same school, and our mothers dragged us along to social events and then forced us to interact. We saw each other regularly, and by force or by nature, we became friends. And then we became more. It started with a kiss on the Fourth of July. After the first kiss, we'd hide out in the rec room at my house and make out on the pool table every chance we got. After a few weeks, I worked my way up to second base. By the end of our first summer together, I'd claimed her virginity. When we started school in the fall, things got awkward…really, really awkward.

Sidney wanted a boyfriend. I wanted a friend with benefits. My fifteen-year-old self tried to explain this to her, but she started crying and then I made out with her just to quell the tears. Then we had sex, and then I had to explain the whole no-dating thing to her again. She slapped me across the face and swore that she was never going to talk to me again.

Not true. She wouldn't stop talking to me. Fifteen-year-old girls are intense—especially when they think they're in love. When she caught me at a popular ice cream place on a date with another girl, she went postal, dumping an entire bowl of dripping chocolate ice cream on my lap.

Sidney Orrico.

Fortunately, for me, she backed off after the ice cream incident. She dated my brother for a while, and then broke up with him for a quarterback. We saw each other randomly after that—holiday parties, prom, the mall. By the time I was dating Olivia, I hadn't seen her in at least a year. She had bypassed college and had gone to real estate school. My mother told me she was working for her father's development company. That's when things got sticky.

I was building Olivia a house. Our house. It was a decision I'd made as soon as I realized I wanted to marry her. I hired an architect to draw up the plans weeks before

I bought the ring and contacted Greg Orrico, Sidney's father.

"The project will take about a year, Caleb. Especially with all of the additional inspections we'll need to pass a widow's walk."

I tapped my pen on the desk. That was fine, as long as the foundation was laid by the time I asked Olivia to marry me. I wanted to be able to take her to see something. The foundation of what we were going to be.

We made plans to meet and sign off on all the paperwork. Before I hung up, Greg told me that Sidney would be my project manager.

"Shit," I said, cradling the phone. If Sidney was anything like I remembered…

Sidney hugged me and pulled a sheaf of papers from her bag. "Are you nervous?"

"Not at all, I propose to the love of my life every day."

She smirked and tapped me on the head with the papers. "Well, let's get to it then."

We spread everything across my desk, and Sidney talked me through each form. I'd just about signed half of them, when Steve wandered into my office in his tux.

"Sidney!" I watched as he hugged her. "You lost all of your freckles, and what happened to all of that metal you used to wear on your teeth?" Sidney and Steve saw each other on a regular basis, but this was their game. I read through my paperwork and waited for it to be over.

"Is that your way of calling me pretty?"

Steve laughed. "Will you stay for the party?"

For the first time I noticed that Sidney was wearing a dress. It looked to me like she had every intention of staying for the party. My mother must have given her a heads-up.

"I am staying," she said. "I was hoping I could get Caleb to have a drink with me before he speeds off on his steed."

"Can't," I said, without looking up. "Olivia is waiting for me."

"Caleb," Steve said. "I need you to make some rounds before you leave. Some of these people are your clients."

"Steve!"

I slammed my laptop closed and stared at him. "I'm proposing to my girlfriend tonight. You can't be serious."

"A few minutes are all I need. Just call Olivia and tell her you're going to be late."

"No." I stood up and grabbed my keys.

Sidney's head bobbed up from where she was reviewing my paperwork. "You're going to hate me."

I sighed. "What did you forget?"

She flushed. "I can just run back to the office and grab it. I'll be back in fifteen minutes."

"What is it, Sidney? Can't it wait until Tuesday?"

She cleared her throat. "The gate keys to the property. You won't be able to get in."

I folded both of my lips in and blinked at her in frustration. *Calm, keep calm.*

"All right. Go! Hurry!" She nodded and jumped up. I turned to Steve. "Thirty minutes, while Sidney is gone. That's it." He patted me on the back. I called my secretary who was already wearing her dress for the night.

"Can you call Olivia, tell her I was held up, but I'll be there as fast as I can?"

She nodded and I went to the small closet in my office where I kept my suit jacket.

I slid my arms into the sleeves, swearing under my breath. This was a bad start to what was supposed to be a huge night. Thirty minutes, that was it. Then I'd be out of here.

By the time she came back, another hour and a half had passed. I'd given up socializing and retreated to my office to wait. I called Olivia twice with no answer. She was probably furious with me.

Sidney walked briskly through the door, holding up her skirt and looking apologetic.

"Traffic, Caleb. I'm so sorry."

I nodded and held out my hand for the key. She looked so forlorn when she dropped it in my palm that I grabbed her wrist before she could pull away.

"Sidney? What's wrong?"

Her bottom lip quivered. She pulled away from me and walked to my desk, leaning up against the side of it.

"Can I see the ring?"

I cocked my head and resisted the urge to look at my watch. Eventually, I nodded and went to get it from the drawer. I opened the box and showed her. Her eyes grew wide.

"It's beautiful," she said. And then she started to cry.

I flipped the box closed and put it in my pocket. "Sidney? What is it? What's wrong?" I gripped her shoulders, and she looked up at me with mascara running down her face.

"I'm in love with you."

Her words rocked me. I brought my forefinger and thumb to my forehead. This wasn't happening right now. I needed to find Olivia. I couldn't deal with this. I didn't want to.

"Sidney, I—"

She shook her head. "It's okay. I've lived with this for a long time. I'm just emotional because you're getting ready to propose and all that…"

I ground my teeth and considered how to proceed. All I could see was Olivia. But, Sidney was my friend. I wasn't in the habit of telling crying women to fuck off. Okay, I could do this quickly. I handed her a tissue and she proceeded to clean up her face.

"Sidney, look at me."

She did.

"I've been lonely. All my life. I was the popular kid. I've always been surrounded by tons of people, but I was indescribably lonely. I didn't know how to cure it. Until the day I saw Olivia. I saw her for the first time standing under this tree." I laughed and rubbed my jaw, remembering. I hadn't shaved. I should have shaved. "When I saw her, I knew she was what was missing. It's crazy, but it's true. I had this flash in my mind, where I saw her sitting at my kitchen table with me, her hair up in this messy bun, drinking coffee and laughing. Right then, I knew I was going to marry her."

Sidney was looking at me with such awe I didn't know if I was doing more harm than good. I had a brief moment when I wished Olivia looked at me like that. I had to fight her to love me. I was in a constant emotional wrestling match with her. I could be with a woman like this, who adored me. I could muster old feelings for Sidney. She was beautiful and kind. I shook my head. *Wrap it up, Caleb.* I told her what I knew to be true.

"When you find him, his name will course through your veins. Olivia courses through mine. She runs through my heart and my brain and my fingers *and* my penis." Sidney laughed through her tears. I grinned.

"You'll find him, Sidney. But, it's not me. I belong to someone else."

I hugged her. She was sitting on my desk and I patted her leg. "Go back to the party, I have to go."

When I looked up, Olivia was standing in my doorway. I felt a rush of blood to my head. Had she heard what I'd told Sidney? Seen the ring box? I had a moment of panic where I didn't know what to do.

She said my name. I watched Sidney hop down from the desk and walk quickly out of the room. She darted a look at Olivia over her shoulder before she closed the door.

Olivia's emotion was frozen on her face. Slowly, it dawned on me what she saw when she walked through the door. How it must have looked. I wrestled with what to tell her. If I explained who Sidney was, I would have to tell her about the ring and the house. I was about to explain the whole thing, anything to get that look off her face, when she told me she loved me for the first time.

"I loved you."

My heart ached. It should have been one of the happiest moments of my life. But, she wasn't telling me because she wanted to. She was telling me to hurt me. Because she thought I did something to hurt her.

I heard my mother's words, about her being too broken. Everything shifted in that moment. I wish it hadn't, but it did. I couldn't fix her. I couldn't love her enough to chip away at the calcified hurt that was affecting everything she did. My thoughts about our life together went from a house in the sunshine and a yard full of children to Olivia crying in a corner, blaming me for rushing her into something she wasn't ready for.

Then she accused me of being like her father.

The hurt was profound. Especially since I'd spent the last year and a half trying to show her I was nothing like him. When she ran out of my office, thinking that I cheated on her, I didn't stop her.

I stood frozen, the ring box pressing against my thigh, the room swinging around me.

I leaned both hands on my desk and squeezed my eyes closed, breathing through my mouth. Five minutes. My whole life just changed in five minutes.

She only wanted to see the bad. Maybe it was for the best. Maybe all I saw was my love and I hadn't weighed the consequences of that love.

Steve walked into my office and stopped short.

"Did I just see Olivia?"

I looked up at him, my eyes burning. He must have seen something on my face.

"What happened?" He pulled the door closed and took a step toward me. I held up a hand to stop him and dropped my head.

"She saw me in here with Sidney. She assumed…"

"Caleb," Steve said. "Go after her."

My head snapped up. That's the last thing I expected to hear. Especially since I wasn't sure how much my mother had turned him.

"She wants out," I said. "Since we first got together. She's always finding a reason for us not to be together. What kind of life can we have if she does that?"

Steve shook his head. "Some people take more work than others. You fell in love with a really complicated woman. You can weigh how hard things can and will be for the two of you, but what you really need to consider is if you can live without her."

I was out the door a second later. *No.* No, I couldn't live without her.

I took the stairs. She'd made a left out of my office instead of going to the elevators. I took them two at a time. By the time I burst through the exit doors, it was dark outside. God, how had I let this day get away from me? If I'd just left when I was supposed to…

Her car was gone. I had to go back upstairs to get my keys. She probably wasn't going to let me explain. If I went to her apartment while she was like this, she wouldn't even open the door. But, if I let the idea that I was cheating sit in her head for too long, it would solidify. She'd believe it, and that would be that. So, what could I do? How did I handle this situation? I paced my office. She wasn't like other women. I couldn't show up and talk her out of her thoughts.

Fuck. This was bad. I had to figure out a way to reach her.

Cammie.

"She's with me," Cammie said, when I called her.

"Let me talk to her, Cammie. Please."

"No, she doesn't want to talk to you. You need to let her cool off."

I'd hung up, thinking that was what I was going to do. But, after a few hours, I was driving to Cammie's. When I got there and didn't see Olivia's car, I knew she'd been lying to me. So I went to the hotel.

THIRTEEN

PRESENT

It's all shadows without Olivia. I feel myself constantly wanting for her light. I haven't heard from her since I left her condo the night she told me about Noah. It's been a month, and I don't know what she's decided. I know what I've decided.

I send her a text.

Divorced?

Her text comes back almost immediately.

O: Fuck off.

You at work?

O: Yes!

I'll be there in ten.

O: No!

I turn my phone off and wait. I was already in the parking lot when I sent the first text. I linger in my car for a minute, running my finger over my bottom lip. I know what she's going to do next, so when I see her walking quickly out of the building, I smirk. She's trying to leave before I show up. I jump out of the car and walk toward her. She doesn't see me until the last minute. She has her car keys out and her heels are snapping on the concrete as she tries to make her escape.

"Going somewhere?"

Her shoulders jerk and she spins around.

"Why are you always so goddamn early?"

"Why are you trying to run away?"

She gives me a dirty look, her eyes darting left and right, as if she's trying to find a way to escape me.

I hold out my hand. "Come on, Duchess."

She tosses a quick glance over her shoulder before she places her hand in mine. I pull her toward me and her little birdlike steps skip to keep up with mine. I don't let go of her hand, and she doesn't try to pull away. When I look down at her, she's biting her lip. She looks terrified. She should.

I stop to open her door then shoot around to mine. She's wearing a red dress with white polka dots. The neckline dips low. She hasn't looked at me since she got in the car; instead she's focused on her feet. Red stilettos, red toenails peeking through. Nice. Her style is a combination of Jacqueline Kennedy and a gypsy—my beautiful contradiction. Her hair is twisted up in a bun, and there is a pen holding it in place. I reach over and slip the pen out. Her hair tumbles around her like black water.

She doesn't ask where we are going. I drive to the beach and pull into a spot a block away. She waits until I walk around to open her door and takes my hand as I help her out. We walk connected, until we reach the sand. She stops there to slip off her shoes, using my shoulder to keep balance. They dangle on the tips of her fingers as she reaches for me with her free hand. I take it and we lace fingers. It is considered winter in Florida, so there is only a handful of sunbathers, most of them from the North and with white hair. The area of beach we are on belongs to a hotel. There are canvas-covered gazebos with lawn chairs underneath them. We find an empty one and I sit down and stretch out my legs. Olivia makes to take the one next to me, but I pull her on my chair. She sits between my legs and leans back against my chest. I put one arm around her and sling the other on top of my head. My heart is racing. I haven't had her in my arms in a long time. It feels so natural to be like this with her. I say her name just to see how it sounds. She jabs me in the ribs with her elbow.

"Don't do that."

"Do what?" I say into her ear.

"Well, talk in that voice for one."

I force myself not to laugh. I can see the goosebumps on her exposed skin. Obviously, my old tricks still work.

"So, you have a hand fetish and you get turned on by the sound of my voice?"

"I never said I had a hand fetish!"

"Really? So you just get turned on by the sound of my voice?"

She wiggles to get away from me, and I have to use both arms to hold her in place while I laugh.

When she finally relaxes again, I gather her hair and swipe it over her left shoulder. I kiss the exposed skin on her neck, and she shivers. I kiss an inch above it and her head tilts to give me better access.

"You shouldn't—we…" Her voice trails off.

"I love you," I say into her ear. She tries to jerk away, but my arms are still wrapped around her.

"Don't, Caleb…"

She's suddenly snapped out of her little daze. Her shapely legs are struggling to gain leverage so she can get away from me.

"Why not?"

"Because it's not right."

"It's not right for me to love you? Or it's not right for you to love me back?"

She is crying; I hear her sniffle.

"Neither." Her voice, which is high on emotion, cracks. Cracks my reserve, cracks my game, cracks my heart.

When I speak, my voice is husky. I stare out at the water. "I can't stay away from you. I've been trying for ten years."

She sobs and drops her head. She is not trying to get away from me anymore, but she's trying to put distance between us. She leans forward and immediately I feel a loss. I've gone so many years without her, I refuse to allow her to try to space me out. I have her trapped and I'm going to take advantage. I wrap my hands in her hair, winding it around my fist, and then I gently pull back until her head is resting against my chest. She allows me to do all of this and doesn't seem to mind the bondage.

Bondage. I'd love to give the love of my life a well-deserved flogging.

I kiss her temple, which is the only thing I can reach, and entwine our fingers, wrapping my arms around her. She snuggles against me and that familiar ache starts in my chest.

"Peter Pan," I say.

There is five seconds of silence before she says, "When I'm with you, every emotion I can possibly feel comes spilling out. I drown in them. I want to run to you, and I want to run away."

"Don't…don't run away. We can do this."

"We don't know how to love each other the right way."

"Bullshit," I say against her ear. "You're full of love that you can't get out. You can't say some things. I'm okay with that now. I know it's there. We've hurt each other. But, we're not kids anymore, Olivia. I want you." I let her go and spin her around so she's kneeling between my spread legs.

I cup her face with my hands, threading my fingers into her hair and laying them flat behind her head. She can't look away from me now.

"I want you." I've said it before, but she's not getting it. She still thinks I'll leave her. Like I did.

Her bottom lip quivers.

"I want your babies, and your anger, and your cold blue eyes…" I choke on my words and I am the one to look away. I bring my gaze back to her face and realize that if I can't convince her now, I'm never going to be able to. "I want to go on anniversary dinners with you, I want to wrap Christmas presents with you. I want to fight with you about stupid things and then hold you down in my bed and make it up to you. I want to have more cake-batter fights and camping trips. I want your future, Olivia. Please come back to me."

Her whole body is shaking. A tear spills down her cheek and I catch it with my thumb.

I grab the back of her neck and pull her toward me so that our foreheads are touching. I run my hands up and down her back.

Her lips are moving, she's trying to formulate words—and by the look on her face I can't tell if I want to hear them. Our noses are parallel, if I bump my head half an inch forward—we'd be kissing. I wait for her.

Our breath mingles. She has my shirt in a vice grip between her fists. I understand her need to clutch something. It is taking every ounce of my self-control to keep from crushing us together.

Both of our chests are rising and falling like the waves. I nudge her nose with mine, and that seems to break her reserve. She wraps her arms around my neck, opens her mouth, and kisses me.

I haven't kissed my girl in months. It feels like the first time. She's up on her knees, leaning over me so that I have to tilt my head back to reach her lips. My hands are under her dress on the back of her thighs. I can feel the material of her panties on my fingertips, but I keep my hands still.

We kiss slowly, just with our lips. We keep pulling back to look each other in the eyes. Her hair creates a curtain between us and the world. We kiss behind it, as it falls around our faces, blocking everything out but each other.

"I love you," she says into my mouth. I smile so big I have to pause in our kissing to recompose my lips. When we start using our tongues, things get heated fast. Olivia likes to bite when she kisses. It really, *really* does something for me.

My heart is in my throat, my brain is in my pants, my hands are up her dress. She pushes away from me and stands up.

"Not until the divorce is finalized," she says. "Take me back."

I stand up and pull her toward me. "All I heard was *take me*."

She laces her arms around my neck, her teeth latching onto her bottom lip. I study her face.

"Why don't you blush? No matter what I say—you never blush."

She smirks. "Because, I'm a fucking badass."

"Yeah, you are," I say softly. I kiss the tip of her nose.

We make our way back to my car. As soon as we shut our doors, Olivia's phone pings.

She lifts it out of her purse, and immediately her face darkens.

"What is it?" I ask.

She looks away from me, her hand frozen midair, still clutching the phone.

"It's Noah. He wants to talk."

FOURTEEN

NOAH

I spin my wedding band on the sticky countertop. It becomes a blur of gold and then does a little dance before falling flat. I pick it up and do it again. The bartender at the shitty dive I wandered into looks at me with his dead eyes before sliding another beer in front of me. I didn't ask, but a good bartender can read his patrons. I pick up the ring, put it in my pocket, and take a long drag of my beer.

She doesn't know I'm back in town. I don't know if I'm ready to tell her. I checked into a hotel near the airport four days ago and have been slumming around at the local bars since. He's back in the picture. I know she's seeing him. I'm not even mad. I left her. What did I expect? It started out slowly. I contracted more and more jobs overseas, leaving for huge chunks at a time. It was financially good for us. But, then I was gone for her birthday, gone for our first anniversary, gone for Thanksgiving. I didn't know that being gone would put such a strain on our relationship. Absence was supposed to make the heart grow fonder. Isn't that what they said? Olivia never complained. She never complained about anything. She was the strongest, most self-reliant person I'd ever met. Despite all my gone-ness, the kicker to her was when I missed the verdict at Dobson's trial.

But, Caleb isn't gone. And he's the first person she ran to when she was afraid. I wanted it to be me, but I'm not even sure I'm emotionally available enough to do that. I'm a career man, first. Always have been. My mother raised my sister and me on her own. I often fantasized about what it would look like to have two parents instead of one. But, not because I was desperate for a father…I wanted my mom to have someone to take care of her, because she took care of us.

For the most part I like being alone. When I turned thirty-eight, I suddenly had this urge to have a family. Not the typical family with kids, I just really wanted a wife. Someone to share coffee with in the mornings and to climb into bed with at night. It was picturesque and beautiful, this image I had in my head—of a house and Christmas lights and dinners together. It was a good dream, except very few women take the child variable out of theirs.

I'm not a romantic, but I can enjoy a good story. When Olivia told me hers on that flight to Rome, I was enthralled. The thought that real people got themselves into these situations where love dominated rational thought was something I was entirely unfamiliar with. She was so honest, so hard on herself. I'm not the type of man who believes in fast love. This is a fast-love culture, where people fall in and out of something so sacred you wonder if it has the same meaning it did a hundred years ago. But, when Olivia said those words "I fell in love underneath a tree," I just about lost it and asked her to marry me right there. She was my opposite, but I wanted to be like her. I wanted to fall in love underneath a tree, fast and hard. I wanted someone to forget me and then remember me in their soul, like her Caleb did.

I immediately thought we were dually matched. Not like souls. Just perfect pieces that needed to fit together in order to see the whole picture. I was a compass to her. And she was the person who could teach me to live. I loved her. God, I loved her. But, she wanted something I wasn't willing to give. She wanted a baby. When arguing turned to bitter fighting, I left. When she wouldn't budge, I filed for divorce. That was wrong. Marriage is compromise.

I take care of my tab and step into the warm air. We can compromise. Adopt. Hell, we could open an orphanage in a third world country for all I care. I just can't do it, have my own. There's too much risk involved.

I need to see her. Enough hiding. I take my phone from my pocket and text her.

Can we talk?

It takes three hours for her to respond with:

O: About what?

You and me

O: Haven't we done enough of that?

I have something new to put on the table.

Twenty minutes go by before her single text comes through.

O: Okay

Thank God. I'm not going to let him take her from me. He let her go in Rome. He broke her heart…again. That night, when Olivia and I parted after dinner, I went back to my hotel and thought about my life. How empty it was. I think I'd already made the decision to change it by the time she called my room, crying. I caught a cab to her hotel and sat with her while she mourned him. She told me it was the last time, that she could only bend and break so many times before the damage was irreparable. She hadn't wanted me to touch her. I wanted to. I wanted to hold her and let her cry on me. But she'd sat on the edge of her bed with her back straight and her eyes closed, and cried silent tears that flowed like rivers down her cheeks. I'd never seen anyone deal with their pain with so much restraint. It was heartbreaking—the way she wouldn't make a sound. Finally, I'd turned on the television and we'd sat with our backs against her headboard and watched *Dirty Dancing*. It was dubbed in Italian. I wasn't sure about Olivia, but I had a sister and I'd seen it enough to know the dialogue by heart. I was still there when the sun came up. I cancelled my appointments, made her get dressed, and took her to see Rome. She fought me at first, saying she'd rather stay at the hotel, but then I'd ripped open the drapes in her room and made her stand in front of them.

"Look. Look where you are," I said. She'd stood beside me and the mist seemed to lift from her eyes.

"Okay," she said.

First the Colosseum, then we ate pizza at a little shop near the Vatican. She cried when she stood in the Vatican underneath Da Vinci's handiwork. She'd turned to me and firmly said, "These are not tears for him. These are because I'm here and I've always wanted to be." Then she'd hugged me and thanked me for taking her.

We parted after that day, but when I got back to Miami I called her. We went out to dinner a few times. Very casually. Things didn't move forward until I kissed her. I hadn't planned on doing it, but we were saying good night outside of a restaurant and I just went in without thinking. It was months before we had sex for the first time. She was timid, hesitant. It took a while for her to trust me. But, she did. And I am not letting that go as easily as he did.

FIFTEEN

PAST

Six months before I saw Olivia at the music store on Butts and Glade, I bought a ring for Leah. It sat next to Olivia's ring in my sock drawer for a week before I moved it. It didn't feel right having them together. I'd bought an antique-style ring for Olivia. It was elegant. When things fell apart, I hadn't known what to do with it. Sell it? Pawn it? Keep it forfuckingever? In the end, I couldn't part with the past and it had stayed exactly where it was. For Leah, I chose princess cut. It was large and flashy and would impress her friends. I planned to ask her while we were on vacation in Colorado. We skied there twice a year. I was getting sick of the skiing circus with her ridiculous friends who named their children things like Paisley and Peyton and Presley. Names without soul. It was my opinion that if you called a child a pattern for long enough, they would become scrambled. My mother named me after a Biblical spy. He was all dash and dare. Needless to say, names meant something.

I suggested we go on a ski trip alone. Initially, she refused to go without "her people," but I think she caught a whiff of engagement ring in the air and quickly changed her tune. The ski trip was a month away when I panicked. It wasn't an inner, hidden panic either. It was a drinking binge panic in which I jogged six miles a day listening to

Eminem and Dre, and googled Olivia's name by night with Coldplay on repeat. I found her. She was working as a secretary at a law firm. I didn't have the chance to find her; I got into a car accident and told my first life-altering lie.

The day I saw her, I was already two months deep in my amnesia lie and just hanging out in the general vicinity hoping to run into her. I'd never actually go into her job—Olivia took herself way too seriously to take that well, but I considered ambushing her in the parking lot. And I might have, had she not walked into the Music Mushroom that day. I was going to tell her the truth—how I'd lied to my friends and family, how it had all been because I couldn't leave her in my past like I was supposed to. And in that split second when I asked her about the damn CD in her hand, she looked so panicked, so stricken that I fell deeper into my lie. I couldn't do it. I watched the whites of her eyes expand, her nostrils flaring as she tried to decide what to say. At least she wasn't swearing at me. That was good.

"Ummm." That's what she decided to say to me. I heard her voice for the first time and I couldn't keep my smile. It rose at the corners of my mouth and ran right into my eyes like it hadn't been lost for the last three years. She was holding a cello-wrapped boy band in her hand. She looked hella confused.

"I'm sorry? I didn't catch that." It was cruel to play on her surprise, but I wanted to keep her talking.

"Err, they are okay," she said. "They're not really your style." I could feel her mentally retreating at that point. Her hand was already placing the CD back on its shelf, her eyes darting toward the door. I had to do something. Say something. *I'm sorry. I was a fool. I'd marry you today, on this very day, if you agreed to it…*

"They're not my style?" I repeated her words while I tried to formulate my own. She looked so forlorn in that moment that I smiled at her beauty more than anything else.

"What exactly do you think my style is?" I immediately recognized my mistake. This was the way we used to flirt. If I wanted to make any headway in her forgiving me, I had to cut the shit and—

"Umm, you're a classic rock kind of guy…but I could be wrong."

She was right, so right. She was breathing through her mouth, her full lips parted.

"Classic rock?" I repeated. She knew me. Leah probably would say my style was Alternative. Not that she knew anything about music; she listened to the top 100 like it was full of Biblical truths instead of clichés. I dragged my bitter thoughts away from Leah and back to Olivia. She looked scared. I saw her expression and it hit me. She wasn't dragging anger around. She was dragging regret. Same as me.

There was a chance for us. Away from the old.

"I'm sorry," I said. And then the lie came. I'd been telling the same one for two months. It came easily, pouring off my tongue like relationship poison.

You're protecting her, I told myself.

I was protecting myself.

I was the same selfish fuck that pushed her too hard in the past. I started to walk out. To run from what I'd just done, when I heard her call after me. That was it. She was going to tell me that she knew me, and I'd tell her that I didn't have amnesia. That the whole fucking charade had been about her. Instead, she took off down an aisle. I watched her dark hair bob as she weaved past people who were in her way.

My heart was beating fast. When she came back, she had a CD in her hand. I glanced at it: Pink Floyd. It was my favorite of their albums. She'd bought my lie and she'd brought me my favorite CD.

"You'll like this," she said. She tossed it to me. I waited for her to tell me that she knew who I was. But, she didn't. I was overcome by every goddamn thing I had ever done to her, every lie, every betrayal.

Here she was trying to heal me with music, and I was lying to her. I walked. Walked. Right out.

I had no intention of ever seeing her again. That was it. I had my chance and I blew it. I went back to my condo and put that CD on, turning the volume all the way up. Hoping it could remind me of who I was. Who I definitely wanted to be again. Then I saw her again. That wasn't planned. That was kismet. I couldn't help myself. It was like every second, minute, hour I'd spent away from her over the last three years came to slap me in the face as I watched her knock over a display of ice cream cones. I bent down to help her pick them up. Her hair was short, barely reaching her shoulders. It was cut at an angle, the front longer than the back. The very tips looked like they could slice your fingers if you touched them.

She wasn't the Olivia I remembered with her long, wild hair and the untamed look in her eye. This Olivia was smoother, more in control. She weighed what she said rather than letting it spill out. Her eyes didn't have the same light they used to. I wondered if I'd taken that from her. That hurt me. God—so much. I wanted to put the light back in her eyes.

I went straight to Leah's. Told her I couldn't do what we'd been doing. She took it as me saying I couldn't be in a relationship with someone I didn't remember.

"Caleb, I know you feel lost right now, but when your memory comes back everything will make sense," she said.

When my memory came back, nothing made sense. That's why I lied.

I shook my head. "I need time, Leah. I'm sorry. I know this is a mess. I don't want to hurt you, but I need to take care of some things."

She looked at me like I was a knock-off purse. I'd seen her do it a million times. Disgust, confusion at how someone could settle. Once she'd made a snide remark in the grocery store while we stood behind a woman sifting through a stack of coupons. She'd had a Louis Vuitton purse slung over her shoulder.

"People who can afford Louis don't clip coupons," she'd said loudly. "That's how you can tell it's a knock-off."

"Maybe people who clip coupons save enough money to be able to afford name brand purses," I'd snapped back. "Stop being so shallow and judgmental."

She sulked for two days, claiming I had attacked her rather than defended her. We fought about how she put things above people. It was a turnoff to me to watch someone place that much value on a thing. After she stormed out, I had two days of peace, during which I seriously considered ending things with her.

Until she showed up at my condo with a pie she'd baked, full of apologies. She brought one of her Chanel purses with her, and I watched in fascination as she pulled scissors from her purse and cut it up in front of me. It seemed like such a sincere and contrite gesture, I softened. She hadn't changed. Neither had I, I guess. I was still in love with another woman. Still faking it with her. Still too unsure to do anything about it.

But, now I was tired.

"I have to go," I said, standing up. "I have to meet someone for coffee."

"A girl?" she asked right away.

"Yes."

Our eyes locked. Where I'd expected to see hurt, maybe tears, she only looked angry. I kissed her on the forehead before I walked out.

I might have been doing this the wrong way, the selfish way, the damn cowardly way—but I was doing it.

SIXTEEN

PRESENT

I drop Olivia off at her office. On the ride over, she barely says two words to me. After what just happened between us I don't know what to say either. I know one thing for sure—Noah wants her back. I could almost laugh. *Join the club, motherfucker.*

He's been gone for three months and is finally getting withdrawals.

It's drizzling when we pull into the parking lot. She opens the door and gets out without a backward glance. I watch her walk toward her car, her shoulders not quite as stiff as they usually are. I suddenly throw my door open and run around the car, jogging to catch up to her. I grab her arm as she reaches for the door and fling her around until she's facing me. Then I press her against the side of her car with my body. She is momentarily stunned, her hands pushing up against my chest, like she's not sure what I'm doing. I put my hand on the back of her head and pulling her toward me, I kiss her. I kiss her deep, the way I would kiss her if we were having sex. Our breathing sounds louder than the traffic behind us, louder than the thunder overhead.

When I pull away from her mouth, she's panting. My hands are planted on either side of her head. I speak softly, looking at her mouth as I do. "Do you remember the orange grove, Olivia?"

She nods, slowly. Her eyes are wide.

"Good," I say, running a thumb along her bottom lip. "Good. I do too. Sometimes I get so numb, I have to remember that so I can feel again."

I back away from her and get in my car. As I pull away, I look in my rearview mirror to catch a glimpse of her. She is still standing where I left her, one hand pressed against her chest.

My competition is good. Undoubtedly he's never lied to her, broken her heart, or married another woman to spite her. But she's mine, and I'm not giving her up without a fight this time.

I wait a few days and then I text her while I'm at work.

What did he want?

I close the door to my office, loosen the top button of my dress shirt, and sling my legs up on my desk.

O: He wants to work things out.

I knew it was coming, but I still get a pain in my chest. Fuck that.

What did you tell him?

O: That I need time to think. Same thing I'm telling you.

No

O: No?

No

I rub a hand over my face, and then type:

You've had ten years to think.

O: It's not that easy. He's my husband.

He filed for divorce! He doesn't want to have children with you.

O: He said he'd be willing to adopt.

I pinch the skin at the bridge of my nose and grind my teeth together.

What I was doing was wrong. I should let them be together—fix things, but I can't.

O: Please, Caleb, give me time. I'm not the person you used to know. I need to do the right thing.

Then stay with him. That's the right thing to do. But, I am the right thing for you.

She doesn't respond after that.

I sit at my desk for a long time, thinking. I am unable to do any work. When my stepfather walks in an hour later, he raises his eyebrows.

"There are only two things that can put that expression on your face." He takes a seat opposite me and folds his hands in his lap.

"And what's that?" I love my stepfather. He's the most perceptive man I know.

"Leah…and Olivia."

I grimace at the first name, frown at the second.

"Ah," he says, smiling. "I see the little raven-haired vixen is back?"

I run my thumbnail across my bottom lip, back and forth, back and forth.

"You know, Caleb…I am very aware of what your mother thinks about her. But, I couldn't disagree with her more."

I look up at him, surprise evident on my face. He very rarely disagrees with my mother, but when he does, it's usually because he's right. He also never shares his personal thoughts unless asked. The fact that he's doing it now makes me sit up straighter in my chair.

"I knew she had you the first time you brought her over. I've had a love like that."

My eyes dart to his face. He never talks about his life before my mother. They've been married for fifteen years. He'd been married once before, but—

"Your mother," he says, grinning. "She's terrible—truly. I've never seen someone as ruthless. But, she's good too. The two sides balance each other out. I think the first time she met Olivia, she recognized a like soul and wanted to protect you."

My mind flashed to that first dinner. I'd brought Olivia home to meet them, and my mother had, of course, made her as uncomfortable as possible. I landed up dragging Olivia out in the middle of dinner—so angry with my mother I never wanted to speak to her again.

"Most men like danger. There is nothing sweeter than a dangerous woman," he says. "Makes us feel a little manlier to be able to call them ours."

He's right…possibly. I lost interest in healthy women shortly after meeting Olivia. It's a curse. After tasting her, I've rarely found a woman who I actually think is interesting. I like her darkness, her ever-present sarcasm, the way she makes me work for every smile, every kiss. I like how strong she is, how hard she fights for things. I love how weak I make her. I might be her only weakness. I earned that spot and I very much want to keep it. Olivia is the type of woman that men write songs about. There are about fifty of them on my iPod that make me think of her.

"Is she available?"

I sigh and rub my forehead. "She's separated. But he showed up again a few days ago."

"Ah." He strokes his beard, his eyes smiling at me.

He's the only one in my family who knows what I did. I went on a drunken binge after Olivia left and landed up punching a cop outside of a bar. I called him to come bail me out. He didn't tell my mother, even when I confessed everything to him about the amnesia. He never once judged me. Only affirmed that people did crazy things when it came to love.

"What do I do, Steve?"

"I can't tell you what to do, son. She brings out the worst in you and the best in you."

It's true and it's hard to hear.

"Did you tell her how you feel?"

I nod.

"Then all you can do is wait."

"What if she doesn't choose me?"

He grins and leans forward in his seat. "Well, there's always Leah…"

My laugh starts in my chest and works its way out.

"Worst joke ever, Steve…worst joke ever."

Just like that, as soon as it began again, she's back together with Noah. I know because she doesn't call me. She doesn't text. She moves on with her life and leaves me in the balance.

SEVENTEEN

PAST

My anger burned. I wanted to kill him, slowly, with my hands.

Jim…he had almost—I didn't want to think about what he'd almost done. And what if I hadn't been around? Who would she have called? Three years she'd lived without me, I had to remind myself. Three years of drying her own tears and staving off assholes with her spiked words. She hadn't fallen apart without me. She'd grown tougher. I don't know if I felt relieved or sore about it. I'd had too much pride to admit my fault in our demise. By not saying more, by not fighting harder for her, I'd allowed her to believe it was her fault. And it wasn't. Her only fault had been her brokenness. Not knowing how to express what she was feeling. Olivia was her own worst enemy. She decided something about herself and then she sabotaged her own happiness with it. She needed the type of love that stayed no matter what. She needed to see that nothing could devalue her in my eyes. *Fuck*, I hated myself. But, I'd been a child. I'd been given something valuable and I hadn't known how to take care of it. I still wasn't sure I knew how. But, one thing was certain—if anyone touched her, I'd kill them. I was going to kill him. Make up for lost time when I hadn't been there to protect her.

I walked calmly to my car because she was watching. As soon as I pulled out of her development, I gunned it. She'd slept against my chest, clinging to me like a child. I'd stayed awake the whole night, torn between wanting to comfort her and wanting to beat the shit out of him. I carried her to her bed, just as the sun was coming up, and went back to the living room to call some hotels. When she woke up, I told her that he'd checked out the night before and left town. But, that wasn't the case. The drunken asshole had gone back to his hotel room and was probably sleeping off his hangover.

I found him at the Motel 6. He was still driving the same 1969 Mustang that he had in college. I remembered him from back then. Skinny kid. One of those emotionally androgynous men who wore skinny jeans and eyeliner and liked to talk about their favorite bands. I never understood what Olivia saw in him. She could have had anyone. His Mustang was parked directly outside room 78. I could see my reflection in it as I passed by. I pounded on the door. It only hit me later that it might not have been his room. I heard a muffled voice and the sounds of something being knocked over. Jim swung open the door, looking enraged. He reeked of alcohol. I could smell it from two feet away. When he saw my face, his expression transitioned from surprise to curiosity…then landed soundly on fear.

"What the—"

I shoved him inside and kicked the door closed. The room smelled.

Slipping my watch from my wrist, I tossed it on the bed. Then I hit him.

He fell back, crashing into the dresser and knocking over a lamp. I was on him before he could stand up. I yanked him to his feet by his shirt, his legs flailing beneath him trying to find ground.

I set him on his feet, and then I hit him again.

"Caleb," he said. He held one hand over his nose, which was bleeding through his fingers, and the other he extended toward me, palm outstretched. "I was drunk, man—I'm sorry."

"You're sorry? I don't give a fuck if you're sorry."

He shook his head.

"Shit," he said. "Shit." He bent over at the waist, hands on his knees and started laughing.

I ground my teeth together until I was sure they'd turn to dust.

"You lied to her about the amnesia." He was laughing so hard he could barely speak. I shoved him.

He staggered back, but he was still laughing. "You're just as bad as me, man. The two of you pretending not to know each other, it's like a fucking—"

I grabbed the front of his shirt and flung him sideways. He landed on the bed, laughing so hard he was holding his stomach. Infuriated, I went after him again.

Before he could say anything else, I pulled him up and held him against the wall.

"You don't know anything about us."

"Don't I?" he hissed. "Who do you think was there for her after you cheated on her and left?"

"I didn't," I said through my teeth, and then I clenched my jaw. I didn't need to explain anything to this little shit.

"You speak to her again, I kill you. You look at her again, I kill you. You breathe in her direction again—"

"You kill me," he finished.

He shoved me, but the guy was like one fifty soaking wet. I didn't move.

"You've been killing her since the day you met her," he spat at me. That hit me hard. I thought about the day I saw her in the record store and how there seemed to be no light left in her eyes. "Why'd you come back? You should have left her alone."

Blood was smeared across his face and his greasy hair was sticking up. I looked down at him impassively. "You think you could have had her if I hadn't?"

My words hit him somewhere deep. His eyes rolled to the side and his nostrils flared. So, he was in love with her too? I laughed, which sent him into a rage. He struggled against my hold, his face clammy and red.

"She's mine," I said into his face.

"Fuck you," he said.

I hit him again.

EIGHTEEN

PRESENT

I don't hear anything from her. How much time goes by? Everything feels so much longer when you're hurting. I am so consumed by thoughts of her, that when a few people from work invite me to go out for drinks, I agree just for the distraction. Among the group is a girl who works in the accounting department and flirts with me relentlessly. Steve raises his eyebrows when he sees me leaving with them.

"A word of advice," he says, as I stop in his office to say goodbye. "When you're in love with a woman, you shouldn't get involved with other women."

"Noted," I say. "Though, I would like to offer that she is probably sleeping with another man as we speak."

"You still think she's coming back to you?"

"Yes."

"Why?"

"Because she always does."

He nods as if that settles things.

We land up at an upscale martini bar in Fort Lauderdale. I leave my suit jacket in the car and loosen a few buttons on my shirt. One of the girls smiles at me as we walk toward the bar. I think her name is Asia spelled Aja.

"Your ass looks great in pinstripes," she says. My buddy Ryan claps me on the back. I've known him since college. Steve gave him a job when we graduated as a favor to me. Turns out he's pretty good at what he does. Ryan looks at Aja with mock sympathy.

"This guy," he smirks, "is not going to sleep with you."

Aja grins. "That would be a new experience for me."

I laugh and really look at her for the first time. She reminds me of Cammie.

"Broken heart?" she asks, ignoring Ryan who is trying to insert himself between us.

"Something like that."

"I specialize in those." She winks at me, and now she reminds me of Leah. I shiver involuntarily. I don't want to be reminded of Leah.

"I've grown attached to my broken heart. I think I'll keep it." I hold the door open for the girls, who file in one by one. Aja waits for me on the other side of the door, and I inwardly groan. I'd rather not spend the night fighting off advances from a woman I'm not interested in. On the other hand, she'd be no work at all. I don't like that. Women hold all the power. They should use it like a whip, not offer it up like a sacrifice.

I haven't done the group bar scene since I was in my early twenties. I buy the first round, hoping that buying drinks will make up for the fact that I'm about to slip away from their group and drink on my own.

Aja finishes her martini in two sips and decides to make me her sole prey for the night. She is joined by Lauren from the accounting department. I've tried for the last ten minutes to have an adult conversation with the two of them, but if I talk about anything other than office gossip and movies, their eyes glaze over. Aja suggests that we leave and go to her place.

A whip, I mentally tell her. *Use it like a whip.*

"Dude," Ryan says when they're distracted by their third round of shots. "You could have both tonight if you wanted to. Loosen up, man. Every time Olivia is around, you become celibate."

I love Ryan, but in that moment, I want to slam my fist into his jaw. I stand up, looking around for the bathroom.

"I didn't mean anything," he says, catching the look on my face. I nod and pat his shoulder as I walk by to show no hard feelings.

My friends never liked Olivia. None of them could understand how a man that went from sleeping with every girl on campus could wait to cash in on a girl's virginity for two years.

Ryan had relentlessly tried to get me to cheat, to the point where I'd eventually stopped hanging out with him.

My other friends had been no less direct.

"She's a fucking cocktease. There are other girls who look like her."

It was true…most of it. She wasn't an intentional cocktease, but that didn't mean that ninety percent of the time I was with her, I didn't have blue balls. There might have been other girls who looked like her, but there was no one who moved like Olivia. She was like water. She moved through everything no matter how hard it was. If there was something she couldn't control, she'd flow right over the top of it and keep going.

I splash water on my face in the bathroom and look at myself in the mirror. She's in my eyes tonight.

I feel ridiculous being here. Clubbing like I'm a kid. I wipe my face and head out. I would say my goodbyes, call a cab, and stop acting like a twenty-year-old douchebag. I am weaving through the suddenly packed bar, when something flashes in the corner of my eye. An emerald green dress curved around a truly magnificent ass. Her hair is up, coiled like black snakes and falling down in places that make her look like walking sex. Two things happen: I get immediately hard, and I get immediately angry. Where the fuck is Noah? I search the crowd for his dark hair and can't find it. Maybe he went to the bathroom. I flinch at the thought of meeting him at a urinal. I'll wait here until he comes back, then I'll call a cab and leave before they see me. I stand glued to my spot for five minutes.

Olivia. I should have known she'd do this. When her life is in turmoil, Olivia hides on the dance floor. I find it disturbing. The girl knows how to move, which makes every male in the near vicinity *move* toward her. I watch as she lifts her arms above her head and sways from side to side. I see Cammie's blonde head bobbing around next to her, and I grit my teeth. I look to the bar where my group is still lingering, and then back to Olivia. In a split decision, I move toward her. I am shaking I am so angry. I want to get to her before she—

She climbs onto a speaker. I stop short. She now has her own stage, and everyone is watching her. Including me, I'm watching her. I stand transfixed. If what just happened in my pants is happening to the other men in the room…I need to get to her before I kill someone. *Where the fuck is Noah?* If he's ever seen her dance, there's no way he'd allow her to go out alone. Maybe they aren't working things out. I brighten up at this. She's dancing so seductively, a guy is trying to climb onto the speaker with her. Cammie smacks his back and shouts something at Olivia—who bends down to hear her. Her dress gapes and I see cleavage.

I shove someone aside and shoulder my way through her admirers. When I reach the speaker, I grab the guy by his shirt collar before he can hoist himself up and shove him to my left. Cammie turns around to see what's happening, her eyes growing wide when she sees me. She tilts her head up to look at Olivia—who is still oblivious. All I can see are legs—toned, tanned. I reach up and wrap both hands around her waist, lifting her down. Her mouth drops open. I make sure to run the full length of her body down my own as I lower her.

She swears at me and smacks my chest. I hold her against me so she can get the full effect of what I'm about to say.

"Do you feel that?" I say into her ear. She glares up at me. "That's what you've done to every man in this room."

It's fairly dark, but I can see the effect my words have on her. She doesn't like to be the subject of sexual fantasy—little prude. I glance over at Cammie who mouths, *Get her out of here.*

I nod and push her in front of me. She's had too much to drink already or she'd be fighting me. The bar is packed, and it's hard to move us both through the throng of bodies. I press her back against my front and wrap my arms around her. We walk that way until we reach the doors. My lips are pressed together as a result of having one of her best assets bumping repeatedly against me. When we reach the fresh air, she's quiet as I take her hand.

"Where's your car?"

"At the office. Cammie drove me."

I swear. Her office is a good eight blocks away from where we are.

I tug her along the sidewalk, her heels making clipping noises as she tries to keep up.

"Where are we going?"

"We're walking to your car."

"No!" She yanks her hand away. "I'm not spending an hour with you."

I stride toward her, grab her face in my fingers, and kiss her roughly on the lips. I don't let go of her face. "Yes, you fucking are. I'm not letting you go back in there to get molested."

Her nostrils flare as she glowers at me.

"What?" I say. "What snarky little comment are you going to make? Keep your mouth shut, and let's go."

We walk two blocks before she starts complaining about her shoes. I yank her into an upscale corner store and snatch a pair of rubber flip-flops from a hook hanging next to the ice cream cooler. Tossing them onto the counter, I reach for the nearest bottle of liquor—which happens to be tequila—and hand that to the cashier who is openly eyeing Olivia.

I hand him my card and watch him watch Olivia. He hands the card back and thanks me without ever moving his eyes from her body.

God, I'm going to fucking kill someone tonight.

Once outside, I bend down in front of her and unstrap her shoes. She steadies herself on my back as I gently pull them off and slide on the flip-flops.

When I stand up she's so much shorter than me, I grin.

She holds out her hand for the tequila bottle. I give it to her. She twists off the cap and lifts the bottle to her mouth, all without taking her eyes from mine. She takes a sip, licks her lips, and hands the bottle back. I take a longer sip, and then we start our long walk.

Sometimes I fall back a little so she's walking in front of me.

"Have I ever told you, that you have the single greatest ass I've ever seen?"

She ignores me.

"Of course, I've only seen it once…"

She stops, snatches the bottle from me, and takes an especially long drink.

"Can you just not flirt with me for five seconds?"

"Fine, let's talk about you and Noah."

She groans.

"You were supposed to be working things out…or thinking…or—"

"I am!"

I scratch my head and look at her out of the corner of my eye.

"Where is he?"

She sniffs. "We had a fight."

"About?"

We cross the street and head west.

"You."

My skin tingles. I don't know whether to feel guilty, curious, or happy that I'm important enough to cause discord.

"You told him that you saw me?"

She nods.

"I can't imagine he liked that."

"He knows everything about us. I never tried to hide things from him. I thought you and I were over, and I wanted to be honest with him."

I grab her hand and pull her to a stop. "Olivia, he knew how you felt about me, and he still married you."

I can't keep the incredulity out of my voice. What man would sign up for that? I rub my hand along the back of my sweat-soaked neck.

"Don't take that self-righteous tone with me when you did the same thing."

"That was different. I stayed with Leah because she was pregnant. I thought it was the right thing."

Olivia's mouth pops open. "Leah was…" She shakes her head. "It's none of my business. And you're right—it was different. Noah is a wonderful person, unlike that black-hearted bitch you married."

We're nearing her office building. She fumbles in her purse until she finds her keys. Instead of going to her car, she opens the door to Spinner & Kaspen and punches the code into the alarm system.

"We were on a cruise when he asked me to marry him. We were taking a walk on the deck, and he just turned to me and said, 'If you weren't in my life anymore, I'd be devastated. I want you to marry me.'"

I search her eyes trying to figure out why she's telling me this.

"He said he knew what I felt for you was real, but he was willing to love me through it."

I swallow. *Damn.* He's a better man than me.

"I forgot you for a year. Noah was good at making me forget."

I interrupt her because I don't want to hear this. "Olivia—"

"Shut up." The door swings shut behind us and we're standing in the dark waiting room. All I can see are the outlines of her face. "I am in love with him, Caleb. I am."

I grind my teeth together.

"But when I won the case, and I went into panic mode, it wasn't him I wanted to talk to." She sounds almost ashamed to say it. I remember how she showed up at my condo. "I just wanted you…and when Dobson escaped from the institution—I wanted you. When I had a miscarriage…" She places a hand over her mouth and sobs into it.

"Duchess…"

"Shut up and let me finish." She uses her fingertips to wipe underneath her eyes. "When I had a miscarriage, I wanted your arms around me," she says again. "Caleb, it hurts him. I don't know whether to scream *I told you so* at him, or to drown myself in the ocean for bringing destruction into everything I do."

She turns and stalks to her office. I follow her blindly. She flings the door open and flicks on the desk lamp instead of the halogen bulbs that hang from the ceiling. Walking over to her filing cabinet, she opens it and pulls out a stack of papers. She hands them to me.

"Why didn't you tell me?"

My eyes water, my throat burns. "I was going to—that night."

Her chin rises and her lips tilt downward. "She was—"

"An old friend—she was in charge of building the house."

"And when I saw you—"

"We were going over the plans. I told her I was going to propose that night. She asked to see the ring."

She sucks in her cheeks and turns her face away until she's looking at the wall to her left.

"You were going to propose to me?"

The tears are already cutting across her cheeks, dripping off her chin, and I haven't even gotten to the worst part.

"Yes."

She looks at the floor and nods. "So what did I see—when I walked in?"

"We were just talking. She told me she had feelings for me. I was trying to reassure her it wasn't mutual."

She punches her fists on her hips and cuts a circle around the room. "So, why didn't you tell me that?"

"You started throwing things at me pretty fast, Duchess. I could barely open my mouth before you'd called me your father, told me you loved me for the first time, and stormed out. I went after you. I waited for a few hours and then went to Cammie's. When you weren't there, I figured you must have gone to the hotel. By the time I got there…"

"So, it's all my fault?"

I grab for her. "No," I say. "It was my fault. I didn't fight hard enough. I should have grabbed you, made you listen."

"You didn't even kiss her?"

"No, but I was attracted to her. I had thought about it."

"Oh God, give me a minute…" She begins pacing between her desk and the window. I slide down the wall until I am sitting, one knee propped up.

Finally, she says, "Noah asked me if I still love you."

I clear my throat. "What did you tell him?"

She sits down, sliding her feet out of the flips-flops and back into her stilettos. I watch as she bends down to tie the clasps on each one, her hair falling over her shoulder and grazing the ground. She's buying time, trying to look busy while she thinks.

"That we're dysfunctional and toxic!"

"We *were* dysfunctional and toxic," I correct her.

She shoots me a dirty look and runs her hands along her thighs. I get the feeling she's trying to wipe me away.

"You and I are in love, baby." I take a swig from the tequila bottle and rest my arm on my raised knee. The liquor is beginning to burn my throat.

"No…nope." She shakes her head. "We're drunk," she informs me, "and drunk people have crazy, sporadic thoughts."

"Very true," I agree. "Sometimes when I'm drunk, I think that loving you is sane."

She throws a clump of sticky notes at me. I move my head to the left and they hit the wall. I take another sip of tequila.

She's working herself into a frenzy. It's sexy. I wait for her to start swearing and am rewarded a minute later.

"There is nothing fucking solid to fucking prove that we fucking work. We've bombed out like—"

I stand up, and her mouth snaps shut.

"Proof…you need proof, Duchess?"

She shakes her head. I drank more than I should have and my emotions are riding a very large tequila wave.

"Because I can show you exactly what you need." I advance toward her and she backs up.

"Don't you dare." She holds up a finger to ward me off. I smack it away and grab her by the waist, yanking her against me. I lower my mouth to her ear.

"Let me do whatever I want to you for one night, and you'll have all the proof you need."

Her eyes glaze over and I laugh, bending my head down to touch our lips together. I run my tongue along the inside of her top lip. She shoves at my chest.

"Don't!" she says, trying to push me away.

"Why not?" I kiss the corner of her mouth and she whimpers. "Peter Pan," I whisper into her ear.

"I'm afraid."

"Afraid of what?" I kiss the opposite corner.

She's not as stiff as she was a minute ago. I kiss her mouth full on and close my eyes at the feel of her lips. *God, I am so whipped by this woman.*

"Of how vulnerable you make me."

She opens her mouth and lets me kiss her. She doesn't kiss back.

"I make you vulnerable because you love me. That's the price you pay for love, baby girl."

We are kissing softly now, pausing to speak, but never moving more than an inch away from each other.

"You have to have real feelings to make love. We made love in the orange grove."

I back her up until the backs of her thighs are flush against the desk.

I move my hands to the hem of her dress and begin sliding them up her legs. "How often do you think about the orange grove, Olivia?"

She's panting.

"Every day."

I grab the backs of her thighs and lift her onto the desk. I stand between her legs and slide the dress over her head. I kiss one shoulder then the other.

"Me too."

Unstrapping her bra, I lower my head and take a nipple in my mouth. Her whole body arches backwards and her thighs clench around my waist.

"Everything you do is sexy. Have I ever told you that?" I move to the other side…repeat the motion until she squirms.

She latches her hands in my hair, and it takes every ounce of my willpower not to take her right then.

"Still the silent lover," I say, moving back to her mouth. Her eyes are closed, but her lips are parted. "But we both know, Duchess, that I have the secret to working your vocal cords."

Her eyes fly open. I trail a finger down her neck. She's trying to formulate a snarky comeback, but I have her body in my hands and she can't seem to make words.

I kiss her neck softly. One of her arms is looped around my neck, and the other is clutching my bicep. Her eyes are smoky blue. She's listening to me seduce her with an almost eager look on her face. I run my hands down her sides and loop my fingers around the thin straps of her panties. As I pull down, she lifts her hips so I can get them off. Now she's naked, perched on the edge of her desk in nothing but three-inch black heels.

"We're going to keep the heels on..." I yank her thighs further apart and trace a hand up the inside of her leg. She watches my hand, riveted. I keep my lips in a straight line, but I want to grin at her obvious hand fetish. She's had one since we were in college. My breath hitches when I touch her.

She's very ready. She folds her lips in and her eyes close. I feel like a teenage boy scoring for the first time. How many minutes, hours, days—have I dreamed about touching her like this? I want to savor the feel of her. I play with her, teasing, rubbing, sliding. I never got to do this the last time, so I take my time. I am so fascinated by the feel of her, by the noises she's making, that I could easily do this for an hour. I could do this every day. I *want* to do this every day. Our foreheads are pressed together, our lips touching but not moving. She has her hand wrapped around the back of my head. I can feel her need in the way her body is tightening. I like that I'm the cause of her untidy breathing and the jerking of her muscles. I like how her body responds to my hands. I still have one finger pressed inside of her when I speak.

"I'm not going to make love to you this time." My voice is husky. She's pushing my pants down, her tongue pressed against her top lip. I bite her tongue and move my mouth to her ear.

"I'm going to fuck you." She stills—or freezes is more like it. I push my own pants down and step out of them. She's eyeing me with wildly glazed eyes.

She lies back, her hair draping over the side of the desk—so long it's sweeping the carpet. Her legs are bent at the knees, heels perched on the edge of the desk—looking every bit like she stepped out of an erotic fantasy. And just when I think I have her, that I've seduced her into submission, she licks her lips and says:

"Hard and fast, Drake—and make it last longer than last time."

Afterwards, we lie on the floor of her office. Me on my back, one arm behind my head, the other wrapped around her waist. She's lying on my chest in the picturesque postcoital position. About halfway through our tangle of hard sex, we started making love. We can't avoid it. Everything with us eventually becomes emotional—even when we try not to make it that way. I am replaying every warm second of it in my head.

"I think I'm sexually addicted to you."

"It's just the newness of it," she says, "because we never did it before."

"Why do you always try to downplay my feelings for you?"

"I don't trust them," she says after a minute. "You claim that you love me, but you've loved other women in between."

"You pushed me away, Duchess. I'm a human being. I was trying to find someone to replace you."

"What about Leah? You married her."

I sigh. "Guilt. I dragged her into something, she fell in love with me, and then I lied to her about the amnesia. I felt like the only way to make up for everything I did was to marry her."

She's very still in my arms. I wish I could see her face, but I want to give her privacy to deal with my words.

My heart. If my heart had knees that's where it would be—doubled over, throbbing from the pain. I pull my arm from behind my head and rub my eyes.

"Olivia…" my voice catches.

I want her to demand the whole story, make me relive the seconds that changed both of our lives, but she pulls her fingers away and darts up to kiss me. Sliding on top of me, she reaches a hand between us, and I forget everything—everything except us.

NINETEEN

PAST

The door was slightly ajar when I arrived. I was about to knock when it swung open and a man came out carrying a garbage bag. I stepped back, too startled to speak. My thoughts spun in a hundred directions. *He wasn't her type. I was going to kill him. Why was he taking out her trash? Did he sleep here often?* I waited for him to look up, thinking every man deserved a chance to explain himself before he got the shit beat out of him.

He was mildly startled to see me standing in front of him. He looked past me to see if I was with someone else, and then said, "Help you?"

He hadn't pulled the door to Olivia's apartment closed, and I could see inside.

Empty.

I felt the air leave my lungs. I closed my eyes, tilting my head back. No, no, no.

I walked away, my hands in my hair, and circled back to where maintenance was looking at me curiously. My instant jealousy had caused me to miss the uniform and name badge. *Why did I leave her? Why didn't I just stay?* I knew she did this. She ran when she was afraid. I thought—what had I thought? That I could keep her because we'd made love? That her demons wouldn't find her in the orange grove where I'd sold my soul to be with her?

I eyed the badge clipped to the front of his shirt.

"Miguel." My voice sounded raw even to my ears. Miguel raised his eyebrows as he watched me struggle with a sentence. "When did she—how long?"

"This one's been open for twenty-four hours," he said, referring to the apartment behind him. "We have a waiting list. Have to make it ready for next tenants."

Twenty-four hours? Where did she go? Did she leave right away? Did something scare her away?

I ran a hand through my hair. I'd left her just two days earlier to go settle my affairs. I danced with her in the parking lot before I left. She tried to tell me the truth, but I stopped her. When she found out about the amnesia, she'd think of every possible reason to run from me. I'd planned on locking her in the apartment, making love to her again, and convincing her that we could make it work. But, first I had loose ends to tie up.

I'd left Olivia and gone straight to Leah's townhouse. When she opened the door, I could tell she'd been crying. It took me thirty minutes to break her heart. It hurt me to do it. She had done nothing to deserve what I was doing to her. I told her I'd met someone. She didn't ask who, though I suspected she knew since she'd followed me to Olivia's apartment a few weeks earlier. Before I left, I kissed her forehead. I didn't tell her about the amnesia. I didn't want to hurt her any more than I already had.

I went to my condo next. As I stood under the shower, I thought of our week together. I thought of the orange grove, the way she tasted, the way her skin felt like cold satin beneath my fingers. When my mind went to that first moment of being inside her, the way her eyes had widened and her lips had parted, I had to blast myself with cold water.

She'd given me everything—everything she'd held back before. She was different. She was also the same. Stubborn, defiant…full of lies.

I tried to break her before. Now, I just wanted her as she was. I wanted every last beautiful flaw. I wanted the witty one-liners and the coldness that only I knew how to warm. I wanted the fight and the friction and the make-up sex. I wanted her to wake up in my bed every morning. I wanted her shitty cooking and her beautiful, complex mind.

I'd gone back on everything I believed, to be with her. I threw truth out the window. I was so afraid she'd forget about me, I'd lied to sneak back into her life. Now, I had inordinate amounts of explaining to do.

I looked at Miguel. He suddenly seemed like my last remaining tie to her.

"Did she leave anything? A note…anything?"

Miguel rubbed the back of his neck. "No, man."

"Did she say where she was going?"

He sucked his teeth. "I'm just maintenance. They don't exactly give me a forwarding address." He looked around to make sure we were alone. "But, if she did leave something it would be in this black garbage bag, which I'm going to set right here while I do a run-through of the apartment."

He dropped the bag on the floor and gave me a look before stepping back into the apartment and closing the door behind him.

I picked it up, weighed it in my hand. It was light. Had she left me something, telling me where she'd gone? Had Jim come back and scared her off? Had he told her? I knelt down and turned the bag over, dumping its contents on the concrete. I was sweating and my hands were damp as I sifted through the trash. Ripped-up papers, broken glass, crushed flower petals…what was I looking for? A letter? Olivia would never write me a letter. It wasn't her style. This was her style—leaving me without notice, throwing me in the fire to burn. I tossed the bag. Half of my heart was breaking; the other half was hell fucking angry. As the bag fluttered to the ground, I heard the slight tinkering of something hitting the floor. My eyes scanned the concrete, desperate for anything that would lead me to her.

I found it lying between my feet.

A penny.

Had she left it for me, or had she just left it? I picked it up, held it between my fingers. The once shiny surface had the slightly green tinge of aging copper. This was her goodbye? I felt anger, and more than anger, I felt confusion. What had I done? The orange grove, the kiss in the parking lot before I left. I'd been so sure of what I felt for her…what she felt for me. There was no way Olivia would have given herself to me if she wasn't sure of us. *Then why? WHY?*

I walked to the edge of the parking lot and lifted my fist, the penny pressing against my palm. *Toss it,* I told myself. My muscles tensed to throw it.

I couldn't do it. My hand dropped to my side. I put the penny in my pocket and drove home.

TWENTY

PRESENT

She drives me to my car just as the sun starts to come up. Neither of us wanted to leave, but we were both afraid that Bernie would decide to come into the office on a Saturday.

"You're going to get depressed later," I tell her when we pull into the Fossy parking lot. "You'll hate yourself and have a good cry, and then you'll go to the grocery store and buy ice cream. Don't."

She looks at me with big eyes, and I can see the guilt is already starting to creep in.

"I don't know what I want," she says. "But, that was very wrong and very unfair to Noah."

"He left you."

"Yes."

"Because you want a baby and he doesn't."

"Yes," she says again.

"And before he left, how often was he around?"

She's quiet for a long time.

"It's like he thought he could be married on his terms. Have you at home for when it was convenient for him, but he's never been there for you."

"Stop."

I grab her wrist and hold it. "Why didn't he come back when Dobson escaped from that damn institution?"

"He said they'd catch him. To sit tight and trust the police."

"Exactly. He was supposed to protect you. That was his job. He should have been on a plane the minute he found out."

"That's not fair," she says, shaking her head. "He knows I'm tough. He knows I can take care of myself."

I make a disgusted noise in the back of my throat. This is sad.

"Listen to me…" I grab her face so she has to look at me when I say this. "I know you don't know this because your dad was a useless shit, and he never did anything to show you how you need to be treated. But you are valuable enough for any and every man in your life to drop everything to protect you. You shouldn't have to be forced to be strong on your own because no one will stand with you. Your dad failed you. Noah failed you. I will not fail you again."

I kiss her on the forehead just as she sheds a tear. Just one.

"Round and round and round we go, Olivia. This is about you and me, not you and Noah. Just take a few weeks. Spend some time with me. No decisions until it's a fair decision."

"The fair decision would be to do what's right—"

I cut her off. "For you. Yes, do what's right for you. Give me some time to show you."

She opens her pink lips to shoot some venom at me.

"Hush," I say. "Pack an overnight bag. There's somewhere I want to take you."

"I can't just take off with you! I have a job!"

"I know you took some time off. Bernie told me."

Olivia looks flabbergasted. "Bernie? When did you talk to Bernie?"

"I ran into her at the grocery store. She was worried about you."

Her mouth is open. She shakes her head like the idea that anyone is worried about her is ludicrous.

"I'm fine," she says firmly.

I grab her wrist and pull her into a hug, kissing the top of her head. "No, you're not. I'm your soulmate. I'm the only one who knows how to heal you."

She slaps me away, and when I let go, instead of pulling away, she buries her face in my chest like she's trying to burrow herself into me. I rewrap her in a hug, trying not to laugh.

"Come on, Duchess. It'll be like the camping trip."

"Yeah, it'll be just like that." Her voice is muffled against my chest. "Except you won't be lying about having amnesia, and I won't be lying about not knowing you, and your redheaded bitch of a girlfriend won't be trashing my apartment while we're gone."

I squeeze her tighter. It makes me sick that Leah did that. The things she's done to keep Olivia and me apart are especially twisted. Almost as twisted as the things I've done to keep us together. I grimace and grip her by the shoulders, pulling her away so I can see her face.

"What do you say? Yes?"

"How long will we be gone?"

I think about it. "Four days."

She shakes her head. "Two."

"Three," I counter. "We have to use one of those days for travel."

She cocks her head and frowns at me. "We're not really going camping, are we? Because, every time we do—we have some type of emotional catalyst, and I really don't think I can handle—"

I put a hand over her mouth. "No camping. Pack something nice to wear. I'll pick you up tomorrow at eight a.m."

"Okay." She tries to act nonchalant, but I can tell she's excited.

I kiss her forehead. "Bye, Duchess. See you soon."

I leave without looking back at her. I have no idea where I'm taking her, and I can't lie and say camping didn't cross my mind. But, as soon as she reminded me that both of our camping trips went to shit, I tossed the idea. She needed something to remind her how good we were together, not about the games we played. I pull out my phone as I climb into my car. I know the perfect place and it's only a few hours away.

I knock on her door at 7:45.

"Always early," she complains when she opens it. Her bag is in her hand. I take it and look her over. She's wearing faded jeans and a fitted Marlins T-shirt. Her hair is wet and loose around her face.

She sees me eyeing her shirt and she shrugs. "I went to a game," she says. I catch the defensiveness in her voice and I smirk.

"What?" she says, slapping me on the arm. "I like sport."

"First of all, I'm the British one, not you. It's *sports*. Second, you hate sports and sport and athletes. As I recall, you once told me that professional athletes were a waste of space."

The corner of her mouth dips in as she frowns. "Noah likes baseball. I was being supportive."

"Ah."

I feel jealous, so I turn away and walk to the elevator with her bag while she locks up.

We ride downstairs in silence, standing so close the sides of our hands are touching. When the doors slide open, we don't immediately step out.

"How long will the drive take?" she asks as she lowers herself into my car.

"We're not driving," I say.

She shakes her head, one eyebrow raised.

"You'll see. Just sit back and relax. We'll be there soon."

She gives me a dirty look and turns on the radio. I hand her my iPod and she scrolls until she finds Coldplay.

"You're crazy and erratic and mean, but I'll never complain about your taste in music."

"I'm sorry," she says, setting down the iPod and staring at me. "Aren't you supposed to be charming me this weekend?"

I grab her knee and squeeze. "That's what I'm doing, Duchess. A compliment with an insult. Just the way you like it."

She smacks my hand away, but she's smiling.

The drive takes twenty minutes. When I pull up at the dock, Olivia looks confused. I get out of the car and grab her bags from the trunk.

"What is this?"

"A marina. It's where I keep my boat."

"Your boat?"

"Yes, love."

She follows me to my slip. I climb on first, setting our bags in the small galley, then I go back for her.

"Peter Pan," she says, not taking her eyes from the boat. "You named it Peter Pan."

"Well, when I first bought it I named it Great Expectations, but Pip doesn't land up with Estella in the end. So I changed it to Peter Pan. Didn't want to jinx myself."

Her nostrils flare. Then she looks at me with those big eyes of hers. "I've never been on a boat. A ship, but they're so much…safer looking."

I hold out my hand and help her on. She wobbles for a minute, and it looks like she is surfing. Then she runs to the cockpit and firmly plants herself on the seat, holding both sides of the padding on her chair. She's such a badass

I forget how little of life she's tasted. I smile and start getting the boat ready to leave.

When we are bouncing forward, the helm of the boat cutting into the waves, she scoots closer to me on the bench. I lift my arm up and around her and she snuggles into me. I can't even smile. I feel so intensely emotional, I steer the boat in the wrong direction for more than thirty minutes before I realize my mistake. At one point, when we are in the middle of nothing but water, I cut the engine and let her look.

"I feel so mortal," she says. "I've collected so much armor over the years: a law degree, money, a hard heart. But, out here I have nothing and I feel naked."

"Your heart isn't so hard," I say, watching the water. "You just like to pretend it is."

I can see her looking at me out of the corner of my eye.

"You're the only one who ever says that. Everyone else believes me."

"I'm the only one who knows you."

"How is it that you always let me go so easily then? Why don't you know that I want you to fight for me?"

I sigh. Here it is. The truth.

"It took me a long time to figure out that's what you were saying. And it seemed that every time one of us came back for the other, we weren't ready. But, ten years later, here I am. Fighting. I'd like to think I've learned from my mistakes. I'd also like to think we've finally made it to the point where we are ready for each other."

She doesn't respond, but I know what she's thinking. Maybe this is finally our time. Maybe.

I start the engine.

We reach Tampa Bay around one o'clock. I park my boat at a marina and call a cab to take us to a car rental place. The only thing they have available is a minivan. Olivia cracks up when we climb in.

"What?" I say. "I kind of like it."

"No," she says firmly. "Don't even say that. I'll lose all respect for you."

I grin and drive us to the hotel. We drop off our bags, and Olivia inspects the room while I call and double check on our dinner reservations.

"Let's go find lunch," I say. She pulls out her makeup bag, but I take it from her.

"Just be all around naked today, feelings and face."

Her mouth twitches to smile, but she won't let it. I see it in her eyes though. That's plenty for me.

We walk to a small restaurant that sells only the fish they catch. It's right on the water. Olivia's nose is sunburned and I see a scattering of freckles across the bridge of her nose and her cheeks. She orders a margarita and swears it's the best she's ever had.

She's chatty after two. We walk into the shops and she tells me about her life in Texas.

"Southern belles," she assures me, "are the deadliest of all creatures on God's earth. If they don't like you, they won't even look at you when you speak to them. And then they'll give you a compliment with the most vicious insult hiding underneath."

I laugh. "How did you deal with that?"

"Not well. I held back on the compliments and just openly insulted them."

"I'm getting uncomfortable just thinking about it," I admit. When Olivia unleashes an insult you feel like you're being assaulted by word bullets. Very uncomfortable experience.

She screws up her face. "Cammie said I was the anti-Texan. She wanted me out of the south because she said I was ruining the integrity of it."

"Oh, Cammie."

She smiles so big. I know how much she values her best friend. I wonder what she'd say if she knew Cammie's part in keeping me away. It doesn't matter. I'll never tell her anyway.

We're looking at goofy Tampa Bay T-shirts when she suddenly says, "I still have my *I'm Cats About Georgia* sweatshirt."

"Me too. Let's get one of these. We can have an entire wardrobe of stolen-getaway clothes."

She chooses two T-shirts with palm trees on them, in the most godawful shade of teal I've ever seen. *Hearts in Tampa Bay*, they say.

I groan. "Look at those nice, fitted ones." I point to a shirt I'd actually feel good about wearing in public, and she frowns.

"What's the fun in that?" She goes to the bathroom and puts on her new purchase, then makes me do the same. Five minutes later, we are walking hand in hand down the boardwalk in matching ugly T-shirts.

I love it.

TWENTY-ONE

PAST

After graduation Cammie moved back to Texas. It was fairly easy to find her all I had to do was follow her brightly lit social media trail. I signed up for Facebook. She ignored my first five messages and then after my sixth attempt, sent one short message back.

WTF, Caleb.

She wants to be left alone.

BACK THE FUCK OFF!

Did you get your memory back?

Fuck it. I don't care.

In other words, Cammie wasn't going to help me. I considered flying to Texas, but I had no idea where Cammie lived. Her profile was set to private and she blocked me. I felt like a stalker. I tried the college next, but even with my connections in the administration office, Olivia hadn't left them with a forwarding address. I went through my other options: I could hire a private detective…or I could leave her alone. That's what she wanted, after all. She wouldn't have left unless she was really done this time.

It hurt. More than the way she left the first time. The first time I had been angry. The anger made me feel self-righteous, which saw me through the first year after our breakup. The second year I felt numb. The third year I questioned everything.

This time felt different. It felt more real, like no matter what we did, we would never be together. Maybe after we had sex, she realized she wasn't in love with me anymore. Maybe I was presumptuous in thinking she ever was. I was in love with her more, if that was even possible. I had to find her. One more time. Just one.

One fake Facebook profile later and I was part of Cammie's extensive network of *friends*. Her entire cache of photos was a click away, and yet I sat staring at my computer screen for a good fifteen minutes before I was able to look through them. I was afraid to see Olivia's life—how easy it was for her to move on without me. I searched anyway, through the endless dragging line of party pictures. Olivia had a special knack for avoiding the camera. I thought I caught her hair sometimes in the corner of a shot, or off in the blurry background, but I was still so drunk off her I was probably seeing her everywhere she wasn't. For all I knew, Olivia was in Sri Lanka with the Peace Corps. Was the Peace Corps in Sri Lanka?

Fuck

Cammie was living in Grapevine. I would go there. Talk to her. Maybe she'd tell me where Olivia was. She couldn't shut me down if I was standing in front of her. I rubbed a hand across my face. Who was I kidding? This was Cammie. She made blonde look like a color of combat. I waited a month, wrestling with the fact that Olivia probably wanted to be left alone, and my need to convince her that she didn't.

Finally, I asked Steve for the time off. He was reluctant to give it to me since I'd taken a four-month leave of absence during the amnesia stint. When I told him it was about Olivia, he relented.

I drove. One thousand, two hundred and ninety miles of Coldplay, Keane, and Nine Inch Nails. I stopped at diners along the way. Places where the waitresses' names were Judy and Nancy, and the bouffant had never gone out of style. I liked it. Florida needed a character makeover. It was wearing on me: the pretentiousness, the heat, the absence of Olivia. Maybe it only felt like home if she was there. I had a feeling she would have liked Nancy and Judy too. If she was in Grapevine and I could convince her to come home with me, I'd bring her back this way. Have her eat fried chicken and macaroni and cheese on a tabletop that was stained with so many coffee cup rings, it was starting to look like a design. We'd eat until we were in a grease coma and then we'd find a cheap motel and argue about where to have sex because she didn't trust the cleanliness of the sheets. I'd kiss her until she forgot about the sheets, and we'd be happy. Finally happy.

I crossed over the Texas state line and decided to hit up a motel before I went to see Cammie. I needed to shave…shower. Look mildly presentable. Then I thought, *fuck it*. Cammie could see me exactly how I was, dirty and miserable. I drove the rest of the way to her townhouse and pulled into her driveway just as the sun was coming up. The townhouse was cream with brick facing. There were flower boxes on the windows, overflowing with lavender. It was too charming for Cammie. I considered waiting a few hours, getting breakfast before I knocked. Cammie was a notorious late riser. In the end, I figured it was best to catch her off guard. She might tell me more that way.

I parked up the block and walked to her front door. I was about to ring the bell when a car turned the corner and headed down the street toward where I was standing. I stopped to look at it and had the eerie feeling that it was headed for Cammie's. I had two options…I could walk back up the driveway and risk passing the car as it turned in, or I could slip around the side of the townhouse and wait. I chose the second option. Cammie had an end unit, and I stood with my back pressed to the side of her house, looking at the neighbors' fence. The neighbors had a Yorkie. I could see it sniffing around the fence.

Yorkies were yappy dogs. If it caught sight of me, it would no doubt bark until someone came outside to see what was wrong.

The car turned into the driveway, just as I guessed. I heard a door slam and the shuffling of feet as they walked up to the door. *It's probably Cammie,* I thought. *Coming back from some guy's house where she spent the night.* It wasn't Cammie. I heard two voices. One of them was Olivia's; the other belonged to a man. I almost launched myself around the side of the house and toward her, when the front door opened and I heard Cammie squeal.

"You guys so had sex!" she said.

Olivia's laugh was forced. The bastard—whoever he was—was laughing along with Cammie.

"It's none of your goddamn business," I heard Olivia snap. "Now, get out of my way. I have to get ready for class."

Class! I felt myself slumping down the wall. Of course. She was in law school. She'd met a guy. Already. She wasn't even thinking about me, and here I was driving thousands of miles to get her back.

What a fucking joke.

Cammie must have retreated back into the house, because I heard Olivia turn around at the door and thank him.

"I'll see you tonight," she said. "Thanks for last night. I needed it."

I heard the distinct sound of kissing before he walked back to his car and drove away. I stayed there for five more minutes, partially seething, partially hurting, partially feeling like a pathetic fucking ass, before I knocked on the door.

Cammie opened the door wearing nothing but a T-shirt with a picture of John Wayne on the front of it. She was holding a coffee mug, but she almost dropped it when she saw me. I lifted it from her limp hand and took a sip.

"Oh. My. God."

She stepped outside, pulling the door closed behind her.

"I want to see her," I said. "Now."

"Are you crazy? Showing up here like this?"

"Go get her," I said. I handed her coffee back, and she stared at me like I was asking her to give me an organ.

"No," she said finally. "I'm not letting you do this to her again."

"Do what?"

"Play games with her head," she snapped. "She's fine. She's happy. She needs to be left alone."

"She needs me, Cammie. She belongs with me."

For a minute I thought she was going to slap me. She took a vicious sip of her coffee instead.

"Uh-uh." She lifted one finger away from her cup and pointed it at me. "You're a lying, cheating scumbag. She needs something better than you."

I mentally backed up a step. That was true, mostly. But, I could be better for her. I could be what she needed, because I loved her.

"No one can love her like me," I said. "Now, move aside, before I move you. Because I'm going in there—"

She considered this for a moment before stepping aside. "Fine," she said.

I opened the door, took my first step into the foyer…

To my left was the kitchen and what looked like the living room, to my right was the stairs. I headed for the stairs. I was three up, when I heard Cammie call after me.

"She was pregnant, you know."

I stopped.

"What?"

"After your little rendezvous under the moonlight."

I looked back at her, my heart suddenly pounding wildly in my chest. My mind went to that night. I hadn't used a condom. I hadn't pulled out. I felt tingling all over my body. *She was pregnant. Was…was…was…*

"Was?"

Cammie pulled her lips tight and raised her eyebrows. What was she suggesting? I felt an ache start in my chest and spread outward. Why would she? How could she?

"It's better that you leave her alone," she said. "There isn't just water under your bridge; there's maggots and shit and dead bodies. Now, get the fuck out of my house before I call the police."

She didn't have to tell me twice. I was done. Done. Forever. Never again.

TWENTY-TWO

PRESENT

We go back to the hotel and get ready for dinner. She showers first and then puts on her makeup and does her hair while I take my turn. So far we haven't kissed. The only contact we've had was when we held hands earlier. I wait on the balcony while she gets dressed. When she comes out to tell me she's ready, my eyes glaze over.

"You're staring," she says.

"Yeah…"

"You're making me feel awkward."

"You're making me hard."

Her mouth gapes.

"Naked feelings, Duchess! You're in a tight black dress, and I know how good it feels to be inside you."

Her face looks even more startled than a second ago. She spins to walk away, but I catch her and pull her against me.

"You're wearing that dress simply because you like it. You don't dress to make men look at you—you hate men. But, your body is ridiculous and it happens anyway. You walk and your hips sway from side to side, but you don't walk that way to get attention, it's just the way you move—and everyone looks. Everyone. And when you listen to people speak, you unconsciously bite your lower lip and then let your teeth slide across it. And when you order wine at dinner, you play with the stem of your wine glass. You run your fingers up and down. You are sex and you don't even know it. Which makes you even sexier. So, when I think dirty thoughts, forgive me. I'm just under your spell like everyone else."

She's breathing hard when she nods. I let her go and lead her out of the room and to our minivan.

She has not lost her childlike awe. When she sees something that has never crossed her vision before, she becomes entranced—parted lips, wide eyes.

We step into the large foyer of the restaurant holding pinkies, and her speaking stills. To our left is the hostess stand, and in front of us the room opens up to two stories of red wall, decorated in gilded gold mirrors. It's a spacious receptacle into the restaurant doors leading off into different directions, and her head swivels around to take it all in. The bulbs they use to light the room are red. Everything glows in red luminescence. The room reminds me of old class and sex.

"Drake," I say to a tall blonde standing behind the desk. She smiles, nods, and looks for my reservation.

Olivia has let go of my pinkie and has grasped my whole hand. I wonder if she's afraid—perhaps intimidated.

I bend down to her ear.

"Okay, love?"

She nods.

"This looks like the red room of pain," she says.

My mouth drops open. My little prude has been expanding her reading horizons. I choke on my laugh, and a couple of people turn to look at us. I narrow my eyes.

"You read *Fifty*?" I ask quietly. She blushes. Amazing!—the woman *is* capable of blushing.

"Everyone was reading it," she says, defensively. Then she looks up at me with big eyes.

"You?"

"I wanted to see what all the hype was about."

She does that *blink, blink, blink* thing with her eyelashes.

"Did you pick up any new techniques?" she says, without looking at me.

I squeeze her hand. "Would you like to try me out and see?"

She turns her face away, pressing her lips together—horribly embarrassed.

"Caleb Drake," the hostess says, interrupting our whispering. "Right this way."

I lift my eyebrows at Olivia, and we follow the hostess through a door at the rear of the room. We are led through a series of dim hallways until we enter another decadently red room—red chairs, red walls, red carpet. The tablecloths are mercifully white, breaking the continuity of the color. Olivia takes a seat, I follow.

The server approaches our table moments later. I watch her face as he guides her through a wine menu that is the size of a dictionary. She is overwhelmed after a few seconds, and I speak up.

"A bottle of the Bertani Amarone della Valpolicella Classico, two thousand and one."

Olivia scans the menu. I know she's trying to find the price tag. The server nods my way in approval.

"A rare choice," he says. "Aged for a minimum of two years, the Bertani hails from Italy. The grapes are grown in soil that is composed of volcanic limestone. The grapes are then dried until they are raisins, which results in a wine that is dry and higher than most in alcohol content."

When he retreats from our table, I smile at her.

"I've already slept with you; you don't have to order the most expensive wine on the menu to impress me."

I grin at her. "Duchess, the most expensive wine on this menu is six figures. I ordered what I enjoy."

She bites her top lip and seems to shrink into her seat.

"What's the matter?"

"I always wanted this—to come to restaurants that raise their own cows and mortgage bottles of wine. But, it makes me feel insecure—reminds me that I'm really just poor white trash with a good job."

I reach for her hand. "Aside from your notably filthy mouth, you are the single classiest woman I have ever met."

She smiles weakly like she doesn't believe me. That's okay. I'll spend the rest of forever convincing her of her worth.

I order her the New York strip. She only ever eats the filet, because that's what she thinks she's supposed to do.

"It's not as tender, but it is more flavorful. It's the steak version of you," I tell her.

"Why are you forever comparing me to animals and shoes and food?"

"Because, I see the world in different shades of Olivia. I'm comparing them to you—not the other way around."

"Wow," she says, taking a sip of her wine. "You've got it bad."

I start singing a rendition of Usher's "U Got It Bad" and she shushes me, looking around embarrassed.

"Singing is something you should never do." She smiles. "But, maybe if you translated some of those lyrics into French…"

"*Quand vous dites que vous les aimez, et vous savez vraiment tout ce qui sert à la matière n'ont pas d'importance pas plus.*"

She sighs. "Everything sounds better in French—maybe even your singing."

I laugh and play with her fingers.

The meal is unparalleled in the state of Florida. She reluctantly agrees that the New York strip is better than the filet. After our meal is over, we receive a tour of the kitchen and wine cellar—which is custom at Bern's.

Our tour guide stops in front of a locked cage, behind which resembles a library of wine bottles. Olivia's eyes grow wide when our guide shows us a bottle of port that is two hundred and fifty dollars an ounce.

"It's a delight in your mouth," he says comically.

I raise my eyebrows. I am standing behind her, so I wrap my arms around her waist and speak into her hair. "Do you want to try some, Duchess? A delight in your mouth…"

She shakes her head no, but I nod at our guide. "Send it to the Dessert Room," I say.

She stares at me in confusion. "The what?"

"Our Bern's experience isn't over. There is a separate part of the restaurant just for dessert."

We are taken up a flight of stairs to another dimly lit area of the restaurant. It is mazelike in the Dessert Room; I'm not sure how we'll find our way out without help. We are taken past a dozen private glass orbs, behind which each individual table sits. Each guest is given their own privacy bubble to eat their dessert. Our table is to the rear of the restaurant and fit for two. It is a strange and romantic setting. Olivia has had two glasses of wine and is relaxed and smiling. When we are left alone, she turns to me and says something that makes me choke on my water.

"Do you think we could have sex in here?"

I return my glass to the table and blink slowly. "You're drunk, aren't you?"

"I haven't had wine in a long time," she admits. "I feel a little carefree."

"Public-sex carefree?"

"I want you."

I am a grown man, but my heart skips a beat.

"No," I say firmly. "This is my favorite restaurant. I'm not getting kicked out because you can't wait an hour."

"I can't wait an hour," she breathes, "please."

I grind my teeth.

"You only do that when you're angry," she says, pointing to my jaw. "Are you angry?"

"Yes."

"Why?"

"Because I really want the macadamia nut sundae."

She leans forward and her breasts press against the table. "More than you want me?"

I stand up and grab her hand, pulling her to her feet. "Can you make it to the car?"

She nods. As we are rounding the corner, our server returns with our two hundred and fifty dollar an ounce port. I take it from him and pass it to her. She shoots it. The server flinches and I bark out a laugh, handing him my credit card.

"Hurry up," I say. He races off and I press her against the wall to kiss her. "Was it a delight in your mouth?"

"It was okay," she says. "I really want to put something else in my mouth…"

"God."

I kiss her so I can taste it. When I turn around, he is back with my card. I quickly sign the receipt and drag her out of the restaurant.

After an intensely memorable fifteen minutes in a pharmacy parking lot in the backseat, we drive to an ice cream shop and eat our cones in the heat outside.

"Doesn't hold a candle to Jaxson's," she says, licking her wrist where the ice cream is dripping.

I grin as I watch the traffic on the street.

"Do you think we'll ever get sick of doing that?"

We switch cones, and I eye her through my haze. She ordered the ice cream shop's version of Cherry Garcia. I ordered something with peanut butter. I watch her eat it. She has that sexed look—flushed skin, ruffled hair. I'm tired, but I could easily go another round.

"I highly doubt that, Duchess."

"Why?"

"Addiction," I say simply. "It can span an entire lifetime if untreated."

"What's the treatment?"

"I don't really care."

"Me neither," she says, throwing the rest of my cone in the trash and dusting her hands on her dress.

"Let's go. Our hotel room has a hot tub."

I don't need to be asked twice.

TWENTY-THREE

PAST

Four months after Leah was acquitted, I filed for divorce. The minute—the very minute I made the decision, I felt a huge weight lifted from my figurative shoulders. I didn't necessarily believe in divorce, but you couldn't stay in something that was killing you either. Sometimes you fucked up enough in life, that you had to bow to your mistakes. They won. Be humble…move on. Leah thought she was happy with me, but how could I make someone happy when I was so dead inside? She didn't even know the real me. It was like sleepwalking—being married to someone you didn't love. You tried to fill yourself with positives—buying houses and going on vacations and taking cooking classes—anything to try to bond with this person you should already have bonded with before you said *I do.* It was all empty, fighting for something that never was. Be it my fault for marrying her in the first place, I'd made plenty of mistakes. It was time to move on. I filed the papers.

Olivia

—That was my first thought.

Turner

—That was my second thought.

Motherfucker

—That was my third thought. Then I put them all together in a sentence: *That motherfucker Turner is going to marry Olivia!*

How long did I have? Did she still love me? Could she forgive me? If I could wrestle her away from that fucking tool, could we actually build something together on the rubble we'd created? Thinking about it set me on edge—made me angry. What would she say if she knew I'd lied about the amnesia? We'd both told so many lies, sinned against each other—against everyone who got in our way. I'd tried to tell her once. It was during the trial. I'd come to the courthouse early to try to catch her alone. She was wearing my favorite shade of blue—airport blue. It was her birthday.

"Happy Birthday."

She looked up. My heart pounded out my feelings, like they did every time she looked at me.

"I'm surprised you remember."

"Why is that?"

"Oh, you've just been forgetting an awful lot of things over the years."

I half smiled at her jab.

"I never forgot you…"

I felt a rush of adrenaline. This was it—I was going to come clean. Then the prosecutor walked in. Truth was put on hold.

I moved out of the house I shared with Leah and back into my condo. I paced the halls. I drank Scotch. I waited.

Waited for what? For her to come to me? For me to go to her? I waited because I was a coward. That was the truth.

I walked to my sock drawer—infamous protector of engagement rings and other mementos—and ran my fingers along the bottom. The minute my fingers found it, I felt a surge of something. I rubbed the pad of my thumb across the slightly green surface of the kissing penny. I looked at it for a full minute, conjuring up images of the many times it had been traded for kisses. It was a trinket, a cheap trick that had once worked, but it had evolved into so much more than that.

I put on my sweats and went for a run. Running helped me think. I went over everything in my head as I turned toward the beach, dodging a little girl and her mother as they walked along hand in hand. I smiled. The little girl had long, black hair and startling blue eyes—she looked like Olivia. Was that what our daughter would have looked like? I stopped jogging and bent over, hands on my knees. It didn't have to be a *would have* situation. We could still have our daughter. I slipped my hand in my pocket and pulled out the kissing penny. I started jogging to my car.

There was no time like the present. If Turner got in the way, I'd just toss him off the balcony. I was soaked in sweat and determined when I turned on the ignition.

I was one mile from Olivia's condo when I got the call.

It was a number I didn't recognize. I hit *talk*.

"Caleb Drake?"

"Yes?" My words were clipped. I made a left onto Ocean and pressed down on the gas.

"There's been an…incident with your wife."

"My wife?" *God, what has she done now?* I thought about the feud she was currently having with the neighbors about their dog and wondered if she'd done something stupid.

"My name is Doctor Letche. I'm calling from West Boca Medical Center. Mr. Drake, your wife was admitted here a few hours ago."

I hit the brakes, swung the wheel around until my tires made a screeching sound, and gunned the car in the opposite direction. An SUV swerved around me and laid on the horn.

"Is she all right?"

The doctor cleared his throat. "She swallowed a bottle of sleeping pills. Your housekeeper found her and dialed 911. She's stable right now, but we'd like for you to come in."

I stopped at a light and ran my hand through my hair. This was my fault. I knew she took the separation hard, but suicide? It didn't even seem like her.

"Of course—I'm on my way."

I hung up. I hung up and I punched the steering wheel. Some things were not meant to be.

When I arrived at the hospital, Leah was awake and asking for me. I walked into her room, and my heart stopped. She was lying propped up by pillows, her hair a rat's nest and her skin so pale it almost looked translucent. Her eyes were closed, so I had a moment to rearrange my face before she saw me.

When I took a few steps into the room, she opened her eyes. As soon as she saw me, she started crying. I sat on the edge of her bed and she latched onto me, sobbing with such passion I could feel her tears soak through my shirt. I held her like that for a long time. I'd like to say I was thinking deep thoughts during those minutes, but I wasn't. I was numb, distracted. Something was agitating me and I couldn't place it. *It's cold in here*, I told myself.

"Leah," I said finally, pulling her from my chest and settling her back onto the pillows. "Why?"

Her face was slimy and red. Dark half-moons camped around her eyes. She looked away.

"You left me."

Three words. I felt so much guilt I could barely swallow.

It was true.

"Leah," I said. "I'm not good for you. I—"

She cut me off, waving my comment away on the frigid hospital air.

"Caleb, please come home. I'm pregnant."

I closed my eyes.

No!

No!

No…

"You swallowed a bottle of sleeping pills and tried to kill yourself and my baby?"

She wouldn't look at me.

"I thought you left me. I didn't want to live. Please, Caleb—it was so stupid. I'm sorry."

I couldn't name the emotion I felt. I was somewhere between wanting to walk out on her forever and wanting to stay and protect that baby.

"I can't forgive you for that," I said. "You have a responsibility to protect something you gave life to. You could have talked to me about it. I'll always be around to help you."

I saw some color come back into her cheeks.

"You mean…help me while we're divorced?" She lowered her head and looked up at me. I thought I saw some fire in her irises.

I didn't say anything. We were locked in a staring contest. That's exactly what I meant.

"If you don't stay with me, I'm not keeping this baby. I have no intention of being a single mother."

"You can't be serious?"

Never did I think she would threaten me with something of this nature. It seemed beneath her. I opened my mouth to threaten her—to say something I'd probably regret, but I heard footsteps. The brisk kind that said *doctor*.

"I'd like some privacy to talk to my doctor about my options," she said quietly.

"Leah—"

Her head snapped up. "Get out."

I looked from her to who I presumed was Doctor Letche. Her face was pale again, all the anger gone.

Before the doctor could say anything, Leah announced that I was leaving.

I stopped in the doorway and without turning around, I said, "Okay, Leah. We'll do it together."

I didn't need to look at her face to know it held triumph.

TWENTY-FOUR

PRESENT

I have a decision to make. I'm pacing it off. That's what my mother would call it—pacing it off. I did it as a kid, across my bedroom. I guess I never grew out of it.

Olivia is making her decision, whether she knows it or not. Noah is going to come back for her, because she's that girl, the one you come back to again and again and again. So, I fight. That's it. That's my only option. And if I don't get her, if she doesn't choose me, I'm going to be *that* guy—the one who spends his life alone and pining. Because I sure as hell am not going to replace her with any more Leahs or Jessicas or any-goddamn-body else. *Fuck it.* It's Olivia or nothing. I grab my wallet and keys and jog down the stairs instead of taking the elevator. I go directly to her office. Her secretary holds Olivia's door open for me as I step in. I smile at her and mouth my thanks.

"Hi," I say.

She's in the middle of sorting through a mound of papers, but when she sees me, she smiles—all the way to her eyes. Almost as quickly, the smile sinks out of her eyes and the lines of her mouth firm into a straight line. Something's up. I walk around her desk and pull her against me.

"What's wrong?" I kiss the corner of her lips. She doesn't move. When I let her go, she drops into her swivel chair and looks at the floor.

Okay.

I grab a chair and pull it up to hers so that we're facing each other. When she spins her chair away from me to look at the wall, I know some type of shit has hit the fan.

Please God, no more shit. I've had about all the shit I can handle.

"Why are you being so cold with me?"

"I don't think I can do this."

"What?"

"This," she says, motioning between us. "It's so wrong."

I rub my fingers over my jaw and start grinding my teeth.

"We are kind of experts on doing what's wrong, no?"

"Ugh, Caleb. Stop it. I'm supposed to be thinking of ways to make my marriage work. Not building a new relationship with someone else."

"Building a new relationship with someone else?" I am confounded. "We're not building anything. We've been in a relationship since before we were actually in a relationship." In actual fact, I tell people we were together for three years, even though it was only one and a half, because I was emotionally *with* her from the moment we met.

"Why are you saying this, now?" I say.

She opens a bottle of water that is sitting on her desk and takes a sip. I want to ask when she started drinking water, but I'm pretty damn sure my non-girlfriend is trying to end our non-relationship, so I stay still and quiet.

"Because it's better for everyone if we're not together."

I can't keep the sneer off of my face. "Better for whom?"

Olivia closes her eyes and takes a deep breath. "Estella," she says.

It feels like someone has reached a hand into my belly and grabbed hold of my organs.

Olivia is chugging her water, her free hand limp in her lap.

"What the hell are you talking about?" I haven't heard her name in a long time. I've thought it plenty, but Olivia's voice wrapping around the syllables is jarring.

Her nostrils are flaring as she breathes. She still won't look at me.

"Olivia…"

"Estella is yours." It's a blurt. I blink at her, not sure where that came from, or why she's saying it.

Being told I had twenty-four hours to live would have been less painful than that statement. I don't say anything. I stare at her nostrils, which are working like fish gills.

She spins in her chair until her knees bump into mine, and she's looking me straight in the face.

"Caleb." Her voice is gentle, yet it makes me flinch. "Leah came to see me. She told me she's yours. She'll take the paternity test to prove it. But, only if we're not together."

My head and my heart are in a battle for who can host the most pain. I shake my head. *Leah? Was here?*

"She's lying."

Olivia shakes her head. "She's not. And you can get a court-issued paternity test. She can't keep Estella from you if you are her father. But Caleb, think about it. She'll use her to hurt you. Forever. It'll affect your little girl, and I know what it feels like to be a parent's weapon."

I stand up. Walk to the window. I'm not thinking about how Leah could use Estella to hurt me. I'm thinking about Estella being mine. How could something like this be true and I not know it?

"She was pregnant before Estella. We were separated, but we had sex once during that time. Anyway, she lost the baby after she swallowed a bottle of sleeping pills and had to have her stomach pumped. That's why we went to Rome. She said that she wanted to reconcile, and I felt so guilty about her sister and the miscarriage."

I look at Olivia when I say that. Her lips turn white as she presses them together.

"Caleb, she wasn't pregnant in the hospital. She lied to you. She told me that too."

I always wondered what Olivia felt when I told her I faked my amnesia. Painful truth is ineffable. It swings you around a couple times until you're dizzy, and then punches you hard in the stomach. You don't want to believe it, but it wouldn't hurt so badly if on some level you didn't know it was true. I run with denial for a few more minutes.

"She bled. I saw her bleed." Denial is such a friendly companion. It's normally Olivia's best friend. Suddenly, I want in on the party.

Olivia looks so distraught.

"Oh, Caleb. It wasn't from a miscarriage. She probably just got her period and passed it off as that."

Dammit. Fuck. Olivia is looking at me like the naive, gullible fool I am.

I remember how Leah chased me out of the room before I could speak to the doctor. How I stood in the doorway and told her I'd stay just so she'd keep my baby. She was clearly trying to get me out of there before the doctor revealed the truth.

I don't need to say anything to Olivia. She can see I'm getting it.

I'm feeling smaller and smaller. During my back and forth time with Leah, Olivia was falling in love with someone else. I could have just walked away with Olivia in Rome and spared us years of this tangled, twisted mess.

"How did Estella come to be?"

"After Rome we made it another month. She was angry with me. She accused me of not being present, and she was right. So I moved out again.

"I was at a conference in Denver and she was on a trip with her friends. We ran into each other at a restaurant. I was friendly, but kind of kept my distance. She showed up at my hotel that night. I was pretty drunk and landed up sleeping with her. A few weeks later she called and told me she was pregnant. I never even questioned it. I just went back to her. I wanted a baby. I was lonely. I was stupid."

I don't tell Olivia that I found out she was seeing someone during that time. That when Leah came to me, I fell into her because I was trying to fill that Olivia hole in my chest again.

"So, she told you Estella wasn't yours? That night you told her you wanted a divorce?"

"Yes. She said she'd slept with someone else before the ski trip. She also told me she only went because she knew I'd be there and she wanted to make me think she got pregnant that night."

"It was all a lie," Olivia says. "Estella is yours."

I see the tear in the corner of her eye. She doesn't swipe it away and it rains down her face.

"She's going to keep hurting you and Estella as long as I'm in your life. I have a husband," she says softly. "I should work things out with him. We've been playing house, Caleb. But, this isn't real. You have a responsibility to your daughter…"

All of it—Olivia, Leah, Estella—ignites a fury in me. I spin and walk to her chair, leaning down and placing both hands on her armrests, and get right in her face. All I want to do is go find my daughter, but first things first. I'll deal with them one at a time. We are breathing each other's air when I speak.

"This is the last time I'm going to say this, so listen carefully." I can smell her skin. "You and I are happening. No one is keeping us apart again. Not Noah or Cammie, and least of all, fucking Leah. You are mine. Do you understand me?"

She nods.

I kiss her. Deep. Then I walk out.

TWENTY-FIVE

PAST

"What's the matter with you?"

She rubbed her hand down my chest. I caught it before it reached the top of my pants.

"Jet lag," I said, standing up.

Olivia.

She puckered her mouth sympathetically.

I'd been lying on the hotel bed for about ten minutes while Leah spoke to her mother on the phone. Now that her phone call was over, she was making her intentions known. I wandered over to the window so I could be out of her reach.

"I'm gonna take a shower," I said. Before she could ask if I wanted company, I closed the bathroom door and locked it behind me. I needed to run to clear my head, but how could I explain a midnight run in a foreign country to my suicidal, overly emotional wife? God, if I started running, I might never come back. I stepped into the shower and stood under the scalding hot water, letting it fill my nose and my eyes and my mouth. I wanted to let it drown me. How was I supposed to do life after what just happened? Leah knocked on the door. I heard her say something, but her voice was muffled. I couldn't look at her right now. I couldn't look at myself. *How did I just do that?* Walked away from the only thing that made sense. I almost had her and I just gave up. I used "had her" loosely, because you can never really have Olivia. She floated around like a vapor, causing friction and then running away. But, I'd always wanted to play the game. I wanted the friction.

You had to do it, I tell myself. It was a *you-made-the-bed* situation. And I was taking responsibility for my actions. Counseling, the endless marriage counseling. The guilt. The need to fix things. The confusion about whether or not I'm doing the right thing. The faking of my amnesia was my one rogue moment, when I stepped away from myself and did what I wanted to do without thought to consequences. I was a coward. I was raised to do what was socially acceptable.

I stood under the water until it turned cold, then I dried myself off and stepped out of the bathroom. My wife—thank God—had fallen asleep on top of the covers. I felt instant relief. I wouldn't have to act tonight. Her red hair was spread out around her like a fiery halo. I tossed a blanket over her, grabbed my bottle of wine, and retreated to the balcony to get drunk. It was still raining when I sat in one of the chairs and propped my feet up on the railing. I never had to "act" with Olivia. We just fit—our moods, our thoughts…even our hands.

Once, during her senior year, she bought a gardenia bush to put outside her apartment. She fawned over that thing like it was a dog—googled ways to take care of it and then made notes in one of those spiral notebooks. She even named it. *Patricia*, I think. Every day she'd squat on her haunches outside her front door and examine Patricia to see if a flower had bloomed. I watched her face when she came back inside—she always wore this look of hopeful determination. *Not yet*, she'd say to me, as if all of her hope for life was tied into that gardenia plant blooming a flower. That's what I loved about her, that grim determination to survive even though the odds seemed to always be against her. Despite all of Olivia's plant nurturing, Patricia slowly started to fade away, her leaves curling at the tips and turning brown. Olivia would stare at that plant, a crease forming between her eyebrows and her little mouth puckered in a frown worth kissing. Florida had an especially cold winter that year. One morning when I got to her apartment, Patricia was clearly dead. I jumped into my car and sped off to Home Depot where I'd seen them selling the same bushes. Before my little love cracked her eyes open, I replaced her dead plant with a healthy one, repotting it over the grass in front of her building. I threw the old one in the dumpster and washed my hands in the pool before knocking on her door. She checked on it when she opened the door for me that morning, and her eyes lit up when she saw the healthy green leaves. I don't know if she ever suspected what I'd done; she never said anything. I took care of it without her knowing, sticking plant food into the pot before I knocked on her door. My mother always put used tea bags in the soil around her rose bushes. I did that a couple times too. Right before we broke up, that damn plant bloomed a flower. I'd never seen her so excited. The look on her face was the same as when I'd missed the shot for her.

If she came back and stood in that same spot beneath my hotel room, I'd probably jump right off the balcony to get to her. *It's not too late,* I told myself. *You can find out where she's staying. Go to her.*

I loved Olivia. I loved her with every fiber of my being, but I was married to Leah. I'd made a commitment to Leah—no matter how stupid that was. I was in. For better or worse. I had a brief moment when I thought I couldn't do it anymore, but that was in the past. Before she'd gotten pregnant with my baby and swallowed a bottle of sleeping pills.

Right?

Right.

I shook the bottle of wine. I was halfway through.

When a woman carried your baby in her body, you started seeing everything a little differently. The impossible became slightly less fucked. The ugly picked up a pretty glow. The unforgivable woman looked a little less stained. Kind of like when you'd been drinking. I finished the bottle and set it on its side on the floor. It rolled away and hit the balcony railing with a *ting*. I was in a baby coma. And I needed to wake the fuck up.

I closed my eyes and I saw her face. I opened my eyes and I saw her face. I stood up, tried to focus on the rain, the city lights, the fucking Spanish Steps—and I saw her face. I had to stop seeing her face so I could be a good husband to Leah. She deserved that.

Right?

Right.

We flew out four days later. We barely had time to recover from the jet lag before it was time to leave again. It's not like I could focus on the trip with my ex floating somewhere around the city. I looked for Olivia at the airport, in restaurants, in cabs that splashed water on my ankles as they drove past. She was everywhere and nowhere. What were the chances that she'd be on our flight? If she was, I'd...

She wasn't on our flight. But, I thought about her for the nine hours it took to fly across the Atlantic. My favorite memories—the tree, Jaxson's, the orange grove, the cake-batter fight. Then I thought about the bad ones—mostly things she made me feel, the constant thought that she was going to leave me, the blatant way she refused to admit that she loved me. It was all so childish and tragic. I glanced at my wife. She was reading magazines and drinking cheap airplane wine. She took a sip and grimaced when she swallowed.

"Why do you order it if you don't like it?"

"It's better than nothing, I suppose," she said, looking out the window. *Telling,* I thought. I opened the book I brought with me and stared at the ink. For nine gracious hours, Leah left me alone. I'd never been so grateful for cheap wine. When we landed in Miami, she dashed to the bathroom to reapply her makeup while I waited in line for Starbucks. By the time we made it to baggage claim, I was in one of the worst moods of my life.

"What's wrong with you now?" she said. "You've been distracted this whole trip. It's really annoying."

I glared at her from behind my sunglasses and grabbed one of her bags off the belt. I flung it down so hard; it wobbled on its fancy fucking rotating wheels. Who traveled with two large suitcases when they went away for five days?

"You're supposed to be working on this with me. You're not even mentally with me right now."

She was right.

"Let's go home," I said, kissing the top of her head. "I want to sleep for twelve hours straight and eat three meals in bed."

She stood on her tiptoes and kissed me on the mouth. It took effort to kiss her back so she wouldn't suspect anything was wrong. When she keened into my mouth, I knew I was every bit as good at lying to her as I was at lying to myself.

TWENTY-SIX

PRESENT

My car tires kick up gravel as I speed out of the parking lot. How could she? I run my hand through my hair. Why wouldn't either of them have told me? They are such vicious, catty women; you'd think they would have come running with the information. All I can think, as I speed on the 95 toward Leah, is of the little girl that still bears my name. The one she told me I was not a parent to. Was that a lie? If Leah lied about Estella's parentage, I would kill her myself.

Estella, with her beautiful red curls and her blue eyes—but she had my nose. I'd been so sure of it until Leah told me that she was someone else's. Then her nose had shifted. I thought that I was seeing things because I wanted so badly for her to be mine.

My mouth feels dry as I pull into her driveway. A million years ago it had been *my* driveway. *My* wife had been in that house. I broke it all apart because of the love I had for a ghost—a married ghost.

God. I think of Olivia now and a peace settles over me. She might not be mine, but I'm hers. It's no use even fighting it anymore. I just keep falling flat on my face and then rolling toward her. If I can't have Olivia Kaspen, then I'll be alone. She is a disease I have. After ten years, I am finally realizing that I can't cure it with other women.

I push the door to the car open and step out. Leah's SUV is parked in her usual spot. I walk past it and up the stairs to the front door. It's open. Walking into the foyer, I close the door behind me. Glancing around, I see that the living room is a mess of toys—a Cabbage Patch doll lays on its head next to a pile of naked Barbies. I step over a tricycle, heading toward the kitchen. I hear my name.

"Caleb?"

Leah stands in the doorway to the kitchen, a dishtowel in her hand. I blink a few times. I've rarely seen Leah hold anything but a martini glass. She dries her hands with the towel and tosses it on the counter, walking toward me.

"Are you okay? What are you doing here?"

My chest heaves with everything that wants to come out. I grind my teeth so hard I'm surprised they don't crumble beneath the pressure. Leah notices what I'm doing and raises her eyebrows.

"Oh," she says. She beckons me to the kitchen. I follow her and watch as she pulls a bottle of tequila from the cabinet. She pours two shots, takes one of them, and refills the glass.

"We fight better with tequila," she says, handing one to me.

I don't want to drink the liquor. Adding it to the fire that is already coursing through me can only mean danger. I look at the clear liquid and bring it to my lips. If Leah wants fire, I'm going to give it to her.

"Where's Estella?"

"Asleep."

I set my glass on the counter.

Good.

I walk toward my ex-wife. She backs up, her nostrils flaring.

"Tell me what you did."

"I've done a lot of things." She shrugs, trying to play it cool. "You'll have to be more specific."

"Olivia."

Her name pings between us, ripping open old wounds and spraying blood across the room. Leah is furious.

"Don't say that name in my house."

"It's my house," I say calmly. Leah's face is pale. She runs her tongue along her teeth, blinking slowly.

"Did you know Turner?"

"Yes."

"And you had him ask Olivia out…to keep her away from me?"

"Yes."

I nod. My heart is aching. I lean over the counter to gather my rising anger before it explodes. I push it down, swallow my contempt, and look her in the eyes. Olivia and I never had a chance. The whole time we were destroying ourselves, someone else was having a go at it too.

"Leah," I say, closing my eyes. "The hospital…after you took those pills—" my voice cracks. I rub a hand across my face. I am so tired. "Were you pregnant?"

She raises her chin and I already know the answer.

Oh God. She lied. If she lied about that baby, what else has she lied about? I remember the blood. All the blood on the bed sheets. She said she was losing that baby and I believed her. It was probably just her period. How long after that had Estella been conceived?

I pace the length of the kitchen, my hands behind my neck. I say her name again; this time it's a plea.

"Is she mine, Leah? Oh fuck." I drop my hands. "Is she mine?"

I watch her face as she takes her time answering. She looks conflicted as to whether or not to tell the truth. Finally, she shrugs.

"Yeah."

The whole world goes quiet. My heart crashes. Rises. Crashes.

Grief cleaves me in two. Two years, I haven't seen her in two years. My daughter. *My* daughter.

The empty glass I drank tequila from sits to the right of my hand. I let my anger come, swiping the glass to the floor. It shatters and Leah flinches. I want to shake her, I want to throw her like that glass and watch her shatter for all the things she's done. I head for the stairs.

"Caleb." She comes after me, grabbing my arm. I yank myself free, taking the stairs two at a time.

She calls my name, but I barely hear her. I reach the top of the stairs and turn left down the hallway. She's behind me, begging me to stop.

"Caleb, she's sleeping. You're going to terrify her. Don't…"

I fling open the door and take in the soft pink light. Her bed is in the corner, a white four-poster. I walk in slowly, my steps muffled by the carpet. I can see her hair fanned out on the pillow, shockingly red and curly. I take another step in and I can see her face—pouty lips, chubby cheeks, and my nose. I kneel next to the bed so I can see her, and I cry for the second time in my life. I cry quietly, my body shaking from my sobs.

Leah's pleas have stopped. I don't know whether she's behind me or not—I don't care. Stella's eyes flutter open. For being woken up in the middle of the night by a stranger, she is surprisingly alert and calm. She lies still, her blue eyes watching my face with the gaze of a much older child.

"Why are you cwying?"

The sound of her voice, raspy like her mother's, startles me. I cry harder.

"Daddy, why are you cwying?"

I feel like someone has just poured ice water over my head. I lean back, suddenly sober. I take in her disheveled curls, her full chubby cheeks, and I melt for my daughter.

"How do you know I'm your daddy?" I ask gently.

She frowns at me, her little lips pouting, and jabs her finger at her bedside table. I look over to see a picture of myself, holding her as a baby.

Leah told her about me? I don't understand. I don't know whether to be grateful or furious. If she wanted to make me think this little girl wasn't mine, why would she bother making Estella think anything different?

"Stella," I say cautiously, "can I give you a hug?" I want to pull her to me and sob into her beautiful red hair, but I don't want to scare *my* daughter.

She grins. When she answers, she lifts her shoulders up and tilts her head all the way to the side.

"Sure." She leans forward, arms outstretched.

I hug her to my chest, kissing the top of her head. I can barely breathe. I want to pick her up, put her in my car, and drive her away from the woman who has kept her from me. I can't be like Leah. I have to do what is best for Stella. I want to hold her to my chest all night. It takes everything I have to separate from our hug.

"Stella," I say, pulling away. "You have to go back to sleep now, but guess what?"

She makes a cute, little kiddie face. "What?"

"Tomorrow, I'm going to come pick you up so we can hang out."

She claps, and again, I'm tempted to pick her up and carry her out tonight. I curb my enthusiasm. "We're going to go eat ice cream, and buy toys, and feed ducks, and kick sand at the beach."

She slaps a hand over her mouth. "All in one day?"

I nod.

I help her snuggle back under her covers and kiss both of her cheeks and her forehead. I kiss her chin for good measure. She giggles, so I pull back the covers and kiss her toes. She squeals, and I have to press my fingertips to the corners of my eyes to stop the tears.

"Night, pretty baby."

I close her door softly. I don't make it five steps when I find Leah sitting against the wall. She doesn't look at me.

"I'll be here first thing in the morning to pick her up," I say as I walk toward the stairs. I want to get out of the house before I strangle her.

"She has school," Leah argues, standing up. I double back and come within an inch of her face. I am breathing hard, my chest heaving. She squares her jaw. I hate her so much in that moment; I don't know what I ever saw. My words are gruff and full of anguish.

"She has a father."

It's then that I hear the sirens.

TWENTY-SEVEN

PAST

"Hey, handsome, what are you doing here?"

I lifted my sunglasses and smiled.

"Cammie."

She smirked and stood on her tiptoes to give me a hug. My eyes darted past her and searched the crowd walking into the mall.

"Is she—?"

She shook her head. "Not here."

I felt myself relax. I didn't know if I could handle seeing her. Out of sight, partially out of mind was what was working for me at the moment.

"So, what are you doing here? Shouldn't you be home with the pregnant wifey witch?"

We fell into step and I grinned at her. "I'm here for a pretzel actually. She had a craving."

"God, that's embarrassing—once the big man on campus, now the bitch's errand boy."

I laughed. Cammie was always good for a laugh. I held the door open for her, and the air conditioning blasted me in the face.

"What are you doing here?"

"Oh, you know me," she sang, stopping at a rack of skirts. "I like to spend money."

I nodded and stuck my hands in my pockets, feeling awkward.

"Actually," she said, turning to me, "I'm looking for a dress to wear to a wedding. Help me?"

I shrugged. "Since when do you need help shopping?"

"Oh, that's right." She tucked her lips in and shook her head. "You have to get back to your pregnant wife. Don't let me hold you up." She dismissed me with a wave of her hand and pulled a slinky white dress off the rack.

I scratched the back of my head. "White makes you look matronly."

She narrowed her eyes and put the dress back, while still looking at me. "Who asked you?"

She held up a blue silk dress for me to see and I nodded. She shoved it at me and I took it.

"So, do you know what you're having…boy…girl…seed of Chucky?"

"We're not finding out."

She tossed another dress my way. I re-shelved it when she turned away.

"I own a nanny agency, you know. So, when the little bundle comes along, I'm sure I can find it a new mother."

She held up a Gucci dress and I nodded. "She'll be fine. You know I'm traditional about those things."

Cammie snorted. "You might be, but I highly doubt your lovely wife will be offering up the breast any time soon."

I ground my teeth together, which she noticed right away.

"Sore subject much? Don't worry, C-Dizzle, I've seen this before. Tell her you'll buy her a new set when it's all over. That should bring her around."

I cocked my head. That wasn't a bad idea.

I followed her to the changing room.

"So," I said, leaning against the wall outside. "How—"

"She's fine."

I nodded, looking at the floor.

"Is she—"

She burst out wearing the blue dress and spun in a circle.

"Don't even bother trying the others on," I said.

She made a kissy face at the mirror and nodded. "You're right."

The door slammed closed. A minute later, she came out dressed and carrying the garment on her arm.

"Well, that was easy."

I walked with her to the register and watched as she plucked out her credit card. "Now a gift and shoes and I'm all set."

"What's the dress for again?"

She leveled her eyes on me, a wicked smile playing on her lips.

"Didn't I tell you?" she said innocently. "This dress is for Olivia's wedding."

A tremor of shock passed through me. Suddenly, all of the colors around me were bleeding together, hurting my eyes. I felt sick, my chest constricting with each second that passed. Cammie's lips were moving; she was saying something. I shook my head to clear it.

"What?"

She smirked at me and tossed her blonde hair over her shoulder. Then she patted my arm sympathetically.

"Hurts, doesn't it, motherfucker?"

"When?" I breathed.

"Uh-uh. I'm not telling you that."

I licked my lips. "Cammie…tell me it's not Turner."

Her face broke into a smile. "Nope."

I felt the pressure in my chest release a little. A little. I hated Turner. I hadn't even met the guy. It was by sight alone.

"Noah Stein," Cammie said, grinning. "Funny story," she said, making her eyes really big. "She met him on that little impromptu trip she took to Rome. You remember?

The one where she came baring her soul, and you turned her away."

"It didn't happen like that."

She cocked the corner of her mouth up and shook her head like she was disappointed in me. "You had your chance, big boy. Fate hates you guys."

"Leah had just lost the baby and her sister tried to commit suicide. I couldn't leave her. I was trying to do the right thing for once."

She jerked to look at me. "Leah was…" her voice trailed off and her eyes glazed over. I cocked my head.

"Leah lost a baby?" she repeated. I saw something in her eyes that made me take a step closer.

"What are you not saying?"

She pursed her lips and shook her head at me. "When you went to Rome with Leah, were you trying to have a baby?"

Cammie was known for asking uncomfortable questions, but this was a little personal, even for her.

"No. We were just taking a break. Getting away from everything. Trying to work on—"

"Your marriage," she finished.

"Why are you asking me this?"

She suddenly looked up from the patch of floor she'd been staring at. "Just interested, I guess. Hey, I've got to get out of here."

She leaned up to kiss me on the cheek, but something wasn't sitting right with me. Cammie was an obnoxious spitfire. When she started acting awkward, something was wrong.

"Cammie…"

"Don't," she said. "She's happy. She's getting married. Leave her alone."

She started walking away, but I grabbed her wrist. "You said that to me once before, do you remember?"

Her face paled. She yanked her arm away.

"Just tell me when?" I pleaded. "Cammie, please…"

She swallowed. "Saturday."

I closed my eyes and dropped my head. "Bye, Cam."

"Bye, Caleb."

I didn't get Leah's pretzel. I got back in my car, drove to the beach, and sat on the sand looking out at the water. Leah called me five times, but I sent the calls to voicemail. Saturday was two days away. She was probably a mess. She always was when there was a big life change on the horizon. I rubbed my chest. It felt so heavy.

I watched the couples for a long time, walking hand in hand along the water. It was too late to swim, but some kids were playing in the surf, kicking water at each other. In a few weeks, I'd have one of my own. The thought was frightening and exciting—the way you felt before getting on a roller coaster. Except this roller coaster ride would last eighteen years, and I wasn't sure if my riding partner really wanted to be a mother. Leah tended to like the idea of things more than the actual things.

Once, when we were first married, she'd come home from work cradling a collie puppy in her arms. "I saw him in a pet shop window and I couldn't resist," she'd said. "We can take him on walks together and get him one of those collars with his name on it."

Despite my skepticism about the duration of the dog's stay in my house, I'd smiled and helped her pick out a name—Teddy. The following day I'd come home from work to find the house filled with dog supplies—squeaking hamburgers, stuffed toys, and tiny, fluorescent tennis balls. *Aren't dogs colorblind?* I remember thinking, picking one up and examining it. Teddy had a fluffy bed, a rhinestone studded collar, and a retractable leash. He even had food and water bowls with his name on them. I studied this all with a sense of dread and watched Leah measure out half cups of food into his dog bowl. For two days she bought things for our new puppy, yet I never once remember seeing her so much as touch him. By day four, Teddy was gone. Given to a neighbor along with his fluorescent balls.

"Too much mess," Leah said. "I couldn't housetrain him."

I didn't bother to tell her that it took longer than three days to housebreak a puppy. And so Teddy was gone before we could ever go on a walk with him. Please, God, don't let a baby be another puppy to Leah.

I stood up, dusting the sand off my jeans. I had to get home—to my wife. That was the life I chose, or what was chosen for me. I didn't even know anymore where my choices started and ended.

Saturday. I told Leah that I had errands to run. I set out early, stopping at the liquor store for a bottle of Scotch I knew I'd need later. Tossing it in the trunk, I drove the twenty minutes to my mother's house. My parents lived in Ft. Lauderdale. They bought their house from a pro golfer in the nineties, something that my mother still bragged about to her friends. When Robert Norrocks owned this house…

She opened the door before I could knock.

"What's wrong? Is it the baby?"

I pulled a face, shook my head. She made a show of looking relieved. I wondered who taught her to make a performance of every emotion she felt. Both my grandparents had been pretty stoic people. As I walked past her into the foyer, her hand fluttered to her neck where her fingers absently found the locket she wore. It was a nervous habit I'd always found endearing. Not today.

I walked into the living room and sat down, waiting for her to follow.

"What is it, Caleb? You're scaring me."

"I need to talk to you about something," I tried again. "I need to talk to my mother about something. Can you do that without being…"

"Bitchy?" she offered.

I nodded.

"Should I be afraid?"

I stood up and walked to the window, looking out at her precious roses. She had every shade of pink and red. It was a mess of thorns and color. I didn't like roses. They reminded me of the women in my life: beautiful and bright, but if you touched them, they made you bleed.

"Olivia is getting married today. I need you to talk me out of going to the church and stopping her."

The only indication that she'd heard me was the slight expansion of white around her irises.

She opened her mouth and then abruptly closed it.

"I'll take that as your blessing." I strode toward the door. My mother jumped up and blocked me. She was pretty stealthy in heels.

"Caleb, honey…nothing good can come out of that. You and Olivia are—"

"Don't say it."

"Over," she finished. "That was my non-bitchy version."

I grimaced. "It's not over for me."

"It's obviously over for her. She's getting married."

She reached up and cupped my face in her hands. "I'm so sorry you're hurting."

I didn't say anything. She sighed and pulled me down on the couch to sit next to her. "I'm going to put aside my extreme dislike for that girl and tell you something that you might find useful."

I listened. If she was putting aside her dislike, I potentially had mind-blowing advice coming my way.

"Three things," she said, patting my hand. "It's okay that you love her. Don't stop. If you turn your feelings off for her, you might turn everything off. That's not good. Second, don't wait for her. You have to live your life—you have a baby on the way." She smiled at me sadly as I waited for the grand finale. "And finally…wait for her."

She laughed at the confused expression on my face. “Life does not accommodate you, it shatters you. Love is mean, but it’s good. It keeps us alive. If you need her, then wait. But, right now she’s getting married. It’s her day and you can’t ruin it.”

Love is mean.

I loved my mom—especially when she wasn’t being a bitch.

I jogged down the stairs to my car. She watched me from the doorway, tugging on her locket. Maybe she was right. I wanted Olivia to be happy. To have the things that were taken from her as a child. I couldn’t give her those things because I was giving them to someone else.

I drove aimlessly for a while before eventually pulling into a random strip mall. Florida was a maze of peach-colored strip malls. Each one bragged a fast food chain front and center like the mast on a ship. Flanking the token McDonald’s or Burger King was always a nail place. I pulled into a spot in front of Nail Happy. The shop was empty except for the workers. When I got out instead of a woman, they looked disappointed. I pulled out my phone, leaning against the door. It was cool outside—not cool enough for a jacket, but Florida cool. My thumbs lingered over the keyboard.

I love you

Delete

If you leave him, I’ll leave her

Delete

Can we talk?

Delete

Peter Pan

Delete

I pocketed my phone. Punched a tree. Drove home with bloody knuckles. Love was fucking mean.

TWENTY-EIGHT

PRESENT

The day after I barged into Leah's, she got a restraining order. If I go anywhere near my daughter, I'll get arrested. I was almost arrested that night. The cops had me handcuffed when my brother showed up. He spoke quietly to Leah for a few minutes before coming over and taking off my cuffs.

"She's not going to press charges, little brother, but she's going to have us file a report, and tomorrow she's going to get a restraining order."

"Was that your idea?"

He smirked at me. We didn't exchange any more words. I just got in my car and drove away. Leah filed a report. She claims that I kicked down the door, threatened her life, and woke Estella up in the middle of the night—drunk. She is also back to claiming that I am not Estella's father. I wonder if she lied to Olivia to torment me. I don't know what goes on in that woman's head. Or what went on in my head for so many years. Either way, Leah's woken the beast. Olivia directs me to an attorney that deals primarily with twisted family issues like mine. She says she's the best in the business. Her name is Moira Lynda. *Ariom*—I like that one. After listening to me speak for ten minutes, Moira holds up her hand to stop me. She has a tattoo on her hand, on the skin between her thumb and pointer finger. It looks like a four-leaf clover.

"You've got to be kidding me," she says. "The woman finds out that you want a divorce and tells you that the child you've been raising for six months isn't yours—and you believe her? Just like that?"

"I didn't have any reason not to. She didn't want a divorce. At that point, it would have only benefited her to let me believe Estella was mine."

"Oh, Caleb." She puts a hand to her forehead. "Didn't you see what was happening? You came out and dropped a couple bombs on her, and at some point in that conversation she decided that she didn't want you, she wanted revenge. And that's exactly what's happening."

I stare out her window at the traffic below and know it's true. But, why hadn't I had the sight to see it? If someone other than myself were telling me this story, I'd laugh at their stupidity. Why do humans have such a hard time seeing their own shit clearly?

"She has you by the balls here, Caleb. There is no proof of what happened that night. But, there is proof that for the last three years of that child's life you haven't seen her, paid child support, or fought for custody. Leah has you at abandonment. And now that she knows that, she's come back to let you know that Estella is yours, and she has the power."

God.

"What do I do?"

"You get a court-ordered paternity test. That's going to take some time. Then we ask for visitation. It'll be supervised at first, but as long as you comply with the rules and show up to see Estella, we can push for joint custody."

"I want full."

"Yeah well, I want to be a swimsuit model. That doesn't change the fact that I'm chubby and ate a cheeseburger for dinner last night."

"Okay," I say. "Do what you need to do. I'm in it. Whatever it is. Is there a way for me to see Estella?"

It's such a stupid question, but I had to ask. There is no way Leah is going to let me anywhere near my daughter. I have no proof, but I'm already thinking of her as my daughter again. Have I ever stopped?

Moira laughs at me.

"No way. Just sit tight and let me do my thing. We'll have you back in her life soon enough, but it's going to be a bit of a fight to get there."

I nod.

I leave her office and go right to Olivia's. She's in shorts and a tank top when I get there, mopping the floors and looking annoyed. I lean against the wall and tell her what Moira said while she works. She's cleaning with gusto, and when that happens I know she's trying to distract herself. There is also a bowl of Doritos on the table, and she keeps walking over to it and pushing chips into her mouth. Something's up, but I know even if I ask, she won't tell me.

"Do whatever she says," is all Olivia tells me. There are a few minutes when we don't speak. Her crunching dominates the room.

"She didn't seem sorry," Olivia says, finally. "It was the strangest thing. She just showed up at my office to tell me all of that. She knew I'd tell you. Seems sinister."

"She's up to something," I agree.

"Maybe she's out of money and she figures she needs to hit you up for child support."

I shake my head. "Her father built an empire. That company was a small portion of what he was dipping his interest into. Leah doesn't need money."

"Then she's out for revenge; Moira is right. What are you going to do?"

I shrug. "Fight for Estella. Even if she wasn't mine I'd want to fight for her."

She stops mopping. A piece of her hair has slipped from the messy pile on her head. She tugs on it then slides it behind her ear.

"Don't make me love you more," she says. "My clock is ticking and you're talking baby."

I grind my teeth to keep from smiling.

"Let's make one," I say, taking a step toward her.

The whites of her eyes explode around her pupils. She hides behind her mop.

"Don't," she warns me. She reaches for the bowl of Doritos, without taking her eyes from me, and finds it empty.

"Do you think we'd have a boy or a girl?"

"Caleb…"

I take another two steps before she dips her mop in the bucket, and whacks me in the stomach with it.

I stare down at my dripping clothes with my mouth open. She knows what's coming next because she drops the mop and runs for the living room. I watch her grab onto furniture as she slips and slides across the wet floor. I go after her, but she's such a cleaning addict she can practically ice skate over wet marble. Amazing. I fall flat on my ass.

I stay there, and she comes out of the kitchen carrying two glass bottles of Coke.

"Peace offering." She extends one toward me.

I grab the bottle and her arm and pull her down on the floor next to me.

She slides around until we are sitting back to back, leaning on each other, our legs extended outward. Then we talk about nothing. And it feels so damn good.

TWENTY-NINE

PAST

My daughter was born on March 3rd at 3:33 p.m. She had a shock of red hair that stuck straight up, like those toy trolls from the 90s. I ran my fingers over it, smiling like a goddamn fool. She was beautiful. Leah had convinced me we were having a boy. She'd stroked my face and looked at me like I was her god and practically purred, "Your father produced two sons, and your grandfather had three sons. The men in your family make boys."

I secretly wanted a daughter. She openly wanted a son. There was a Freudian element to our gender preferences, which I didn't express to my wife as she bought and decorated the nursery in greens and yellows "just to play it safe." Though she wasn't playing it safe when I noticed a teether in the shape of a dump truck appear in the mounds of baby things, or the tiny baseball-inspired onesie. Since I played basketball in college, the baseball selection could only have been a salute to her father, who never missed a Yankees game on TV. Her lying, playing-it-safe ass was cheating. So, I cheated too. I bought baby girl things and secretly hid them in my closet.

On the day she went into labor, we were planning on going for a walk on the beach. She wasn't due for another few weeks, and I had read that most first-time pregnancies went past the due date. Leah was climbing into her side of the car when she made a noise in the back of her throat. Her hands were tan; I watched them clutch her stomach, the white fabric of her dress bunching between her clawed fingers.

"I thought they were just Braxton Hicks, but they're getting closer together. We might want to go to the hospital and save the beach for another day," she panted, closing her eyes.

She leaned across the center console, started the car, and positioned all three air conditioning vents at her face. I'd watched her for a minute, unable to comprehend that this was actually happening. Then I ran inside and grabbed her hospital bag from the bedroom.

I was shocked when the doctor loudly announced "Girl" before tossing her onto her mother's chest. Not shocked enough to keep the stupid grin off my face. I named her Estella from *Great Expectations*. That night when I went home to take a shower, I pulled a box from the top of my closet. It had shown up in the mail a month earlier, with neither a note nor a return address attached. I was baffled, until I opened it.

I sliced the tape open with scissors and pulled a lavender blanket out of the box. It was so soft; it felt like cotton between my fingertips.

"Olivia?" I said softly. But, why would she send me a baby gift? I shoved it back in the box before I could overthink things.

I stared at it with a smirk on my face. Had she known Leah desperately wanted a boy and sent a girl gift to spite her? Or had she remembered how much I wanted a daughter? You could never really get a firm grip on Olivia's motives. Unless you asked. But, then she'd just lie.

I carried the blanket with me to the hospital. When Leah saw me with it, she rolled her eyes. She would have done more than roll her eyes if she'd known where it came from. I wrapped my daughter in Olivia's blanket and felt euphoric. *I am a father. To a little girl.* Leah seemed less excited. I chalked it up to the disappointment of the missing boy child. Or maybe she had the baby blues. Or maybe she was jealous. If I'd said the thought that my wife would be jealous of a daughter hadn't crossed my mind, I'd be lying.

I held Estella a little tighter. I'd already wondered how I would protect her from the ugly things in the world. I never thought I'd be wondering how to protect her from her own mother. *But, that's the way of things*, I thought sadly. Leah's parents were emotional black holes for most of her childhood. She'd get better. I'd help her. Love fixed people.

She was in better spirits when we drove home from the hospital. She laughed and flirted with me. But, when we got to the house and I handed her the baby for a feeding, her back stiffened like she'd been punched between the shoulder blades. My heart dropped so deeply in that moment, I had to turn away to hide my expression. This was not what I had hoped for. This was not what Olivia would have done. For all of her decorated hardness, she was kind and nurturing. With Leah, I always thought there was good in her…somewhere beyond what her parents had done to bring out the bad. Maybe I thought she was capable of more than she really was? But as it was said, if you had faith like a mustard seed, one could move mountains…or soften hardness…or love someone into healing. *God. What had I done?*

THIRTY

PRESENT

Later that night, I'm going for a jog. When I reach the lobby in my building, my steps die. At first I don't recognize him. He's not as put together as the last time I saw him. What is it about men refusing to shave when their hearts are breaking? *Fuck. How is this happening?* I run a hand along the back of my neck before taking the necessary steps toward him.

"Noah."

When he turns, he looks surprised. He glances at the elevator, then back at me.

Man, the guy looks ragged. I've looked like that a couple times in my life. I almost feel bad for him.

"Can we talk?" he asks.

I look around the lobby and nod. "There's a bar on the corner. Unless you want to come up to my place."

He shakes his head. "Bar's fine."

"Give me ten. I'll meet you there."

He nods and walks out without saying another word. I go back up to my place and call Olivia.

"Noah's in town," I say as soon as she picks up. "Did you know?"

There is a long pause before she says, "Yeah."

"Has he been to see you?"

I feel the tension creep into my shoulders and spread to my hands. I grip the phone a little tighter as I wait for her answer.

"Yeah," she says again.

"That's it? That's all you're going to say?"

I hear her shifting things around, and I wonder if she's in court today.

"Did he come to see you?" she whispers into the phone. I can hear her heels clicking as she walks.

Fuck. She is in court, and I'm dropping this on her.

"It's fine. I'll call you later, yeah?"

"Caleb—" she starts to say.

I cut her off. "Focus on what you're doing right now. We'll talk tonight."

Her voice is breathy when she says, "Okay."

I hang up first and head back downstairs. I walk along the crowded sidewalk, barely seeing anything. My mind has latched onto her voice—or maybe her voice has latched onto my mind. Either way I can hear it. And I know something is wrong. I'm not sure I can handle all of this at once. Estella is my priority, but I don't think I can do this without Olivia. I need her.

Noah is sitting at a small table to the rear of the bar. It's an upscale place, and like everything in this neighborhood, you pay dearly for its services. There are only two other patrons aside from him at this hour; one is old and one is young. I walk past both of them, my eyes adjusting to the dim light. When I pull the chair back and take a seat, the bartender approaches me. I wave him away before he can reach us. Noah is drinking what looks like a Scotch, but my only interest is being in full control of my mind.

I wait for him to speak. I really don't have anything to say to him.

"I told you to stay away from her," he says.

I lick my lips as I watch the poor son of a bitch. He's scared. You can see it all over him. I am too.

"That was before you left your wife alone to deal with a stalker."

He cracks his neck before he looks up. "I'm here now."

I want to laugh. He's here now. Like it's okay to just be part of a marriage part-time and show up when you please.

"But, she's not. That's what you don't know about Olivia. She doesn't need anyone to take care of her. She's tough. But, if you don't force yourself in and do it anyway, she moves on. She's moved on. You fucked up."

Noah's eyes flash. "Don't talk to me about my wife."

"Why not? Because I know her better? Because when you were gone on one of your damn trips and she needed help, she called me?"

We both stand up at the same time. The bartender sees the commotion and slams his fist on the counter. The bottles around him rattle with the impact.

"Hey! Sit down or get out of here," he says. He's a big fucking guy, so we both sit down.

We take a moment to calm down—or to think—or whatever men do when they are compelled to beat the shit out of each other. I'm about to leave when Noah finally speaks up.

"I was once in love with a girl, the same way you're in love with Olivia," he says.

"Hold on right there," I cut him off. "If you were in love with a girl the same way I'm in love with Olivia, you wouldn't be with Olivia. You'd be with this girl."

Noah smiles, but it doesn't reach his eyes. "She's dead."

I feel like an asshole.

"Why are you telling me this?"

"Think about what you're doing, Caleb. She's not yours anymore. We made a commitment to each other, and it's like you said—I fucked up. We need to be able to work on what we have without you showing up every five minutes getting her high on nostalgia."

Nostalgia? If only he knew. You couldn't sum Olivia and me up to nostalgia. The day I met her under that tree, it was as if I breathed a spore of her into my lungs. We kept coming back to each other. The distance between our bodies grew wider over the years as we tried to live separately. But that spore took root and grew. And no matter the distance or circumstance, Olivia is something that grows inside of me.

His nostalgia comment pisses me off so much; I decide to go with a low blow.

"So, you're going to have a baby then…"

The shock that passes through his eyes is enough to tell me I've struck a nerve.

I rotate my phone between my fingers as I watch his face and wait for the answer.

"That's none of your business."

"She's my business. Whether you like it or not. And I want to have a baby with her."

I don't know why he doesn't hit me. I would have hit me. Noah is a classy guy. He rubs his hand across his stubble, which hosts mostly grey, and finishes his Scotch. His face is wiped of emotion, so I can't tell what he's thinking.

"My sister had Cystic Fibrosis," he says. "I used to go with her to her support groups. That's where I met Melisa. She had it too. I fell in love with her and then had to watch her die before she had the chance to turn twenty-four. My sister died two years after her. I've seen two women that I love—die. I don't want to bring a child into this world with the chance of passing them the gene. It's not fair."

I order a Scotch.

I try to rub my headache away. This is becoming more complicated by the minute, and the last thing I want to do is feel sorry for this guy.

"What does Olivia want?" I don't know why I'm asking him that instead of her, but all I can think about is the way her voice sounded on the phone. What is she going to tell me?

"She wants to save what we have," he says. "We met last night to talk about things."

I've felt so many forms of pain in my years with Olivia. The worst was when I walked into the hotel room and saw the condom wrapper. It was a jealous, ripping pain. I'd failed her. I'd wanted to protect her, she wanted to self-destruct, and I couldn't stop her no matter what I did or how hard I loved her. The only thing that came close to that pain was when I showed up at her apartment and found out that she'd left me again.

What I feel now may be worse than that. She's leaving me, and she has every right to. There is nothing I can do to morally justify her walking away from her marriage for me. Noah is right, but that doesn't mean I am able to accept it.

The last few months we've gotten to know each other as adults, made love as adults, seen into each other as adults. And Olivia can deny it until her snobby face turns blue, but we work together as adults. How can she walk away from me again? We were in love. We are in love.

"I have to talk to her."

I stand up and he doesn't try to stop me. Had they planned this together? Noah would come tell me what her choice was? I'd have to deal? She's obviously forgotten what I'm willing to do to have her. I drop a twenty on the bar and walk out.

THIRTY-ONE

PAST

One week before my baby came into this world, I received a call from Olivia's office. Not Olivia. Just her secretary. It was a new secretary, thank God. The one she had when she first started at Bernie's firm was a psycho. The new girl's name was Nancy, and in her clipped, professional voice, she informed me that Ms. Kaspen had asked her to make the call. Three weeks ago—she said—a woman named Anfisa Lisov contacted Olivia, claiming to have seen an American news story on CNN in Russian. She said she was the mother to the woman in the picture with Olivia, Johanna Smith. I almost dropped the phone.

She wanted contact with the woman she suspected was her daughter. I collapsed into a chair and listened to Nancy talk. No one knew Leah was adopted. We kept it out of the press; we were careful—so careful not to let that information be released. It would have jeopardized Leah's testimony, or at least that's what the partners said. I think it would have jeopardized her mental health. And nothing had changed. Courtney was in an assisted living facility, a vegetable. Her mother was an alcoholic. Leah was balancing a fine line of sanity. And she was having my baby. Whoever this woman was, I couldn't let her near my wife.

"She said she gave up her baby while working as a prostitute in Kiev when she was sixteen."

Fuck fuck fuck.

"She is flying to America to meet Johanna," Nancy said. "Ms. Kaspen tried to deter her, but she was insistent. She wanted me to call and warn you."

Fuck. Why hadn't she told me sooner?

"All right. Give me all the contact information you have for her."

Nancy gave me the hotel and flight times and wished me good luck before hanging up.

Anfisa was flying into New York first and catching a flight a day later to Miami. No doubt she was who she said she was. Who else knew Leah's real mother was a sixteen-year-old prostitute in Kiev? Her parents certainly wouldn't have told anyone. When I tried sending an email to Anfisa using the address Nancy gave me, it came back saying the email had a faulty address. The phone number had been disconnected. I googled Anfisa's name and the search came back with a picture of a striking woman with short, red hair, cut no longer than my own. She had written and published three books in Russia. I put the titles into Google Translate and they came back as: *My Scarlet Life*, *The Blood Soaked Baby*, and *Finding Mother Russia*. She hadn't published a book in four years. I booked a trip to New York right then and there. I would fly out to meet this woman, send her away, and be back in time for my baby's birth. I had no idea what she wanted to gain out of this reunion, but the fact that Leah came from a wealthy family was at the forefront of my thoughts. She wanted a new story to tell. Reuniting with her daughter would either give her plenty of money to take a writing hiatus or it would give her the story she was looking for. There was no way Leah would want to meet this woman—mother or not. I needed her to focus on being a mother, not have a mental breakdown about her own. I'd take care of it. I'd give Anfisa money if I had to. But, then Estella came early.

I'd told Leah that I had a business trip. She was upset, but I arranged for her mother to come for the days I would be away. I didn't want to leave Estella, but what choice did I have? If I didn't stop this woman from boarding a plane to Miami, she'd be knocking on our door in a few days.

I packed a small bag, kissed my wife and daughter goodbye, and flew to New York to meet Anfisa Lisov, Leah's birth mother. I could barely sit still on the plane ride. I'd asked Leah on our honeymoon—just a few days after she told me she was adopted—if she'd ever want to meet her birth mother. Before the last word was out of my mouth, she was already shaking her head.

"No way. Not interested."

"Why not? Aren't you curious?"

"She was a prostitute. My father was a disgusting pig. What is there to be curious about? To see if I look like her? I don't want to look like a prostitute."

Well then…

We hadn't spoken about it again. Now here I was, doing damage control. I probably drank too much on the plane. When I got off, I booked into my hotel and caught a cab to hers. She was staying at a Hilton close to the airport. Nancy hadn't known which room she was in. I asked the front desk to call her and tell her that her son-in-law was there to see her. Then I sat in one of the lounge chairs near a fireplace and waited. She came down ten minutes later. I knew it was her by the picture I'd seen of her on the Internet. She was older than in the picture, more worn around the eyes and mouth. Her hair was dyed, no longer naturally red, still spiky and short. I eyed her face, looking for traces of Leah. It might have been my imagination, but when she spoke, I saw my wife in her expressions. I stood up to greet her, and she stared up in my face with complete calm. My little surprise trip hadn't rattled her at all.

"You are Johanna's husband? Yes?"

"Yes," I said, waiting for her to take a seat. "Caleb."

"Caleb," she repeated. "I saw you on television. During the trial." Then— "How did you know I was here?" Her accent was thick, but she spoke English well. She was sitting ramrod straight, her back not touching the chair. She looked more like Russian military than former Russian prostitute.

"Why are you here?" I asked.

She smiled. "We are going to have to answer each other's questions if we want to get anywhere, no?"

"Her attorney's office called me," I said, leaning back in my chair.

"Ah, yes. Ms. Olivia Kaspen."

God. Her name even sounded good with a Russian accent.

I didn't acknowledge or deny.

"Should we go to the bar? Order a drink," she said.

I nodded, tight-lipped. I followed her into the hotel bar, where she sat at a table near the front. Only after the bartender brought her vodka and my Scotch, did she answer my question.

"I've come to meet my daughter."

"She doesn't want to meet you," I said.

She narrowed her eyes and I saw Leah.

"Why not?"

"You gave her up a long time ago. She has a family."

Anfisa scoffed. "Those people? I didn't like them when they took her. The man didn't even like children, I could tell right away."

"That doesn't speak very highly of you, giving your baby to people you didn't even like."

"I was sixteen years old and I slept with men to survive. I didn't have much choice."

"You had a choice to give her to people you liked."

She looked away. "They offered me the most money."

I sat my glass down harder than I intended. "She doesn't want to see you," I said firmly.

My statement seemed to jar her a little. She slouched some and her eyes darted around the empty bar like she couldn't hold it together anymore. I wondered if this whole stiff-backed thing was an act.

"I need money. Just enough to write my next book. And I want to write it here."

That's what I thought. I took out my checkbook.

"You never come to Florida," I said. "And you never try to contact her."

She downed the rest of her vodka like a true Russian.

"I want a hundred thousand dollars."

"How long will it take you to write the book?" I scrawled her name onto the check and paused to look up at her. She stared at that check with hunger in her eyes.

"A year," she said, without looking at me. I held my pen above the amount line.

"I'll divide it by twelve then. I'll put money in an account every month. You contact her or leave New York, you don't get your deposit."

She eyed me with something I didn't recognize. It could have been contempt. Hate for a situation that left her dependent on me. Annoyance that her blackmail wasn't working as well as she wanted it to.

"What if I say no?"

I saw Leah in her defiance too.

"She won't give you money. She will slam the door in your face. Then you'll get nothing."

"Well then, son-in-law, sign my check and be done with it."

And so I got done with it.

I changed my flight. Went home early. I didn't ever hear much from Anfisa. I sent her money even after Leah and I separated and got divorced. I didn't want her presence to hurt Estella, even if she wasn't mine. When her year was up, she went back to Russia. I ran an Internet search for her once and saw that her book was a huge seller. Leah might hear from her eventually, but I was done with her.

THIRTY-TWO

PRESENT

I go straight to her condo. If she's not home already, I'll be waiting there when she arrives.

She is home. When she opens the door, it's as if she was expecting me. Her eyes and her lips are swollen. When Olivia cries, her lips double in size and turn bright red. It's the most beautifully fragile and feminine thing about her.

She stands to the side to let me in, and I walk past her into the living room. She closes the door softly and follows me.

She wraps her arms around her body and stares out at the ocean.

"When you left and went to Texas, after we..." I break to let her catch up to what I'm saying. "I came after you. It took me a few months to get past my initial wounded pride, and to find you, of course. Cammie didn't want to tell me you were there, so I just showed up on her doorstep."

I tell her about how I waited at the side of the house when I saw the car coming, and how I heard the exchange between her and Cammie. About how I knocked on the door when she went upstairs to shower. I tell her all of it and I can't tell if she can hear me, because her face is unmoving, her eyes unblinking. Her chest doesn't even rise and fall with breath.

"I was on my way up the stairs, Duchess, when Cammie stopped me. She told me that you got pregnant after our night together. She told me about the abortion."

Finally, the statue springs to life. Her fierce eyes turn on me. Blue fire—the hottest kind.

"Abortion?" The word tumbles out of her mouth. "She told you that I got an abortion?"

Now…now, her chest is rising and falling. Her breasts straining against the fabric of her shirt.

"She inferred it. Why didn't you tell me?"

She opens her mouth, runs her tongue along her bottom lip. I don't know why I'm doing this to her now. Maybe I think that if I remind her of how much history we have, it'll stir her to choose me.

"I didn't have an abortion, Caleb," she says. "I had a miscarriage. A goddamn miscarriage!"

She swims in and out of focus as I grasp her words.

"Why wouldn't Cammie tell me?"

"I don't know! To keep you away from me? She was right to! We are bad for each other!"

"Why didn't you tell me?"

"Because it hurt! I tried to pretend it never happened."

I don't know what to do with myself. It's like the whole world is determined to keep us apart. Even fucking Cammie who'd had a front-row seat to our relationship for all these years. *How could she?* Olivia is struggling not to cry. Her lips move as she tries to form words.

"Look at me, Duchess."

She can't.

"What are you going to tell me?"

"You know…" she says softly.

"Don't do this," I say. "This is our last chance. You and I were made for each other."

"I choose him, Caleb."

Her words ignite anger—so much anger. I can barely look at her. I breathe through my nose, her announcement reverberating across my brain, burning my tear ducts, and landing somewhere in my chest, causing such incredible heartache, I can't see straight.

Through my crash, I lift my head to look at her. She's pale, her eyes wide and panicked.

I nod…slowly. I'm still nodding ten seconds later. I'm calculating the rest of my life without her. I am contemplating strangling her. I am wondering if I did everything I could…if I could have tried harder.

There is one last thing I have to say. Something I said before and was so terribly wrong about.

"Olivia, I once told you that I would love again, and that you would hurt forever. Do you remember?"

She nods. It's a painful memory for both of us.

"It was a lie. I knew it was a lie, even as I said it. I've never loved anyone after you. I never will."

I walk out.

Walk away.

No more fighting—not for her, or with her, or with myself.

I am so sad.

How many times can a heart be broken before it is beyond mend? How many times can I wish to not be alive? How can one human being cause such a crack in my existence? I alternate between periods of numbness and inconceivable pain all in the span of—an hour? An hour feels like a day, a day feels like a week. I want to live, and then I want to die. I want to cry, and then I want to scream.

I want, I want, I want…

Olivia.

But, I don't. I want her to suffer. I want her to be happy. I want to stop thinking altogether and be locked in a room without thoughts. Possibly for a year.

I run. I run so much that if the zombie apocalypse were to happen, they'd never be able to catch me. When I run I don't feel anything but the burning in my lungs. I like the burn; it lets me know I can still feel when I'm having a numb day. When I am having a day of pain, I drink.

There is no cure.

ONE MONTH GONE

TWO MONTHS GONE

THREE MONTHS…

FOUR

Estella isn't mine. The paternity test comes back. Moira makes me come into her office to deliver the news. I stare at her blankly for five minutes while she explains the results—there is no way, no chance, no possibility that I am her biological father. I get up and leave without saying anything. I drive and don't know where I am going. I land up at my house in Naples—our house in Naples. I haven't been here since the issue with Dobson. I leave all the lights off and make some calls. First to London, then to my mother, then to a realtor. I fall asleep on the couch. When I wake up the next morning, I lock up the house, leaving a set of spare keys in the mailbox, and drive back to my condo. I pack. I book a ticket. I fly. As I sit on my flight, I laugh to myself. I've become Olivia. I'm running away, and I just don't give a fuck anymore. I trace the rim of my plastic cup with my fingertip. No. I'm starting over. I need it. If I can help it, I'm never going back there. I'm selling our house. After all these years. The house where we were supposed to have children and grow old together. It will sell fast. I've received offers for it over the years and there are always realtors leaving their cards with me in case I decide to sell. In the divorce I gave everything to Leah so long as she left the Naples house alone. She hadn't put up much of a fight, and now I can see why. She had something much crueler planned for me. She wanted to give me back my daughter and then take her away again. I close my eyes. I just want to sleep forever.

THIRTY-THREE

OLIVIA • PAST

Birthday parties made me uncomfortable. Who the hell even invented them? Balloons, presents you didn't want...cake with all that fluffy, processed frosting. I was an ice cream kind of girl. Cherry Garcia. Cammie bought me a pint of that and handed it to me as soon as I blew out my candles.

"I know what you like," she said, winking at me.

Thank God for best friends who make you feel known.

I ate my ice cream perched on a barstool in Cammie's kitchen while everyone else ate my cake. There were people everywhere, but I felt alone. And every time I felt alone, I blamed it on him. I set my ice cream on the counter and wandered outside. The DJ was playing Keane—sad music! Why the hell was there sad music at my birthday party? I slumped in a lawn chair and listened, watching the balloons bob. Balloons were the worst part of parties. They were unpredictable; one minute they were happy little balls of emotion, the next they were exploding in your face. I had a love/hate relationship with unpredictability. He-who-must-not-be-named was unpredictable. Unpredictable like a boss.

When I dutifully started opening presents, my husband standing to my left, my best friend jiggling her breasts at the cute DJ—I was not expecting the blue-packaged delivery.

I'd already opened twenty presents. Gift cards mostly—thank God! I loved gift cards. Don't give me shit about gift cards not being personal. There's nothing more personal than buying your own gift. I'd just put the last gift card I'd opened on the chair next to me, when Cammie took a break from flirting with the DJ to hand me the last of my presents. There was no card. Just a simply wrapped electric-blue box. To tell you the truth, my mind didn't even go there. If you work really hard at it, you can train your brain to ignore things. That shade of blue was one of them. I sliced the tape with my fingernail and pulled away the wrapping, balled it up, and dropped it in the paper pile at my feet. People had started to drift away and talk, getting bored with the present unwrapping show, so when I opened the lid and stopped breathing, no one really noticed.

"Oh fuck. Ohfuckohfuckohfuck."

No one heard me. I saw a flash. Cammie took another picture and moved away from the DJ to see what was making my face contort like I'd sucked on a lemon.

"Oh fuck," she said, looking into the box. "Is that?"

I slammed the lid shut and shoved the box at her. "Don't let him see," I said, glancing at Noah. He was holding a beer in one hand, his face turned away from me and talking to someone—it might have been Bernie. Cammie nodded. I stood up and bolted for the house. I had to walk around people who were still eating cake around the island in Cammie's kitchen. I made a right and darted up the stairs, choosing the bathroom in Cammie's bedroom, rather than the one downstairs that everyone was using. I kicked off my shoes, closed the door, and stood bent over the sink, breathing hard. Cammie came in a few minutes later, shutting the door behind her.

"I told Noah you felt sick. He's waiting in the car. Can you do this, or do you need me to send him home and tell him you're staying the night?"

"I want to go home," I said. "Just give me a minute."

Cammie slid down the door until she was sitting on the floor. I sat on the edge of her tub and traced the lines of the floor tile with my toe.

"That was uncalled for," she said. "What's with you two sending each other anonymous packages?"

"That was different," I said. "I sent him a fucking baby blanket, not…that." I eyed the box that was sitting next to Cammie on the floor. "What's he trying to do?"

"Umm, he's sending you a pretty clear message."

I tugged at the collar of my dress. *Why is it so damn hot in here?*

Cammie pushed the box across the bathroom tile until it nudged my toe.

"Look again."

"Why?"

"Because you didn't see what was underneath the divorce papers."

I flinched at the word *divorce.* Bending down, I retrieved the box from the floor and lifted out the stack of papers. Divorce was heavy. It wasn't official, but he'd obviously filed. Why did he need to tell me this? Like it made a difference anymore. I put the papers next to me on the lip of the tub and stared down at the contents underneath.

"Holy hell."

Cammie tucked her lips in and raised her eyebrows, nodding.

The Pink Floyd CD from the record store—the case cracked diagonally across, the kissing penny—green from age and flattened, and one deflated basketball. I reached out a finger and touched its bumpy skin, and then I dropped everything on the floor and stood up. Cammie quickly scooted out of the way, and I opened the door and stepped into her bedroom. I needed to go home and sleep forever.

"What about your fucked-up birthday present?" Cammie called after me.

"I don't want it," I said. I stopped when I reached her doorway, something eating at me. Turning back, I strode into the bathroom and crouched down in front of her.

"If he thinks this is okay, he's wrong," I snapped. She nodded, her eyes wide. "He can't do this to me," I reiterated.

She shook her head in agreement.

"To hell with him," I said. She gave me a thumbs-up.

While our eyes were still locked, I reached out a hand and felt along the floor until my fingers found the penny.

"You didn't see me do this," I said, tucking it into my bra. "Because I don't give a fuck about him anymore."

"Do what?" she replied, dutifully.

"Good girl." I leaned over and kissed her on the forehead. "Thank you for my party."

Then I walked to my car, walked to my husband, walked back to my life.

I was in bed an hour later, turned toward the ocean, even though it was too dark to see it. I could hear the waves rushing against the surf. The ocean was choppy tonight. Fitting. Noah was watching television in the living room; I could hear CNN through the walls. CNN was a lullaby to me at this point. He never came to bed when I did, and every night I fell asleep listening to the drone of the news. Tonight, I was grateful to be alone. If Noah looked too carefully—which he often did—he would see through my hollow smiles and pretend illness. He'd ask me what was wrong and I wouldn't lie to him. I didn't do that anymore. I was betraying him with my rogue emotions. I had the penny clutched in my fist; it was burning a hole through me, but I couldn't put it down. First Leah had come to me, throwing those deed papers in my face. Papers that, until that moment, I knew nothing about. Now, him. Why couldn't they just leave me alone? Ten years was a long time to grieve a relationship. I'd paid for my stupid decisions with a decade. When I met Noah, I finally felt ready to put my broken love to rest. But, you couldn't put something to rest when it kept coming back to haunt you.

I stood up and walked to the sliding glass doors that led to my balcony. Stepping out, I walked lightly to the edge of the railing.

I could do this. I kind of had to. Right? Exercise the ghosts. Take a stand. This was my life, dammit! The penny wasn't my life. It had to go. I lifted my fisted hand and felt the wind wrap around it. All I had to do was open my fist. That was it. So easy and so hard. I wasn't the type of girl to back away from a challenge. I closed my eyes and opened my fist.

For a second my heart seized. I heard my voice, but the wind quickly took it away. There. It was gone.

I stepped back and away from the railing, suddenly cold. Backwards I walked to my bedroom, one step, two steps…then I lurched forward, throwing myself against the railing to peer over into the space between me and the ground.

Oh my God. Had I really done that?

I had, and my heart was aching for a goddamn penny. *You're an idiot*, I told myself. *Until tonight you didn't even know he still had the penny*. But, that wasn't really true. I'd seen inside his Trojan horse when I'd broken into his house. He'd kept it all those years. But, he had a baby, and babies had a way of making people throw out the past and start new. I walked back into my bedroom and shut the door, and climbed into bed, and climbed into my life, and cried, cried, cried. Like a baby.

The next morning I took my coffee out there. I was dragging, and I told myself the fresh air would be good. What I really wanted was to stand at the site of where I murdered my penny. God, would I ever stop being so melodramatic? I was halfway to the balcony with my coffee clutched in my hands, when my foot passed over something cold. I backed up a step, looked down, and saw my penny.

Gah!

The wind. It must have blown it back toward me when I threw it. I didn't pick it up until I was through drinking my coffee. I just sort of stood there and stared at it. When I finally crouched down to retrieve it, I knew. You couldn't get rid of the past. You couldn't ignore it, or bury it, or throw it over the balcony. You just had to learn to live beside it. It had to peacefully co-exist with your present. If I could figure out how to do that, I could be okay. I took the penny inside and pulled my copy of *Great Expectations* off the bookshelf. I taped the penny to the title page and slid the book back in. There. Right where it belonged.

THIRTY-FOUR

PRESENT

I kiss her as I slide my hand up her skirt. She pants into my mouth and her legs tense as she waits for my fingers to push past her panties. I let my hand linger at the place where the material meets her skin. I enjoy the chase. I don't have sex with easy women. She says my name, and I tug at the material. I'm going to have sex with her. She's beautiful. She's funny. She's intelligent.

"I'm sorry," I say. "I can't do this."

I pull away from her and drop my head in my hands. *God.*

"What is it?" She scoots closer to me on the couch and puts an arm around my shoulders. She's nice. That makes it worse.

"I'm in love with someone," I say. "She's not mine, but this still feels like I'm cheating on her."

She starts to giggle. My head jerks up to look at her.

"I'm sorry," she says, covering her mouth. "That's pathetic and a bit romantic, yeah?"

I smile.

"She in America, this girl?"

"Can we not talk about her?"

She rubs my back and pulls her dress down.

"It's okay. You're not really my type. I've just always wanted to bang an American. Like in the movies."

She gets up and wanders over to my fridge. "This is a nice flat. You should buy some furniture." She takes out two beers and carries one over to me. I look around the room guiltily. I've been here for two months and the only thing in the room is a couch the last owner left behind and a bed I purchased the day I got here. I need to make some purchases.

"We can be friends," she says, sitting down next to me. "Now, tell me her name so I can Facebook stalk the girl who cockblocked me."

I run a hand across my face. "She isn't on Facebook. I don't want to say her name."

"Caleb…" she whines.

"Sara."

"All right," she says, standing up. "I'll see you at the gym then. Call me if you want to get drinks. No sex attached."

I nod and walk her to the door. She's a nice girl. Even nicer to take that whole situation with such good humor.

When she's gone, I pull out my computer. I order a kitchen table and a living room set. Then I go through my emails. Almost everything in my inbox is work related. My mother emails me daily, but I've yet to respond to any of them. When I see my father's name, I start. My mother must have told him I was back in London. I click on his name.

> *Caleb,*
>
> *Heard you were back in town. Let's get together for dinner. Call me.*

That's all he wrote to the son he hasn't seen in five years. Eh. Why not? I pull out my phone and text the number in the email. Might as well get the reunion over with. Maybe he'd surprise me and be less of an asshole than the last time I had dinner with him and he spent the entire two hours texting on his Blackberry.

He texts back almost immediately and says he'll meet me at a local pub tomorrow night. I wander over to my bed and fall into it, still dressed.

My father hasn't changed much in the five years since I've seen him. He's greyer…maybe. And what grey he's chosen to keep is probably as planned out as his tan—which I know has to be spray because he turns bright red in God's sun.

"You look like me!" he says, before embracing me in a man hug.

I pat his back and sit down, grinning. God, I hate this bastard, but it's good to see him.

He acts like we've been together every day for the last five years. It's all an act. My father is a salesman. He could make a terrorist feel at home in an electric chair. I let him do his thing and drink heavily.

Finally, he gets down to why I'm here.

"It's right up your alley, actually," I tell him. "A woman I wanted who didn't want me, and a kid I wanted to be mine and wasn't."

He grimaces. "That's not up my alley, son. I get the women I want."

I laugh.

"She must have had quite an effect on you to chase you out of your beloved America."

I don't answer that.

Suddenly, he sobers up. "I wanted to see my granddaughter. When I thought she was my granddaughter, that is."

I watch his face for lack of sincerity but find none. He's not blowing smoke up my ass or saying something to be polite. He's aging and getting a taste of his mortality. He genuinely wanted to meet Estella.

"I heard your ex-wife is worst than my first ex-wife." He smirks. "How did you manage that deal?"

"I'm the same type of fool as you, I guess."

He smirks.

"Come over to the house for dinner. Meet my new wife."

"Sure," I say.

"She has a younger sister…"

"Ugh. You're so sick." I shake my head and he laughs.

My phone rings. It's an American number. I look at my father, and he motions for me to take the call. "I'll be back," I say, standing up. When I answer, I immediately recognize the voice.

"Moira," I say.

"Hello, my dear. I have news."

"Okay…" My mind is spinning. I glance at my watch. It's around two o'clock stateside.

"Are you sitting down?"

"Out with it, Moira."

"When your ex-wife took Estella into the clinic to get the blood work done, she used Leah Smith on her paperwork instead of Johanna. There was another Leah Smith in the database—"

I cut her off. "What are you saying?"

"You got someone else's results, Caleb. Estella is yours. Ninety-nine point nine percent yours."

"Oh my God."

It turns out Leah was in the process of getting another test when the clinic found their mistake. She hadn't wanted me to think Estella wasn't mine. That would ruin her long-term plan of making me battle her in court for custody, all the while looking like I abandoned my daughter. And I had abandoned her. I hadn't fought to know the truth. I had been so blinded by my hurt that I never looked at the situation hard enough. I hate myself for that. I've missed so many important milestones in her life, and why? Because I'm an idiot.

Since I'm living in another country, Moira tells me I won't have to be there for all the court dates. I fly back anyway. Leah looks genuinely surprised to see me in court. I fly back three times in three months. I signed a one-year contract with the company in London, or I would have moved back already. When the judge sees me appear at all three hearings, he grants me three weeks a year, and since I am living in England, he will allow Estella to spend the time there as long as she is accompanied by a family member. It's a small victory. Leah is pissed. Three weeks. Twenty-one days out of three hundred and sixty-five. I try not to focus on that. I get my daughter for three uninterrupted weeks. And the year is almost over. Next year Moira will go for joint. I just have to finish out my contract and I can move back. It's settled that my mother will fly with Estella to London. When I ask if I can see Estella before I fly back, Leah says she has the stomach flu and it would be too traumatic for her. I'm forced to wait. I fly home and start getting things ready. I buy a twin bed and put it in the spare bedroom. I'll only get her for a week the first time, but I want her to feel like my flat is her home. So, I buy little girl looking things—a duvet with ponies and flowers, a dollhouse, a fluffy pink chair with its own ottoman. Two days before my mother is scheduled to fly in with her, I fill my fridge with kid food. I can barely sleep. I am so excited.

THIRTY-FIVE

PRESENT

I spend forty minutes in a toy store trying to decide what to get Estella. In the movies when parents are reunited with their children, they have a pastel-colored stuffed animal in their hands—usually a bunny. Since a cliché is the worst thing a person can be, I browse the aisles until I find a stuffed llama. I hold it in my hands for a few minutes, smiling like a fool. Then I carry it to the register.

My stomach is in knots when I climb onto the Tube. I take the Piccadilly line to Heathrow and mistakenly get off at the wrong terminal. I have to double back and by the time I find the correct gate, my mother has texted that the plane has landed. What if she doesn't remember me? Or if she decides not to like me and cries the entire trip? *God.* I am an absolute mess. I see my mother first, her blonde hair in a perfect chignon even after the nine-hour flight. When I look down, I see a chubby hand attached to my mother's slender one. I follow the length of the arm and see messy, red curls bouncing excitedly around a face that looks exactly like Leah's. I smile so hard my face hurts. I don't think I've smiled since I moved to London. Estella is wearing a pink tutu and a cupcake shirt. When I see that she's smeared lipstick all over her face, my heart does the most peculiar thing: it beats faster and aches at the same time. I watch my mother stop and point toward me.

Estella's eyes search me out. When she sees me, she pulls free of her grandmother's hand and…runs. I drop to my knees to catch her. She hits me with force—too much force for such a little person. She's strong. I squeeze her squishy little body and feel the ducts in my eyes burn as they try to summon tears. I just want to hold her like this for a few minutes, but she pulls back, smacks both hands on either side of my face, and starts talking a mile a minute. I wink at my mother in greeting and direct my gaze back to Estella, who is recounting a detail-by-detail version of her flight while clutching the llama underneath her arm. She has a forceful little voice, slightly raspy like her mother's.

"And then I ate my butter and Doll said it was gonna make me sick …" Doll is what she calls my mother. My mother thinks it's the greatest thing in the world. I think she's just relieved to have escaped the normal "Granny" or "Grandma" monikers that would make her feel old.

"You're a genius," I say while she's taking a breath. "What three-year-old speaks like this?"

My mother smiles ruefully. "One who never stops speaking. She gets unfathomable amounts of practice."

Estella repeats the word *unfathomable* all the way to baggage claim. She gets the giggles when I start chanting it with her, and by the time I pull their luggage from the belt, my mother's head looks ready to explode.

"You used to do that when you were little," she says. "Say the same thing over and over until I wanted to scream."

I kiss my daughter's forehead. "Who needs a paternity test?" I joke. Which is the absolute wrong thing to say, because my small person starts chanting *paternity test* all the way through the airport…until we climb into the cab outside and I distract her with a pink bus that's driving by.

During the cab ride home, Estella wants to know what her bedroom looks like, what color blankets I got for her bed, if I have any toys, if she can have sushi for dinner.

"Sushi?" I repeat. "What about spaghetti or chicken fingers?"

She pulls a face that only Leah could have taught her, and says, "I don't eat kid food."

My mother raises her eyebrows. "You'd never need a maternity test," she says out of the corner of her mouth. I have to stifle my laughter.

After taking them to my flat to drop off their things, we head out to a sushi restaurant where my three-year-old consumes a spicy tuna roll on her own, and then eats two pieces of my lunch. I watch in amazement as she mixes soy sauce and wasabi together and picks up her chopsticks. The waiter brought her a fixed pair, one with the rolled-up paper and the rubber band to keep the sticks together, but she politely refused them and then dazzled us with her chubby-fingered dexterity. She drinks hot tea out of a porcelain cup, and everyone in the restaurant stops to comment on her hair and ladylike behavior. Leah's done a good job teaching her manners. She thanks everyone who passes her a compliment with such sincerity; one elderly lady gets teary eyed. Estella passes out on my shoulder in the cab on the way home. I wanted to take her on the Tube, but my mother will have nothing to do with dirty underground trains, so we hail a cab.

"I want to ride the twain, Daddy." Her face is pressed into my neck and her voice is sleepy.

"Tomorrow," I tell her. "We'll send Doll off to visit friends, and we'll do lots of gross things."

"All wight," she sighs, "but Mommy doesn't like me to do…" and then her voice drops off and she's asleep. My heart beats and aches and beats and aches.

I spend the next week alone with my daughter. My mother visits friends and relatives, giving us plenty of time to bond and do our own thing. I take her to the zoo and the park and the museum, and upon her request, we eat sushi every day for lunch. I talk her into spaghetti one night for dinner, and she has a meltdown when she drops the noodles on her clothes. She wails, her face turning as red as her hair, until I put her in a bath and feed her the rest of her dinner sitting on the edge of the tub. I don't know whether to be amused or mortified. When I get her out of the bath, she rubs her eyes, yawns, and falls asleep right as I get pajamas on. I'm convinced she's half angel. The half that isn't Leah, of course.

We stop by my father's house one evening. He lives in Cambridge in an impressive farmhouse with stables out back. He carries Estella from stall to stall where he introduces her to the horses. She repeats their names: Sugarcup, Nerphelia, Adonis, Stokey. I watch him charm my daughter and feel grateful that she's a continent away from him. This is what he does. He gets right down on your level—whoever you are—and shines his attention on you. If you like to travel, he'll ask where you've been, he'll listen with his eyes narrowed and laugh at all your jokes. If you're interested in model cars, he will ask your opinion on building them and make plans to have you teach him. He makes you feel like you're the only person worth having a conversation with, and then he goes a year without having a conversation with you. The disappointment is vast. He will never build that model car with you, he will cancel dinner plans and birthday plans and vacation plans. He will choose work and someone else over you. He will break your charmed, hopeful heart time and time again. But, I'll let my daughter have today, and I'll protect her the best I can in the tomorrow. Broken people give broken love. And we are all a little broken. You just have to forgive and sew up the wounds love delivers, and move on.

We go from the stables to the kitchen where he makes a show of making us huge ice cream sundaes, and then squirts whipped cream into Estella's mouth right from the can. She announces that she can't wait to tell Mommy about this new treat, and I'm fairly certain my ex-wife will be shooting me nasty emails in the coming weeks. She loves him. Like I did. It's heartbreaking to watch what kind of dad he could have been had he tried. The last two days of her visit, I feel sick to my stomach. I don't want her to go. I want to be able to see her every day. In a year she will start pre-K. Then kindergarten and first grade. How will we wing weeklong visits to the UK then? *It'll all work itself out,* I tell myself. Even if I have to bribe Leah to move to London.

Estella cries when we part at the airport. She's clutching the llama to her chest, her tears dripping into its fur, begging me to let her stay in "Wondon." I grind my teeth together and hate every decision I've ever made. *God. What am I even letting her go back to?* Leah is a vicious, conniving bitch. She left her at a daycare to get drunk when she was a week old for God's sake. She kept her away from her father just to hurt me. Her love is conditional and so is her kindness, and I don't want her anger to touch my daughter.

"Mum," I say. I look into my mother's eyes, and she gets it. She grabs my hand and squeezes.

"I pick her up from school twice a week, and I have her on weekends. I'll make sure she's okay until you have her back with you."

I nod, unable to say anything else. Estella sobs into my neck, and the pain I feel is too complex to put into words.

"I'm going to pack up and come home," I say to my mother over my daughter's shoulder. "I can't do this. It's too hard."

She laughs. "Being a daddy suits you. You have to finish out your contract with them. Until then, I'll keep bringing her to see you."

My mother has to pick her up and carry her through security. I want to jump past the barriers and snatch her back.

I'm so fucking depressed on the Tube ride home; I sit with my head in my hands for most of it. I drink myself into a stupor that night and write an email to Olivia that I never send. Then I pass out and dream that Leah takes Estella to Asia and says she's never coming back.

THIRTY-SIX

PRESENT

Since the court appointed all my custody dates with Estella, I get to have her with me every other Christmas—which makes it *this* Christmas. It'll be my first Christmas with my daughter. Leah called me seething when our court-appointed mediator gave her the news.

"Christmas is important to me," she said. "This is wrong. A child should never be away from her mother on Christmas."

"A child should never be away from her father on Christmas either," I shot back. "But you made sure that happened for two years."

"This is your fault for moving away. I shouldn't have to pay for your asinine decisions."

She was right to a degree. I didn't have anything for her, so I told her I had to go and hung up.

Christmas isn't important to Leah. She doesn't value family or tradition. She values being able to put our daughter in a Christmas dress and carting her to the numerous Christmas parties she attends. All the wealthy mothers do that. Tis the season to show off your children and drink low-fat, liquored-up eggnog.

I go shopping for her presents the day I find out I'm getting her for Christmas. Sara goes with me for reference. We've had drinks a couple times and I land up telling her everything about Olivia, Leah, and Estella, so when I ask her to come shopping with me, she jumps at it.

"So, no dolls," she says, holding up a Barbie. I shake my head.

"Her mother buys her dolls. She has too many."

"What about art supplies? Nurture the inner artiste."

I nod. "Perfect, her mother hates her to be dirty."

We head over to the art aisle. She dumps play dough, paints, an easel, and crayons into the cart.

"So, any word about Olivia?"

"Can you not?"

She laughs and grabs a box of chalk. "It's like a soap opera, mate. I just want to know what happens next."

I stop at a tie-dye T-shirt kit. "Let's get this, she'll like it."

Sara nods in approval.

"I haven't reached out to any of our friends. She told me to leave her alone and that's exactly what I'm doing. As far as I know—she's knocked up and living fuckily ever after."

Sara shakes her head. "Unfinished business is a bitch."

"Our business is finished," I say more sharply than I intend. "I live in London. I have a daughter. I am happy. So fucking deliriously happy."

We both laugh at the same time.

I talk to my mother the day before she flies out with Steve and Estella. She's acting odd. When I ask her about it, she stumbles over her words and says she's stressed about the holidays. I feel guilty. Steve and my mother are foregoing their usual plans to bring Estella to me. I could have gone home, but I'm not ready. She's everywhere—under every twisted tree, in every car on the road. One day, I tell myself, the sting will subside and I'll be able to look at a fucking orange and not think of her.

Or maybe it won't. Maybe life is about living with the hauntings.

I buy a tree and then scour the city for pink Christmas ornaments. I find a box of tiny ballerina shoes to hang on the tree and pink pigs with curly silver tails. When I grab two armfuls of silver and pink foil, the sales clerk grins at me.

"Someone has a daughter…"

I nod. I like the way that sounds.

She points to a box of pink flamingos and winks. I throw those on the counter too.

I set everything up in the living room so that when she arrives we can decorate together. My mother and Steve are staying at the Ritz Carlton a few blocks away. I figure I'll let Estella choose what we eat for Christmas dinner, though if she asks for sushi or a rack of lamb, I'm screwed. The following day, I arrive at the airport to collect them an hour early.

I wait, sitting on the edge of one of the baggage claim carousels that aren't in use. I'm anxious. I wander off to buy an espresso and drink it, looking out at an empty runway. I don't know why I feel like this, but something ugly is curling in my stomach.

People start walking through the gate, so I get up and wait near the front of the crowd, trying to spot my mother's hair. Blonde is a hard color to miss on a woman. My brother once told me that he remembers her having red hair when he was little, but she firmly denies it. I pull out my phone to check if there are any missed calls or texts from her and see none. She always texts when she lands. My stomach does the sick lurch. I have a really strange feeling about all of this. What if Leah has done something stupid? There is nothing I'd put past her at this point. I am about to dial my mother's number, when my phone starts flashing. I see a number I don't recognize.

"Hello?"

"Caleb Drake?" The voice is a woman's, breathy and quiet, like she's trying not to be overheard.

I get chills. I remember the last time I got a call like this.

"My name is Claribel Vasquez. I am a counselor at Boca South Medical Center." Her voice drops off and I wait for her to continue, my heart beating wildly.

"There's been an accident," she says. "Your parents…your daughter. They—"

"Are they alive?"

She pauses. It feels like an hour, ten hours. Why is she taking so long to answer me!

"There was a car accident. A semi—"

"Estella?" I demand.

"She's in critical condition. Your parents—"

I don't need her to say anything else. I sit, except there is nothing to sit on. I slide down the wall I am leaning against and hit the ground, my hand covering my face. I can barely hold the phone to my ear I am shaking so much.

"Is her mother there?"

"No, we haven't been able to contact your ex-wife."

"Estella," I say. It's all I can manage. I'm too afraid to ask.

"She came out of surgery about an hour ago. There was a lot of internal bleeding. The doctors are monitoring her now. It would be best if you came back right away."

I hang up without saying goodbye and walk straight to the ticket counter. There is a flight in three hours. I have just enough time to go home and get my passport and come right back. I don't think. I just throw a few things in a bag, catch a cab back to the airport, and board my flight. I don't sleep, I don't eat, I don't think. *You're in shock,* I tell myself. *Your parents are dead.* And then I remind myself not to think. I need to get home, get to Estella. I'll mourn them later. Right now, I don't need to think about anything but Estella.

I take a cab from the airport. I call Claribel directly as soon as the door closes. She tells me Estella's condition hasn't changed and says she will be waiting for me in the hospital lobby. When I run through the doors, Claribel is waiting for me. She is childlike in size, and I have to bend my neck down to look at her.

"She's still critical," she says right away. "We still haven't managed to get in touch with Leah. Are there any other numbers we can call?"

I shake my head. "Her mother, maybe. Have you tried her?"

Claribel shakes her head. I hand her my phone. "It's under *in-law*."

She takes it and walks me to the elevator.

"You might want to call Sam Foster. If anyone knows where she is, he does."

She nods and steps inside with me. We take the elevator to the critical care unit. I watch the floors light up as we pass them. When we reach the fifth floor, Claribel steps out first and swipes an access card through a keypad next to the door. It smells like antiseptic, though the walls are painted a warm tan color. It does little to lighten the mood, and somewhere off in the distance, I can hear crying. We walk briskly to room 549. The door is closed. She pauses outside and places a small hand on my arm.

"It's going to be hard to see her. Just keep in mind there is still a lot of swelling on her face."

I breathe deeply as she opens the door, and I step inside. The light is dim and a symphony of medical equipment is playing around the room. I approach her bed slowly. She is a tiny lump under the covers. When I stand above her, I start crying. A tiny piece of red hair sticks out from the bandages on her head. That is the only way I can identify her. Her face is so swollen that even if she were awake, she wouldn't be able to open her eyes. There are tubes everywhere—up her nose, down her throat, snaking into her tiny, bruised arms. How did she survive this? How is her heart still beating?

Claribel stands at the window and politely looks away while I cry over my daughter. I am too afraid to touch her, so I run my pinkie over her pinkie, the only part of her that isn't bruised.

After a few minutes, the doctors come in to speak to me. Doctors. She has multiple because of all the injuries she sustained. By the time the 747 touched down on American soil with me in its belly, my three-year-old daughter had survived surgery on hers. I listen to them talk about her organs, her chances of recovery, the months of rehabilitation she's facing. I watch the back of their white coats as they're leaving the room and I hate them. Claribel, who had slipped out a few minutes earlier, comes back into the room with her phone in her hand.

"I spoke with Sam," she says softly. "Leah is in Thailand. It's why no one has been able to reach her."

My eyes narrow. It's almost second nature when Leah's name is mentioned.

"Why?"

Claribel clears her throat. It's a tiny, chirping sound.

"It's all right," I tell her. "I don't have ties to her emotionally."

"She went with her boyfriend. Since you were supposed to have Estella for Christmas."

"God, and she just didn't tell anyone? Was he able to contact her?"

She pulls on her necklace and frowns. "He's trying."

I cover my eyes with the heels of my hands. I haven't eaten or slept in thirty hours. I glance at Estella.

"Her mother should be here. Let me know as soon as you hear something."

"I'll get them to send a cot up. You should eat. You need to be strong for Estella," she says.

I nod.

I don't eat. But, I do fall asleep in the chair next to her bed. When I wake, there is a nurse in the room checking her vitals. I rub a hand across my face, my vision blurry.

"How is she?" I ask. My voice is hoarse.

"Vitals are stable." She smiles when she sees me rubbing the back of my neck. "Your wife went to get a cot sent over."

"I'm sorry. Who?" Had Leah made it back that quickly?

"Estella's mother," she says. "She was just here."

I nod and start walking toward the door. I want to know where the hell she was while our daughter almost lost her life. You don't just leave the country without telling any family when you had a child. She could have made it here before I did if anyone had been able to contact her. Why she didn't bother leaving a number with my parents…I stop walking. Maybe she had. They weren't here to confirm it. Maybe that's why my mother had sounded so strange on the phone. Or maybe my mother had known who Leah left the country with, and that's what made her upset. *My mother. Think about that later,* I tell myself for the thousandth time today. My feet kick-start and I'm walking again. Around the corner, into the main corridor where the nurses' station is. Beeping…beeping…the smell of antiseptic…I can hear muffled footsteps and hushed voices, a doctor's pager going off. I think about the crying I heard earlier and wonder what happened to the patient. Had it been tears of fear or mourning or regret? I could cry the trifecta of those emotions right now. I look for red hair and see none. Rubbing my hand across the back of my neck, I stand in the middle of the corridor, not sure where to go. I feel detached, as if I'm floating above my body instead of being inside of it. *A balloon on a string,* I think. *Is this what exhaustion looks like, everything muted and blurry?* Suddenly, I'm not sure what I came out here to do. I turn around to go back to Estella's room and that's when I see her. No more than a few yards away, we're both still, watching each other, surprised—and yet, not—to have fallen into this same corridor together. I feel the balloon pop and suddenly, I'm being pulled back into my body. My thoughts regain their sharpness. Sounds, smells, colors—they all come into focus. I am living in high definition again.

"Olivia."

She walks slowly toward me and doesn't stop a few feet away like I think she will. She comes right into my arms, molding herself against me. I hold her, pressing my face into her hair. How does such a tiny fleck of a woman have so much power that I can be restored just by looking at her? I breathe her in, feel her under my fingertips. I know, I know, I know that I am the match and she is the gasoline and without each other we are just two objects void of reaction.

"You were in the room earlier?"

She nods.

"The nurse said that Estella's mother was here. I was looking for red hair…"

She nods again. "She assumed and I didn't correct her. Sam called Cammie, Cammie called me," she says. "I came right away." She touches my face, both hands on either cheek. "Let's go back in and sit with her."

I blow air through my nose trying to quell the overwhelming emotions, the relief that she's here, the fear for my daughter, and the anger at myself. I let her lead me back to Estella and we sit on either side of her, saying nothing.

THIRTY-SEVEN

PRESENT

Olivia stays with me for three days. She coaxes me into eating, brings me clothes, and sits with Estella while I shower in the little bathroom attached to the room. In the days that she is there, I never ask why she came, or where her husband is. I leave out the questions and allow us to exist together in the worst few days of my life. Besides Leah, another person missing in action is my brother, Seth. Steve had mentioned that he was going on a deep-sea fishing trip the last time I spoke to him. I wonder if Claribel had managed to contact him and if he knew that our mother and stepfather were dead? Then, the strangeness of the situation hits me. Leah and Seth both missing at the same time, and how strangely my mother was behaving days before they were supposed to fly to London with my daughter. Had my mother known that Seth and Leah were together? I try not to think about it. What they do now is their business.

On day two, Olivia quietly reminds me that I have to make funeral arrangements for my parents. I'm on the phone with the funeral director late in the afternoon when Olivia walks in holding two cups of coffee. She refuses to drink hospital coffee and has been making the pilgrimage across the street to get Starbucks twice a day. I take the cup from her and she sits down opposite me. Albert—*Trebla*—the funeral director is asking questions, but I can't focus on what he's saying. Flowers, religious preferences, email notifications. It's all too much. When she sees me struggling with the decisions, she sets her coffee down and takes the phone from me. I hear her speak in the voice she reserves for the courtroom.

"Where are you located? Yes, I'll be there in forty minutes."

She is gone for three hours. When she gets back, she tells me that everything is taken care of. She is just in time to see Estella wake up. I've been looking at her eyelids for days, so I almost cry when I see the color in my daughter's irises. She whimpers and asks for her mommy. I kiss her nose and tell her that Mommy is on her way. Leah had trouble getting a flight out of Thailand. We've done nothing but fight over the phone. Last I spoke to her was a few hours ago, and she was in New York switching planes. She blames me, of course. I blame me too.

When the doctors and nurses leave the room, Estella falls asleep holding my hand. I am so grateful she didn't ask about her grandparents. Long after her fingers go limp, I'm still gripping her little hand, my heart beating a little easier.

Olivia is standing at the window watching the rain late in the day. She left earlier to go home and shower. I expected her to be gone for the night, but she came back two hours later, wearing jeans and a white tunic shirt, her hair still wet and smelling of flowers. I watch her silhouette and for the tenth time that day, am overtaken with the grief/regret cocktail I've been drunk on.

"This is my fault. I shouldn't have left. I shouldn't have made my parents bring my daughter halfway across the world to see me…" It's the first time I've said any of this out loud.

She looks startled, turning away from the window and glancing my way. She doesn't say anything right away. Just walks over and sits in her usual chair.

"The day I saw you in the music store it was raining too, do you remember?"

I nod. I remember everything about that day—the rain, the drops of water clinging to her hair, the way she smelled like gardenia when she furtively approached me.

"Dobson Scott Orchard was standing outside of the music store. He offered to walk me to my car with his umbrella. I don't know if I was one of the ones he watched, or if he decided on the spot, but I had a choice: hightail it out of there under his umbrella, or go inside and talk to you. It would seem that I made the right choice that day."

"My God, Olivia. Why didn't you tell me?"

"I've never told anyone." She shrugs. "But, that moment—that one, ever-changing moment—has made a profound impact on me. My entire life would have been different had I not walked toward you. The next time you would have seen me would have been on the news." She nods, staring at the floor, her little mouth pulled off to the side. When she continues, her voice is lower than before. "The sum of all the things we shouldn't have done in our lives is enough to kill us with the weight, Caleb Drake. Neither you, nor I, nor anyone else in this life could possibly know the chain reaction our decisions cause. If you're to blame, then so am I."

"How?"

"If I'd done what my heart said and said yes to you, you wouldn't have left for London. Luca and Steve would be alive and your daughter wouldn't be in the hospital in a medical-induced coma."

We are quiet for a few minutes as I think over her words. Everything she has said is frightening.

"So why did you take his case?"

She breathes deeply. I hear the air leave her in a great sigh.

"Brace yourself, this is going to sound really sick."

I mock grab the arms of my chair, and she snickers.

"I felt a connection to him. We were both dealing with our obsessions that day, Dobson and I." She makes her eyes wide when she says the last part. "We were both looking for someone. We were both so goddamn alone that we took a risk not to be. Are you disgusted with me?"

I smile and run my pinkie along Estella's. "No, Duchess. Your ability to see outside the box and mentally align yourself with the scum of the world is why I love you."

The minute the words are out of my mouth, I regret them. I glance at her face to catch her reaction, but there is none. Maybe she's used to me professing my love by now. Maybe, she didn't hear me. Maybe—

"I love you too."

I catch her eyes and hold them, my heart pounding.

"Well, isn't that beautiful. All the fucking inappropriate love."

Our heads spin toward the door as Leah strides into the room. She doesn't look at either of us as she walks past our chairs. She goes right to Estella. At least her priorities are right; I'll give her that. I hear her intake of breath when she sees Estella.

"Shit," she says. Both of her palms are pressed against her forehead, her fingers splayed out above them. If the situation weren't so dire, I would have laughed. She lowers herself to her haunches, says "shit" again, and then stands back up too quickly. She wobbles on her heels then steadies herself on the bed.

She spins toward me. "Has she woken up? Has she asked for me?"

"Yes, and yes," I say. On the other side of the room, Olivia stands up like she's going to leave.

I mouth *wait* and turn back to Leah who has started to cry. I put a hand on my ex-wife's shoulder. "She's out of the forest. She's going to be okay."

Leah looks at my hand, which is still on her shoulder, and then at my face.

"You mean *the woods*," she says.

"What?"

"The woods," she repeats. "You said *forest.* Except you're not in England anymore, you're in America, and in America, we say WOODS!" Her voice rises and I know what's coming next. "And if you'd stayed in America, this never would have happened. But, you had to run away because of her!" She points a finger at Olivia. If her finger were an arrow it would have wedged in Olivia's heart.

"Leah," Olivia says quietly, "if you point at me again I'm going to break that manicured finger right off your hand. Now, turn around and smile, your daughter is waking up."

Leah and I both spin toward Estella, whose eyes are fluttering open.

I give a quick thank-you glance at Olivia before she slips out the door.

The funeral is three days later. Sam comes to sit with Estella while we are gone. I have a sneaking suspicion that something is going on between him and Leah, but then I remember he told Claribel that Leah was in Thailand with a man. I wonder again bitterly if that man was my shithead brother and then I kill the thought. I am a hypocrite. I slept with Olivia while she was still legally married. To each his own. I toast my bottle of water to the ceiling of my car and press down on the gas. I asked Olivia to come to the funeral a few days ago.

"Your mother hated me," she said, on the phone. "It would be disrespectful."

"She didn't hate you. I promise. Besides, your father would have hated me, and I still would have gone to his funeral."

Her breath hissed across the line.

"Fine," she said.

I've pushed every thought of my parents from my mind in order to give Estella what she needs, but when I walk through the doors of the funeral home and see their coffins, side by side, I lose it. I excuse myself from an old neighbor who is approaching me with condolences, and walk briskly to the parking lot. There is a low-hanging willow to the rear of the property. I stand underneath it and breathe. That's where she finds me.

She doesn't say anything, just comes to stand next to me, taking my hand and squeezing it.

"This isn't happening," I say. "Tell me it's not."

"It's happening," she says. "Your parents are dead. But, they loved you. They loved your daughter. You have so many good memories."

I glance down at her. She saw two parents die and no doubt only one of them provided decent memories. I wonder if she had anyone to hold her hand after Oliver and Via died. I squeeze her hand.

"Let's go in," she says. "The service is about to start."

When we walk into the chapel, every eye is trained on us. Leah is sitting next to my brother. When she sees me with Olivia, it is a mixture of jealousy and rage. She quickly averts her eyes and steams privately. For now.

Doesn't she know Olivia isn't mine? What does it even matter that an old friend is comforting me? She'll just drive home to her husband afterward. I take my seat near the front.

My mother's favorite roses are—were—English Garden. There are several tasteful arrangements around her casket, as well as next to the blown-up picture of her face, which is sitting on a large easel. Both caskets are closed, though Olivia told me that she had her dressed in a black Chanel dress that she chose from my mother's closet. Steve had always jokingly said he wanted to be buried in his old baseball uniform. She blushed when she told me she took that and a suit to the funeral home, and when she got there, she left the suit in the car. I reach out and squeeze her hand. She's so fucking thoughtful, it's ridiculous. I wouldn't have even been able to walk in my mother's closet, never mind choose an outfit I'd think she'd like. When the service is over, I flank one side of the door, and my brother takes the other. We don't speak to each other, but do plenty of speaking to the people offering their condolences. It makes me sick. All of it. That they died. That Estella won't know them. That it's all my fault.

When the room clears out, we move to the gravesite. It's so sunny, everyone is hidden behind sunglasses. *It feels like a Matrix funeral*, I think jokingly. My mother hated *The Matrix*. When my parents' boxes are lowered into the ground and covered in dirt, Leah starts the fight.

THIRTY-EIGHT

PRESENT

It might have been seeing me with Olivia, walking so closely our arms were touching. Or maybe every once in a while, someone with that much venom can't hold it in anymore and it just erupts out of their person, burning everyone around them. Whatever the fuck it was, it came.

"Caleb?"

I stop, turn. Leah is standing next to my brother's car, just a few spaces back. I was walking Olivia to her car before I drove back to the hospital. I had a feeling I wouldn't be seeing her for a while, and I wanted to thank her for taking care of me. Olivia keeps walking for a few feet and then turns around to see why I'm lagging. The wind blows, flattening her dress against her and causing her hair to whip around her face. We are all spaced evenly apart. Leah and I are in the middle, with Olivia and Seth flanking us.

I feel it coming. I swear to God, confrontation has a taste. I hesitate before answering.

"What is it, Leah?"

Her red hair is up. I always thought that when she wore her hair up, she looked more innocent. I glance at my brother, who is looking at her with just as much curiosity as I am. His thumb is poised over the unlock button on his car keys, his arm extended outward. If we were all freeze-framed, we'd look like a scene from a Quentin Tarantino movie. She opens her mouth, and I know it's not going to be good.

"I don't want you coming to the hospital. You're a shitty, irresponsible father. And don't think Estella will be making any more trips to see you." She punctuates her sentence with, "I'm taking you to court for full custody."

My retort is hot on the tip of my tongue, when I feel a slight breeze to my right. I see a flash of black and Olivia moves past me. I watch as she approaches Leah. She moves like an angry river, flowing across the black tar of the parking lot. I look on in frozen astonishment as the angry river lifts her hand and slaps Leah across the face. Leah's head snaps to the side from the force and when it straightens, I can see a red handprint.

"Fuuuuuck." I lunge toward them the same time as Seth. For a moment, my brother and I are united in an effort to stop Leah's retaliation. Leah is screaming in anger, writhing to get out of Seth's grip. That's when I notice that Olivia is calm and still. My hands are on her shoulders, so I lean down to speak in her ear.

"What the hell are you doing, Duchess?"

"Let me go," she says. "I'm not going to do anything." She's still staring toward Leah and all I can see of her is the back of her head.

I let her go and she reaches across the space and slaps Leah again. Seth curses loudly. Luckily the parking lot is empty except for us.

"I'm going to sue you, you stupid bitch!" Leah screams.

Seth lets her go and she lunges for Olivia. Before she can get to her, I push Olivia behind my back and block Leah's path.

"No," I say. "You don't touch her."

Seth starts laughing. Leah spins on him. "You saw that, right? You saw her hit me?"

"Doesn't matter," I say. "It's our word against yours. And I didn't see anything."

Leah pulls out her phone and takes a picture of the red mark on her face. I shake my head. Was I really married to this woman? I'm distracted enough for Olivia to get past me and snatch Leah's phone out of her hand. She throws it on the ground and stomps on it with her heel, cracking the screen. Once…twice…three times—I grab her.

"You really have a death wish today, Olivia," I say between my teeth.

Leah's mouth is open. "I'm going to destroy you," she says.

Olivia shrugs. I can't believe she's being so calm about this. "You already did. There is nothing more you could do to me. But, I swear to God, if you fuck with Caleb, I'm going to put you in prison for one of your *many* illegal activities. Then you won't see your daughter."

Leah closes her mouth. I open mine. I'm not sure who is more shocked by this fierce defense of me.

"I hate you," Leah spits. "You're still the same worthless piece of white trash you always were."

"I don't even hate you," Olivia says. "You're so pathetic, I can't. But, don't think for a minute that I won't revive your indiscretions."

"What are you talking about?" Leah's eyes are shifty. I wonder what Olivia has on her. It must be pretty good if she thought she could get away with two good slaps.

"Christopher," Olivia says quietly. Leah's face drains of color. "You're wondering how I know about that, yes?"

Leah doesn't say anything, just continues to stare.

"It won't get you locked up for pharmaceutical fraud, but boy would this be better…"

Seth looks at me and I shrug. The only Christopher I know is a thirty-year-old transgender who works—worked—for Steve.

"What do you want?" Leah says to Olivia.

Olivia swipes the dark hair out of her face and points a finger at me. Actually, she jabs a finger at me.

"You don't mess with his custody. You mess with his custody, I mess with yours. Understand?"

Leah doesn't nod, but she doesn't fight it either.

"You're a criminal," Olivia says. "And you're actually looking kind of chubby."

With that last bit, she turns on her heels and marches the rest of the way to her car. I don't know whether to stay and watch Leah's mortified face or chase after her. Leah *is* looking a little chubby.

Seth nods to me, then tugs at my ex-wife's arm, pulling her toward their car. I watch them go. I watch Olivia go. I stand for thirty minutes after they've gone and watch the empty parking lot.

Who the fuck is Christopher?

"Who the fuck is Christopher, Duchess?"

I hear music on the other end of the line. She must turn off the radio because a second later it's gone.

"You really want to know this?"

"You just made Leah's face turn as red as her hair. Yeah, I want to know this."

"All right," she says. "Hold on, I'm in the drive-thru at Starbucks."

I wait while she orders. When her voice comes back on the line it sounds professional, like she's briefing a client.

"Leah was having sex with her housekeeper's son."

"Okay," I said.

"He was seventeen at the time."

I let go of the steering wheel to run ten fingers through my hair.

"How do you know?"

We're heading in two different directions down the 95, but I can feel her smirking. See it.

"Her housekeeper came to see me. Actually, not me—Bernie. Bernie ran a couple billboards last year in Miami, urging sexual harassment victims to come see her. You know, one of those godawful advertisements where the lawyer is looking all serious and there is a gavel in the far right corner to symbolize your coming justice?"

I know exactly the type.

"Anyway, Christopher's mother—Shoshi—happened to see it and scheduled an appointment at the office. When she filled out her client information, I noticed that she listed your address as her own. So, I pulled her in before Bernie could get to her. She wanted to talk to someone about her teenage son. She'd sometimes take him with her to work and pay him to do some of the harder things. Apparently Leah was so impressed with his work ethic, she asked Shoshi to bring him on weekends and she paid him to do stuff around the house. After a few months of that, Shoshi found condoms in his wallet and a pair of panties that she said she'd seen a hundred times since she folded them."

I groan. Olivia hears it and laughs into the phone. "What? Did you think she was normal after that little *Who's my baby daddy?* stunt she pulled on you?"

"Okay, so why was this Shoshi character coming to you about sexual harassment? Why not call the police and get Leah jailed for statutory rape?"

"This is where it gets complicated, my friend. Shoshi said her son was denying the whole thing. He refused to get Leah in trouble for sleeping with a minor since he was over eighteen by the time she came to me, but his mother did get him to agree to nail her for sexual harassment."

"What did you do, Olivia?"

Her eyebrow was up. I knew it was.

"Nothing. Before I could do anything, Shoshi changed her mind. Sounds like Leah paid them off. But I could still get him to testify and she knows it."

"Ah," I say. "Well, thank God you're cunning."

"Thank God," she repeats.

"You slapped her, Duchess."

"Mmmm," she says. "And it felt so damn good." We both laugh.

There is a long, awkward silence. Then she says, "Noah and I are divorced."

The world freezes for one second…two seconds… three seconds…

"Remember that coffee shop? The one we went to after we ran into each other at the grocery store?"

"Yeah," she says.

"I'll meet you there in ten minutes."

When I walk into the coffee shop, she's already there. She's sitting at the same table we sat at years earlier. In front of her are two cups.

"I got you a tea," she says when I sit. I grin at the irony. This time it's me asking about her breakup.

"So, what happened?"

She tucks the hair that has fallen into her face behind her ears and looks at me sadly.

"I got pregnant."

I try to pretend that I'm unfazed by this little piece of news, but I can feel the awkwardness all over my face. I wait for her to go on.

"I lost it."

Agh! So much pain in her face. Our hands are both resting on the table, so close, that I reach a finger out and stroke her pinkie with it.

"He agreed to have a baby with me, but when I lost it, he looked so relieved. Then—" she pauses to hide her watery eyes and take a sip of coffee, "—then he said maybe it was for the best."

I flinch.

"We made it a few more months after that, then I asked him to leave."

"Why?"

"He wanted to go back to life as he knew it. He was happy and laughing. In his mind, we tried and it wasn't meant to be. I couldn't go back after that. It was my second miscarriage." She looks up at me and I nod.

"Whoever thought the cold, heartless Olivia Kaspen would want to have children?" She smiles bitterly.

"I knew you would," I say. "It was just a matter of time and healing."

We finish our drinks in silence. When we stand up, I stop a few feet away from the trash can with my coffee cup in my hand.

"Olivia?"

"Yeah?"

"If I make this shot, will you go out with me?" I hold my cup like it's a basketball and look from her to the trash can.

"Yeah," she says, smiling. "Yeah, I will."

I make the shot.

THIRTY-NINE

PRESENT

This is the start of our life. This is our choice. We barely have our shit together. I terminated my contract in London, moved home, and sold my condo. She sold hers too, and we moved into an apartment near both of our jobs. It's not even a nice apartment—there is too much linoleum and our neighbors fight constantly. But, we don't care. We just wanted to ditch the past and be together. We'll figure it out. Might take some time. We don't have a plan yet; we barely even have furniture, but we are both okay with the surrender. We have little fights all the time. She hates that I don't throw away my trash—water bottles, cookie bags, candy wrappers. She finds them all over the apartment and makes a big show of crinkling them up and throwing them in the trash. I hate the way she soaks the bathroom floor. The woman doesn't dry herself. Goddamn if it's nice to look at her soaking body as she walks from the bathroom to the bedroom, but use a fucking towel already. She always makes the bed. I always do the dishes. She drinks milk straight from the carton and that kind of pisses me off, but then she reminds me that she has to live with my snoring and I call it even. But, holy hell is she fun. How did I not know that we could laugh this much? Or sit in absolute silence and listen to music together? How did I live without this for so long? I watch her sit on one of our two chairs, one from her house, one from mine—her fingers clipping lightly across her keyboard. It still feels like I'm dreaming when I come home to her every night. I love this dream!

I lean over her neck as she works and kiss her on her sweet spot. She shivers. "Stop it, I'm trying to work."

"I don't really care, Duchess…"

I kiss her again, my hand sliding down the front of her dress. Her breath catches. I can't see her face, but I know her eyes are closed. I step around the front of her chair and I extend my hand to her. She looks at it for a long moment. The longest moment. Without looking away from me, she sets her computer down and stands up. We are still getting to know each other sexually. She's a little timid, and I'm afraid of being too aggressive and chasing her away. But, here we are. I struck my match, she poured out her gasoline. We burn now. All the time.

I lead her to my bed, stopping at the foot to pull her against me. I kiss her for a long time. I kiss her until she's leaning into me so much I have to hold her up.

"Do I make you feel weak?" I say this against her mouth.

"Yes."

"How?"

"You take away my control."

I unzip the back of her dress and slip the sleeves from her shoulders. Every single sexual encounter with Olivia is a balancing act: part seduction, part psychoanalysis. I have to wrestle with her demons to get her legs to open. I love it and I hate it.

"Why do you always need to have control?"

"So, I don't get hurt."

I don't make a big deal of anything she's saying. I work at taking off her clothes. When I reach her bra, I pull down the cups instead of taking it off completely. I hold one of her breasts with one hand. My other arm is wrapped around her waist so she can't get away. Not that she would try. I think by now, I have her.

"Do you like feeling weak?"

If I look over her shoulder, I can see the entire rear of her in our dresser mirror. She is wearing a white lace panty.

I eye her legs as I wait for her answer. My heart is pounding; the rest of me is aching. I already know her answer. I know she likes to feel weak. It is a thrill for her to yield, though it costs her something every time she does. I want to eliminate the emotional fear and get her to the point where she just enjoys it.

"Yes."

"I won't leave you," I say. "I won't ever love another woman."

I let go of her breast and let my hand trail between her legs. Pulling the material aside, I touch her. I've learned that leaving her underwear on until right before I take her helps the process. You have to strip this woman's defenses away slowly.

She falls back on the bed, and I slide on top of her. She unclasps her own bra and throws it to her left.

"Wanna try something new?"

She nods.

I make her straddle me, and then turn her around so she's facing away. She can see herself in the mirror this way. I'm curious to see if she'll watch.

She leans forward, putting her hands flat on the bed between my knees, and begins to roll her hips in a circular movement. It's times like these that I am unsure of who is really made weak by whom. This woman was made for sex. She's so inhibited, but when she lets go, I am given the most sensual ride of my life.

Without prompting, she turns around, placing both of her hands flat on my chest. She rocks back and forth as she rides me. She throws her head back and her hair is so long it sweeps my knees. I have never seen anything more erotic and beautiful in my life. When her head rolls forward, her hair cascades into her face. I wrap it around my hand and pull her to kiss me. While I'm playing with her tongue, I shift her body off mine. She protests and I nip her on the shoulder, which seems to shut her up. I am behind her and I have her on her knees, but instead of bending her over, I run my hands down her arms and grab her wrists, guiding her hands to the frame of the bed so she's half upright.

I swipe her hair over one of her shoulders, kiss her neck, and place my hands on her hips. I lean forward to speak into her ear.

"Hold on tight."

"You can't deny we do that right."

She smiles up at me, her eyes soft and hazy. The only time Olivia's eyes are not alert and pointedly cold are when she's pinned beneath me—or when she's recovering from being pinned beneath me. I've trained her to say *I love you* when she orgasms. If she doesn't say *I love you*, she doesn't get an orgasm—she learned that the hard way. It's payback for all the years she wouldn't tell me. Afterward, it takes her at least an hour to return to her normal spitfire mode. But, for an hour after sex, I have her soft and submissive. I like to call it the "temporary taming of the shrew." I live for those hours, where she's looking up at me like I'm the man. Sometimes, I can even get her to say it.

You're the man, Caleb. You're the man.

"As opposed to doing it…wrong?" Her eyebrows lift. "Is there a wrong way to do that?"

"Everything that's not you feels wrong, Duchess."

I can tell she's pleased by my words. She scoots closer, throwing her leg over my waist. I trail my fingers lightly along her spine, and when I reach the "world's greatest ass" I lay my hand flat and stay there.

She wiggles and I know what she wants.

"Again?" I suck on one of her fingers and she shivers.

"Again," she says. "And again, and again, and again…"

EPILOGUE

Olivia and I never marry. We took too many casualties in our struggle to be together. It seems almost wrong to get married after what we did to love. One night while we're in Paris, we make vows to each other. We're in our hotel, sitting side by side on the floor in front of the open window. Our view is of the Eiffel Tower, and we're wrapped in the blanket we just made love on. We are listening to the sounds of the city, when suddenly she turns to face me.

"Mormons believe that when they get married in this life, they stay married in the next. I was thinking that we should convert to Mormonism."

"Well, that's most certainly a viable option for us, Duchess. But, what if we're married to our first spouses in the next life?"

She grimaces. "I'd definitely be less fucked than you."

I laugh so hard we both fall over backwards onto the carpet. We shift our bodies until we are lying with our faces inches apart. I reach out to touch the small oval she wears on a chain around her neck. It's our penny. She had it made into a necklace that she never takes off.

"Wherever we go in the next life, we'll be together," I say.

"Let's not go to hell then; that's where Leah will be."

I nod in agreement, then I look in her eyes and say, "I'll do whatever I have to do to protect you. I'll lie, cheat, and steal to make you okay. I'll share your suffering, and I'll carry you when you're weighed down. I'll never leave you, not even when you ask me to. Do you believe me?"

She touches my face with the tips of her fingers and nods.

"You're strong enough to protect your heart and mine, and your heart from mine. I'll give you everything I have because from the day I met you, it's belonged to you."

I kiss her then I roll on top of her.

And that's it. Our hearts are married.

We fight. We make love. We cook huge meals and fall into food comas for days. After she defends a murderer and wins the case, she sells her share of the business and we move into our house in Naples. She says if she keeps defending criminals, she's going to go to hell and she really doesn't want to spend eternity with Leah. She opens up her own practice, and I work from home. We have a vegetable garden. Olivia has a black thumb and kills all of the plants. I nurture them back to life when she's not looking and then convince her she has a green thumb. She's very proud of her (my) tomatoes.

We try to have a baby, but Olivia miscarries twice. When she is thirty-five, she is diagnosed with ovarian cancer and has to have a hysterectomy. She cries for a year. I try to be strong, mostly because she needs me to be. But, during that time it wasn't Noah I was afraid to lose her to, or Turner, or herself, it was cancer. And cancer was a foe I didn't want to fuck with. Most days I just begged God to keep her alive and make it go away. That's what I asked him—make it go away—like I was five years old and there was a boogeyman in my closet. God must have heard my prayers, because the cancer never came back and the boogeyman was vanquished. My hands still shake when I think about that time.

I wish I could have given her a baby. Sometimes, when she's at the office late, I sit in what would have been the nursery and think about the past. It's a pointless game of torture, but I suppose it's a consequence of being a flawed, stupid man. Olivia doesn't like it when I think. She says my thoughts are too deep and they depress her. She's probably right. And I would hate for her to see what I see—the fact that if we'd just done things right, if I'd fought harder, if she'd fought less, we would have been together sooner. We could have had our baby before it was too late—before her body made it impossible. But, we didn't, and we're both a little broken because of it.

I've come to the conclusion that there are no set rules in life. You do what you have to do to survive. If that means running away from the love of your life to preserve your sanity, you do it. If it means breaking someone's heart so yours doesn't break, do it. Life is complicated—too much so for there to be absolutes. We are all so broken. Pick up a person, shake them around, and you'll hear the rattling of their broken pieces. Pieces our fathers broke, or our mothers, or our friends, strangers, or our loves. Olivia has stopped rattling quite as much as she used to. *Love is a God-given tool,* she tells me. *It screws things back in place that were loose, and it cleans out all the broken pieces that you don't need anymore.* I believe her. Our love has been fixing each other. I hope to only hear a tiny jingle when I shake her in a few years.

Leah remarries and has another baby. Luckily, it's a boy. When Estella is nine, she comes to live with us. Despite the "stepmother" status, Estella loves Olivia. They share the same sense of humor, and too often, I find myself the target of their jokes. Some nights I come home and they're sitting side by side on the sofa, legs propped on the coffee table, MacBooks open, stalking boys. Olivia wishes she'd had Facebook when we were young. She says so every day. I'm not sure who's more confused by their immediate chemistry—me or Leah.

Leah still hates Olivia. Olivia is grateful that Leah gave us Estella. Fortunately, Estella is nothing like her mother, aside from her red hair, of course. It's a joke in the family that no one has the same hair color. Raven, red, and blonde. We're an odd sight in public.

We are raising a really beautiful little soul. She wants to be a writer and tell our story someday. We are gonna be okay. That's what happens when two people are meant to be together. You just work it out until you are okay.

We make love every single day—no matter what. She is the only woman I've seen that gets more beautiful with age. She is the only woman I see.

THANKS BE

And the journey is over. After eight years and loving my characters through their lies, I can finally move on. To mothers, and fathers, and friends, and foes—I steal snippets of your words and lives to thread through my stories.

I owe all to my readers: passionate, dedicated, mildly insane. Just like me! Thank you. I wrote this for you. I will never forget the book signings, the gifts, the scrapbooks, the emails, and the harassment. Thank you to the blogs for empowering the writer. And to the writers who empower other writers through their intoxicating words. I am ever so grateful for all of it.

Tarryn

CONTACT

www.tarrynfisher.com

www.facebook.com/authortarrynfisher

www.instagram.com/tarrynfisher

http://twitter.com/DarkMarkTarryn

CPSIA information can be obtained
at www.ICGtesting.com
Printed in the USA
JSHW021400060420
5008JS00004B/1314